# SAMANTHA RANSIER

# Murderess of the Midnight Raven

## A Tale from the Midnight Raven

S.R.

MIDNIGHT
RAVEN
PUBLISHING

First edition

Cover art by Juniper Hartman
Editing by Matt Stone
Illustration by Mew.Munn

This book was professionally typeset on Reedsy.
Find out more at reedsy.com

# Contents

# Dedication

To all of you who feel unworthy of love, trapped in systems you cannot escape, and those of us who enjoy wearing our hearts on our sleeves and a hand-shaped necklace around our throats.

For:
Reeka, Azira, Kaja, Juniper, Skylar, Katy, and Gemma

# Trigger Warnings

Hello Reader!

I wanted to start this off by extending a massive thank you to YOU for picking up my work in the first place. I personally believe in complete and total transparency when it comes to understanding what you will face when it comes to reading, so please have a good read through of the following triggers and get yourself accustomed to the material before we settle in for the ride! This is a Dark Contemporary Urban Romance that follows Sex-Worker, Valentine and her Driver, Cain. Because of the nature of her work, there will be plenty… and I mean plenty of spice. Some more fuzzy than other bits. Here is a list of potential triggers:

- Sex Work and Prostitution (which includes morally ambiguous approaches to sex)
- Scenes which may allude to nonconsensual intercourse or assault
- Physical Assault
- Sex Addiction, and the highs and lows which come from that

- Mentions of murder
- Mentions of abuse
- Scenes which depict graphic details of death/dying
- An unfair amount of horniness from the slow burn
- Use of sex toys: Dildos, vibrators, etc.
- Depictions of domestic violence/ Domestic breakdown
- Addiction and addictive behaviours
- Depictions of self-harm and panic attacks

Did I mention this is a book about a sex-worker? If the idea of selling your body for money or for some other form of payment, makes you uncomfortable, this is not the novel for you. Murderess of the Midnight Raven delves into the mental health awareness behind sex addiction and the negative effects that sex has on the body, mind, along with the ensuing psychosocial stressors.

There will be depictions of sex that are expressed as morally corrupt, but it only makes the character all that more real. This is something that real men and women (and all our amazing friends in between and outside) put themselves through, and it should be highlighted in raw form.

Saying this, the relationship between Cain and Valentine will hopefully demonstrate that even when you feel hopeless; like the world takes advantage of you, there is someone who will kill to keep you from harm. You are still worthy of having your story written. Things can change for the better. I like to say that, though I write Dark Romance, it is the world around them which carries the darkness and not the romance itself.

This book also features a strong, stoic male character who expresses genuine emotions. Cain cries, as all men are allowed to do.

If you or anyone you know is struggling with sex addiction, are under duress to provide these services, or just need a helping hand, please reach out to your local mental health resources. In the UK: MIND, The Samaritans, and much more are available to help, judgement free.

You're worthy of being heard <3 Thank you for taking the time out of your day to read my story. The first of many to come!

# To Be Loved...

*

⁓⋯⁓

*"you are a horse running alone
and he tries to tame you
compares you to an impossible highway
to a burning house
says you are blinding him
that he could never leave you
forget you
want anything but you
you dizzy him, you are unbearable
every woman before or after you
is doused in your name
you fill his mouth
his teeth ache with the memory of taste
his body just a long shadow seeking yours
but you are always too intense
frightening in the way you want him
unashamed and sacrificial
he tells you that no man can live up to the one who*

*

*lives in your head*
*and you tried to change, didn't you?*
*closed your mouth more*
*tried to be softer*
*prettier*
*less volatile, less awake*
*but even when sleeping you could feel*
*him travelling away from you in his dreams*
*so what did you want to do, love,*
*split his head open?*
*you can't make homes out of human beings*
*someone should have already told you that*
*and if he wants to leave*
*then let him leave*
*you are terrifying*
*and strange and beautiful*
*something not everyone knows how to love."*
**Warsan Shire**

# The Escort's Escort

# VALENTINE

Rain pattered lightly on the single-paned window of my downtown Atlanta apartment. It was a sound that would have usually filled me with bliss on any other day. Tonight, however, I stared at myself in the makeup-smudged hand mirror that leaned haphazardly against peeling wallpaper behind my vanity. Products lined the messy top of the desk, splaying out to clutter it even further.

I examined my face for imperfections, studying my sharp blush-smoothed cheekbones and full lips that I had painted a beautiful deep crimson, and then lined with a deep, almost black, maroon liner.

I hated this part of the job.

It was the only part I could never feel good enough at. It was easy to shake your ass or suck a dick… but makeup… makeup was a whole different ballgame.

After searching my foundation, for a few grueling seconds, I resigned to sigh softly and continue on with the eyeshadow that I had been putting off.

For some reason, midnight blue was calling to me today. I wasn't quite sure how well it would match with this darker lip color, but I had an inexplicable craving.

Maybe it was the rain… The way the sound of the pattering droplets across the condensation-dripping window reminded me of happier days.

Tar tainted, cigarette smoke stained walls flashed with the light of a far-off lightning strike, and the soft rumble of the following thunder sounded briefly after. I pushed a swift breath of air from my nostrils, glaring a piercing stare out the window as if to curse God himself for threatening my only light source.

A soft buzz startled me, a low rumble emanating from the watch on my wrist. A crease knitted itself between my perfectly manicured brows as I narrowed my eyes at the name that scrawled itself across the screen:

**Incoming Call:
Cain**

A scoff made its way up my throat, and I rolled my eyes, ignoring the call and allowing it to slowly fade from buzzing…

No joy.

No hope for peace.

It began to buzz again the second that the previous call declined.

I rolled my eyes and mashed the green phone-shaped icon beneath his name.

"What?" I snap, returning my attention to my eyeliner.

This look was turning out better than I had expected; more than likely to the chagrin of the man whose voice sounded a sharp response to my question.

"Where are you?" Cain's low voice rumbled from behind the screen that currently situated itself on my wrist.

The desire to roll my eyes filled my mind and I stuck my tongue out childishly at the watch as if he could see me. *He's such a dick.*

"Val?" He sounded impatient.

I sighed and threw down the makeup brush that had just completed my perfect look for the night, "I am literally at home right now. I'm getting ready."

He growled a low grumble. I could practically see him pinching the bridge of his nose in his exacerbated attempt to control his temper.

"You were supposed to meet me at the plaza twenty minutes ago. You're going to be late."

My eyes settle upon the letters of his name as they glow on the rounded watch. A slow heat ascended up to my cheeks from my chest, and I sighed again.

"No. Lorenzo told me that we were meeting at seven... it is currently..." I swiped his call away and stared at the plainly obvious starch white numbers that revealed my error, 7:25. "Shit..." I swiped back through to his call and mashed the red button to end it.

I leapt from my seat and grabbed a tattered black leather duffle bag, slinging it over my shoulder aggressively as my wrist began to vibrate yet again from another impatient call from my driver. I threw open the door to my bedroom and rushed quickly through the small, cramped apartment, pushing behind the couch where my roommate currently splayed across the messy cushions in some sort of drugged slumber, and dashed through the door.

The corridor was empty, dark, and damp.

Rain pelted down at the city sidewalks around my building, and I felt a curse raise from my chest once more as I realized that all my hard work would be for naught with the impending drenching in my near future.

I raced down the three flights of concrete stairs, my bag bouncing off my shoulder as I ran.

Just as I reached the ground floor, I saw him there.

*Cain.*

He stood at the edge of the awning holding an umbrella outstretched above his head that was scarcely big enough to cover him in its entirety. His facial features were mostly obscured by the darkness that was cast upon him by the dark concrete surroundings of the corridor, but I could feel his deep blue eyes burning holes into me.

He wore what he always wore: dark black jeans held securely to his waist by a leather belt with an oval shaped, black titanium belt buckle. (It had some inscriptions that I had never gotten close enough to read, etched into the metal on ribbons around a pattern of roses.) Cain's customary top-wear was a black leather jacket that fit him well, accentuating his broad shoulders and thick biceps that entertained chords of braided muscle beneath the layers of skin, fabric, and leather.

Tonight, like almost any other night, a black knit beanie pulled tightly over his ears, flattening down the top of his shaggy brown hair.

I hated that fucking beanie.

I twisted my face into a disgruntled grimace as I stared at him, crossing my arms before myself as I looked at him, "I would have met you at the plaza."

"You would have ruined your hair and makeup." He retorts with a snort of annoyance, "Come along, Val. You're making us late. The other girls will be pissed." The monolithic creature at the end of the hall began to turn away from me to face a slick black Dodge Charger that rumbled at the curb, the soft roll of its engine hummed through the cascading sound of falling rain.

Cain's hand extended backwards to offer the umbrella and rain began to soak into the knit fabric of his hat.

I slipped my fingers around the base of the handle, below the grasp of his hand as though I avoided the mere idea of gracing him with my touch.

Before I could blink, Cain had slipped back into his precious car, sinking into the driver's seat without another word.

The handle of the umbrella was still warm from his grasp, and a hint of his deep earthy cologne swirled in the air around me, dissipating the longer that I stood still. The car growled before me as Cain revved the engine impatiently.

I rolled my eyes and stamped through the puddle laden pathway toward the car, slipping into the passenger side seat with no less than a graceful thud. I closed the umbrella and tossed it to the floorboards, and then placed the leather bag beside.

"You're a pain in my ass, you know?" Cain grumbled,

rubbing the bridge of his nose in annoyance as he peeled away from the curb.

"You could have always picked Sasha and Mags up first." I spat back.

He didn't respond, deciding instead to stare straight ahead as he rushed through the lower streets of downtown Atlanta.

Cain always picked me up first. Ever since the day we met, it had always been the same. Methodical to a fault.

Everyone else in the agency seemed to believe that it was because he had a thing for me. They called me "His Valentine" or "Cain's Valentine". The name made me sick to my stomach.

When we first met, sure, I thought he was eye candy. But his true nature has since shown itself, and I've never been able to look at him the same since... *that* night...

That night when he watched as one of the guests at a sleezy frat party gig pull me into a room.

I stared him straight in the eyes and called out my safe-word...

But he simply watched with that fucking vacant, brooding stare.

I guess it was his way of punishing me for being such a bitch to him. I *was*, after all, a bitch. Told him he was nothing more than a man with a big dick and a shiny car and boy did I learn my lesson.

I was drunk. It was stupid.

I was always so fucking stupid.

This thick silence weighed heavily throughout the cab of the car; it was a tension that burned a hole in my chest. Cain was a broody, self-obsessed asshole with a proclivity for doing everything exactly as he saw fit. If I didn't trust him with my life, it would be so much easier to just up and ask Lorenzo to switch me to another driver.

The car grumbled to a slow halt outside another apartment complex. Two girls with thick, professional makeup stood at the entrance of the building with annoyed sneers on their faces. They raced through the rain toward the Charger and fought to pull the back door open, then they threw themselves inside hopelessly with complaints lacing their every word.

Mags was the first to speak. She was a tall woman with ebony black skin and piercing brown eyes. Her hair was styled in tight box braids that reached just beyond her ass that must have cost her a fortune in appointments. A long white trench coat concealed everything... if anything... that she was wearing beneath, but her legs showed ruby red fishnets with faux diamonds sprinkled throughout and matching red high heels about six inches in height.

"What the fuck, Cain?" She scowled, adjusting one of her false eyelashes as she stared into her reflection at her neon-colored makeup.

Cain shot her a glance in the rear-view mirror, noting that she was far too transfixed by her own reflection to notice his glance, "Val was late."

My head snapped in his direction, and I felt a heat flowing to my face as I glared daggers into his stupid beanie covered head.

"Don't blame Val. You should have picked us up first," Sasha chirps in a hushed tone, sitting peacefully behind my seat. A soft-spoken girl with red hair that was shaved on one side and cut to a sharp bob on the other. Today her longer hair was curled lightly, stings of silver hair tinsel strung throughout. She had on a grey hooded sweater and matching sweatpants with tacky white tennis shoes on, a duffle bag propped in her lap.

Her makeup was by far the best of all three of us. Thick black eyeliner that flicked up into beautiful wings, with black lipstick, and red eyeshadow. Her cheeks were adorned with shimmering body gems, like the twinkles of starlight captured on her rosy cheeks.

Her response signaled a grunt from the driver, and Mags snickered as she peeled her eyes away from her reflection.

"You know he always picks Valentine up first. That's his girl."

"I'm not his girl," I snorted, a display of disgust rolling over my expression as I turned to face them in the back seat.

Cain tapped the accelerator, speeding the car up just enough for us to notice.

He remained silent, the streetlights occasionally painting warm yellow light across his pale face. His white knuckles stood out amid the darkness of the car; like he had something weighing on him that he didn't want to verbalize just yet.

I turned back to face the front and crossed my arms. There was a desperate attempt within me to keep my gaze to myself, and I resigned myself to staring at the tattered fabric of my duffel bag sitting on the floor.

"Did you bring the gear?" I asked in a mutter.

"I always bring the gear," Sasha piped up, patting the duffle bag in her lap with a grin, "don't worry. I made sure to add the spicy lube this time."

A smirk rose to Mags' face as she jabs an elbow into Sasha's side. The pair burst into fits of giggles, and I couldn't help but feel the energy in the car brighten around me. The tension seemed to be slowly melting away…

That was until I turned my glance to Cain and saw that

he was surrounded by his own personal haze of conflict and frustration.

"You could at least pretend to like us," I complained, my eyes narrowing in his direction.

His eyes remain glued to the road before him, "My job is to drive, drop off, and protect. *Liking* you doesn't cross into that description."

Despite my general annoyance with him, the words still kinda stung. I rolled my eyes, fixing them to the distant scenery in stubborn silence instead.

"Seems like trouble in paradise," Mags mused, never looking up from scrolling on her phone.

Sasha laughed as she pulled a tube of lipstick from her bag, "what do you mean? I have *never* seen them get along." She tapped the black ink to her lips, pursing them together to smooth the pigment into her skin.

"Exactly!" Mags cheers, "That means that as soon as we are behind closed doors, they can't stop themselves from wanting to hate-fuck one another."

I turned my head over my shoulder to send a disgruntled look to Mags, but she simply grinned, waving her slender fingers at me playfully.

The revving of the engine began to soften as Cain pulled up to a college campus, and the energy zipped from the car once more. He came to a rolling stop outside of the frat house we would be visiting. There was already a mess of chaos over the front lawn with drunken college kids running amok.

I bit the back of my lip, "Classy venue."

Mags groaned, "I thought Lorenzo said no more frat parties after what happened to-"

"It is a high-profile client's birthday." Cain shut off the

words that Mags had voiced before she could even finish her train of thought. There was a sharpness to his tone, protective.

Any complaints we felt had been immediately silenced, and despite our disagreement, we each exited the car.

Cain led the way, with Mags and Sasha in the middle. I trailed behind, my black shoes squelching beneath me in the muddy grass. It was a fitting visual to match the way my brain felt in this very moment.

As we grew nearer, a gaggle of inebriated college-aged men began to wolf whistle and whoop. It summoned feelings of rage within me but I silenced the thoughts. I was here for a job, one that I was damn good at.

Cain did most of the talking, asking for a room to be cleared out for us to change and store our belongings in for the duration of the party. He then led us down a small corridor to a bedroom that had seen better days. It would do though, at least for the few hours that we would be here.

Each of us set our bags on the bed, and Cain perched himself at the door with his arms crossed over his chest.

I scoffed, "You know better than to stand and stare at us. Make yourself useful and guard the *outside* of the room, you brute."

His eyebrow lifted as he stared into my soul for a moment.

I won't lie… A rush of fear fell over me… and it turned me on.

Eventually, he nodded without a single word and exited the room, pulling the shitty plywood door closed behind him with a rattling thud. With his presence now vanquished, so too was the inexplicable inability to catch a full breath of air, so I pulled one in deeply for the first time since he had gathered me.

I turned to Mags, who had removed her trench coat to reveal a stunning red leather lingerie set that perfectly accentuated her full hips and her round ass. She had a knowing look in her eyes as she stared at me.

"Who told you that color of eyeshadow would go with that lip?" she asked in her kindest possible mothering tone.

A spatting of red dusted across my cheeks, darkening the synthetic blush further and warming my face, "Does it really look that bad?"

Sasha stepped in front of me, her sweats now removed to reveal a pleated tartan skirt with no coverage of her ass. She pulled me to sit on the bed and gently retrieved out a makeup wipe from the duffel bag on her left, "It is actually really pretty, but your lipstick clashes… and the blue doesn't match your outfit." Sasha drags the wipe across both of my eyelids in a very professional manner.

Sasha used to be a lead makeup artist for a local movie studio, but she was laid off when her boss tried to sleep with her, and she rejected him. I wasn't quite sure how she figured working as an escort under Lorenzo's thumb would be any better than that, but I greatly appreciated her presence.

Her and Mags were my best friends… my only friends in this world. She diligently worked on my eyes, quickly finishing me off with a dazzling eyeshadow and eyeliner that rivalled her own.

When she was done, she lifted a compact mirror to show me.

It was beautiful… too beautiful.

A pang of insignificance droned in my chest. I nodded and smiled gratefully at her, then unzipped my duffel to remove a slick black faux leather two-piece lingerie set. I removed my clothing and slipped the black fabric over my skin, tightening the multitude of straps. Then stooped to put on a pair of black platform boots that had chains hanging from them.

The other two girls perfected their own looks: Sasha had now removed her sweater to reveal a very oversized, somewhat sheer white top with a red frilly bralette beneath it. I smiled at each of them and then glanced down to Sasha's duffel. There was a smaller waterproof bag inside which contained numerous silicon sculptures that ranged in size and shape. I smirked at her and then stepped toward the door, rapping the back of my knuckles twice against the wood.

In an instant, the door swung open and Cain slipped inside.

"Are you ready?" he asks, his eyes falling respectfully on each of our faces.

We each nodded in unison and Mags and Sasha began to exit the room with their matching white dressing gowns tied closed around them.

I reached to tie my own gown around myself when Cain stepped closer to me, "Are you going to be okay, Val?" his eyes focused on my own. For some reason, I thought that there was a glitter of concern in those blue orbs.

A flutter of indecision churned in my chest as I forced myself away from thinking too hard about the memories. I stiffened, squared my shoulders and straightened my spine.

"I don't really have a choice."

He seemed displeased by this answer, but his steely blue eyes remained heavy on mine, "You know the code word. Say it and I bring everything to a halt." He assured me, then turned and left the room.

A burning warmth lingered on my cheeks, but I shook it away, assuming it was the nerves that bubbled in my belly like every other time we did these events. I pulled the fastener of my robe closed and joined the other two girls in the lounge.

I noted the raised platform where we would be performing most of our acts.

"Thank you for your invitation tonight, I want to introduce my girls: The Varsity Vixens." Cain's voice took a saccharine softness, deepening intentionally on our name to churn the hearts of the few women who speckled the room. "We have a real treat for you, our first lady of tonight, Madam Magnolia Bites. A woman who can take a man to his knees with just a single glance."

Mags pressed the tips of her fingers to her full, luscious lips and blew a kiss into the audience. The crowd oo's and aa's, filling with a lusty air that we were all too used to.

"Miss Sasha Sins, will make you quiver... in fear or pleasure? That is up to you to decide."

Sasha made a flirty bow, slipping a hand through her meticulously styled hair. Claps and shouts rang out just as they had for Mags.

"And finally, per special request. Our finest, most skilled temptress this side of the Blue Ridge Mountains, Our Lady Valentine Valore." Cain's voice rolled in a deep, seductive tone as my name rolled off his lips.

I fanned my face with one hand, my eyes narrowing into sultry slits as I pretended to be disinterested in the audience. Men crave what they cannot have, and although the cheers didn't sound as loudly as they had for the other girls, the room felt heavier with seduction.

"Before we begin, we have a few rules." Cain broke through the air with his typical voice returning. Despite the crowd booing and jesting, he continued. "Rule Number One. Do not touch the girls unless they permit you to. This act of denial is part of the act itself.

Rule Number Two. Absolutely no kissing the girls on their mouths.

Rule Three. Each girl has the agency to tell you to stop, if you persist, they will have a signal word that is unique to them. The second that word is shouted; the entire show is over. Don't ruin the fun for the whole group."

A roar of boos crashes through the audience, but some of the stronger and more sober men hushed the rowdy ones.

"Finally, there will be toys that you will be permitted to use during the show. You are *absolutely* not to use anything on the girls other than the toys supplied by them personally." Cain finished, then glanced at us. "Are you ready girls?"

"Yes, Daddy!" Sasha called out to him, her lively curls swaying with each bounce.

Without further ado, the music began, and we each took our places. On beat, we pulled open our dressing gowns one by one and allowed them to slink down to our forearms. Then in unison we pulled them off and tossed them into the crowd. A few men cheered, having caught the forlorn clothing.

Mags and Sasha stepped down from the slightly raised platform, leaving me alone on the stage to saunter through the crowd of horny intoxicated people. They would run their hands over shoulders, teasingly sit in laps, and more while I danced. This was a dance I had done a million times. It flowed out of me; I could feel an energy of control washing over me and I stepped down from the stage to the man seated in the very first row.

"Hello, birthday boy," I cooed in a raspy tone into his ear, my legs perching on either side of his hips as I clasped his face in my hands.

"I heard you've been… a little lonely" the words rolled from my lips in an intoxicating chant as I felt his length harden beneath his trousers.

He inhaled sharply through his nose, biting at his lip as his hands hovered anxiously inches away from my hips, barely heeding Cain's warnings.

I laughed, thrusting my chest upwards and pulling his face into my leather restrained breasts, "You sorry sap. You must love being tortured."

The crowd began to grow in excitement as Sasha returned to the stage, taking control of the audience while I had the guest of honor's face stuffed into the ample flesh of my breasts.

Sasha pulled open a few of the buttons from her shift as the song swiftly changed to her own. She started to dance seductively, reaching behind the stage to remove a long white stick with a silk ribbon that extended from it. As she danced, she twirled the ribbon. It danced around her in a blindingly beautiful display, and the audience watched in awe.

As Mags stepped back onto the stage, she held a bottle of champagne. Her dark fingers clasped around the neck as she popped the cork, and the bottle sprayed a wave of foam all over Sasha's sheer white top. The fabric began to stick to her, becoming more sheer by the second until it was clinging to her skin tightly, showing the tiny bralette and her pierced belly button beneath.

Mags then tossed the bottle at the nearest audience member and moved to stand behind Sasha. Her hands traced Sasha's sternum, unfastening buttons slowly until the wet shirt hung listlessly from her shoulders. Mags placed a few kisses along Sasha's neck and then slipped her free from her shirt before tossing it too into the audience.

I rolled my hips along the length of the Birthday Boy, then pushed myself away from him. His hands twitched as if he wanted to grab me and pull me back, but he didn't. He knew better. Cain's eyes could be sensed burning holes into anyone who came too close to any one of us.

I stepped back onto the stage just as Mags ripped off her lingerie to reveal sparkling nipple pasties and a thin red thong beneath her fishnets. She and Sasha both turned to bare their visible asses toward the crowd and I stood between them, unzipping the leather restraints which confined my breasts. As pressure released, my tits spilled from within and the crowd reveled in it. I slipped the leather top off and threw it directly back to the birthday boy, and then Sasha knelt on the ground before me.

The crowd roared as Sasha tugged at the leather bottoms from around my waist and finally pulled them down to my ankles. She then crawled between my legs, her own ass showing clearly to the audience as Mags pushes me to my knees, my thighs framing either side of Sasha's face. Mags then pulls my arms behind my back and binds them in thick chorded rope.

Sasha perched her hands on my ass cheeks and lifts her face toward my pussy, her tongue grazing lightly against my clit as her own legs lay spread open for the whole audience to see. They waited on bated breath as Sasha begins to lick my clit. Mags retrieved a large purple dildo from the bag and walked over to the special guest. She extended the silicon toy to him and pointed to Sasha's open legs with a wordless demand.

His eyes glazed over and I watched as he stared between the toy and the woman beneath me. Mags then stepped back onto the stage with a steely gaze that searched the eyes of each audience member. They cheered for their friend as he stood and sank to his knees between Sasha's legs, pressing the tip of the toy at her entrance. She let out a slightly excited groan and her hips wiggled.

The audience members drew closer, the fifteen or so men and women fighting to watch as the birthday boy slipped the toy into her pussy all the way. At the same time, Sasha licked my clit just enough to signal me toa moan.

Mags pushed my shoulders forward and I leaned over Sasha, pressing my face down to place kisses against her clit in return. I could hear the trembling breaths of the man before me as he watched, slowly moving the dildo in and out of Sasha. She returned his grace in my direction, sucking lightly on my own clump of nerves. I whimpered, trying to avoid grinding my hips into her face. This wasn't for my pleasure. It was for theirs. All of them, as they watched.

Mags retrieved a second dildo from the case and walked it over to a tall handsome man with dark features, handing it to him and then pointing wordlessly to me. The tall man smirked and then practically ran over to me. He crouched behind and pushed the silicon length deep inside of me without hesitation. He must have thought it would feel nice. It didn't.

Dildos take a touch of technique… which he clearly didn't have.

Despite this, I choked back with my own annoyance as whatever pleasure Sasha had given me faded, and I made direct eye contact with the birthday boy, letting out a loud and helpless moan.

"God, I'd fuck her if I were you, Kev!" One of his friends shouted behind him, but Kev's eyes stayed locked on mine.

He began to speed up the thrusts of the toy within Sasha, and she moaned against my pussy.

Our ebony friend took care of the shouting man, approaching him and pulling him onto stage where she made him peel back her fishnets and start to perform oral on her.

The audience began to grow wild and before I could really tell what was happening, Kevin had reached to lightly brace his hand around my throat.

Panic burned in my chest, but I didn't yet sound the alarm. I moaned lightly, staring into his eyes. If I just gave in to what he wanted, he would probably move on from me soon.

I was wrong.

With my next moan, I could feel his grip around my throat tighten, his eyes darkened as he slammed the toy into the girl beneath me. Sasha was growing uncomfortable and had stopped licking my clit. He was getting more aggressive with her, and suddenly I was thrust into a reality which was far too sinister for my liking, my eyes frozen as if he had locked them in place. I could see the seething desire in his terrifying orbs.

In an instant… everything stopped. The music cut silent, the lights flashed on, and the burning warmth of Kevin's tight clutch on my throat disappeared. As my senses returned to me, I glanced down to see tears on Sasha's face. He had been too rough with her; she'd given Cain her code word.

Cain shut everything down and then removed the men from the stage, ushering us into the room where we had gotten ready before.

It felt like I was floating.

It felt ike the world was running on a speed that my brain couldn't cope with. The next few minutes were a blur as we quickly changed out of our skimpy, lube and alcohol-soaked clothing, back into our transitional clothing.

The ride home was silent.

That eerily thick air of tension was strong in the car, but as Sasha and Mags got out, Mags dipped her head low to peer into the cab of the car. She grumbled, "If Lorenzo ever sends us to a frat party again, I quit on the spot," And then slammed the door.

Now alone once more with Cain, I could see his knuckles gripping tightly to the wheel. There was something on his mind, but he didn't say anything. Even as we approached my apartment, he sat in complete silence.

I looked at him one more time as I reached for the door handle, but he didn't even spare me a glance. That pissed me off. His stupid beanie covered head faced away from me, even as I slammed the door to his precious car and stomped upstairs.

I burst through the front door of my apartment to find my roommate/ex-boyfriend, Finn, still asleep on the couch. Probably drugged out of his mind.

I groaned and kicked my shoes off before slamming my bedroom door shut and sinking to the ground behind it.

Tears welled in my eyes and then spilled down my cheeks in waves. I hated this. I hated everything about this. The other girls always threatened to quit when a gig was difficult… To leave me by myself, knowing that I can never escape from Lorenzo's grasp… and that bastard, Cain!

He was meant to protect me, but all he ever did was brood and complain, and brood some more, and now when I think he might offer me some semblance of sympathy…he ignores me like the memories I had weren't shared with him. As if he didn't know what happened to me.

I pulled my phone out of my bag to see a number of notifications that I couldn't care less about, swiping them all away. I then checked my hidden inbox to see if Lorenzo had emailed me... but nothing.

Solitude is horrid. Solitude pushes people to the brinks of their own destruction... and I think I am on that brink. Maybe I should just give in and let Lorenzo win...

But then my phone rang...

And that fucking prick's name flashed across my screen.

"Pain in my ass," I grumbled in a swift exhale of the breath I had just savored, rolling my eyes.

She never answered my calls. She never replied to my messages. What was the fucking point?

Resigned, I twisted at the ignition of my car and revved the engine a few times, drawing disgruntled glances from nearby pedestrians. Their displeasure summoned a deep smirk to my face, and I flipped through the options on my phone before settling on the Bluetooth button.

In seconds, the cab of my car filled with the up-tempo beat of drums, then the heavy strum of an electric guitar. I revved one more time, then removed my break and sped off into the night with the sound of Black Sabbath to coax me onwards to face the main man of this whole fucking operation.

As I approached the up-town mansion, I swore I could taste bile. It was a Victorian multilevel home with white marble pillars. Everything that could be encrusted in gold, WAS encrusted in gold. The lawn was meticulously manicured and sprinkled with anti-vermin poison, enough to kill anyone who dared fuck around with Lorenzo's perfectly green grass.

What I wouldn't give to fuck with Lorenzo's perfectly green fucking grass.

I pulled into the driveway and shut off the engine, thankful for the heavy rain as it pelted down on the windshield before me. The walls of falling rain obscured this Midas-wannabe's palace in the northern affluence of Atlanta.

That same rain coated my skin and soaked into the knit fabric of my beanie as I climbed from within the car, leaving my phone strapped to the dashboard. I pressed the keyfob and waited to hear two solid clicks to ensure the car was locked.

Lorenzo was already stood at the door. His belly protruding

over the threshold despite his position a pace or two within it. He had oily black hair that was thinning at the crown, slicked back haphazardly as if he didn't care. His round belly was enwrapped by a bright white dress shirt with buttons that struggled to cope with the strain at the stomach's roundest point.

"Cain!" He called out, his mezzo tone hitting me like a ton of bricks.

I glanced over at him, narrowing my eyes as I drew closer to the door, taking the few steps up to join him on the marble patio.

Lorenzo laughed, stepping through to clap me hard over the shoulder with his big, meaty palm. "Come in! Tell me about the show that the Vixens put on tonight!"

A pang of annoyance rang in my ears as a stitch knit itself between my eyebrows. "We had to pack up early."

Lorenzo's pleasant demeanor immediately shifted, he gritted his teeth and groaned dramatically, stepping across the brightly lit foyer toward a drinks cabinet where he poured himself a cocktail. "Why does this keep happening?"

I narrow my eyes, pulling my arms from my side to rest folded over one another in front of my chest, "Your *guest of honor* started getting aggressive with the girls. He was so rough that Sasha had to use her safe-word."

The stubby man turned to face me, a geometric glass of liquor now in his hands, but was mostly hidden by... well... his hand. "I will reprimand her. She cannot be so easy to break. This is money we are talking about!"

That stitch between my brows creased further as I felt my eyes narrow. This man was everything I hated about the world, but I was stuck with him.

"She should be more like our Valentine!" Lorenzo muses, taking a thick swig of his drink, "now she is a true Vixen. Through and through. She never breaks!" A menacing smile grew on the lips of this ornery old bastard, and I could feel the surge of rage bubbling within me.

Val was a special breed, indeed, but not for the reasons that our boss believed. She had a stubborn habit of choking on the things she feared, and then blacking out.

"I don't think she has ever said her safe-word!" Lorenzo beams, turning from me to enter his main lounge.

His words forced the wind from my chest, and I stood there like a statue, quiet and fucking pissed.

She had…once…

And the worst part is that it was the one time I didn't listen. The one time I didn't intervene.

The memory flooded my mind. She was extra sassy that day when I picked her up that day. Her boyfriend had recently dumped her because he didn't like her lifestyle, and she had taken to drinking heavily to cope with whatever the fuck was going on in her fucked up life. The Vixens were performing at a frat party, some stupid 90s themed shindig. I don't remember what happened, but she got mad at me and got in my face, telling me I was a piece of shit and that all I did was bitch and moan.

She was right, too. All I ever really did was bitch and moan. But can one really blame me? After all, I am literally a chauffeur for the biggest pimp in the Peach State, and the girls I drive around couldn't be grateful for anything that didn't come with six figures or diamonds.

That night I saw her disappear into a bedroom with the client. I thought she was just doing it to piss me off, she knew better than to go behind closed doors. Especially when I had two more girls to watch over. I swore that as she turned to me before the door closed to seal her within, she mouthed a big fat "Fuck off" right at me.

I won't lie, I was pissed and annoyed. I let my pride get the better of me. It wasn't until later when she emerged from the bedroom in shambles and darted to the makeshift dressing room that the realization hit me... she hadn't told me to fuck off. Val made direct eye contact with me and mouthed her safe-word: *Focus*. I can see it now clearly, burned into the recesses of my brain. The way her lips parted, and her eyes were blatantly full of fear.

After that she stopped accepting my calls.

Her bubbly attitude turned sour.

She started accepting fewer gigs unless the other girls were there with her, and Lorenzo had no idea what Val was actually like... and he had no idea that I had ruined his prized girl.

Now, when I think of Val, I think back to that moment. The moment where I let her down. The moment when I failed to protect her. She hated me now, and although I don't blame her... I wish more than anything that I could change it.

"Are you gonna keep standing there like a lout or are you going to come in here and get your next assignment?" Lorenzo shouted, an echo through the vast.

I grumble out a groan and sauntered through to join him, coming to stand alertly at the end of the couch where his wife Zophia and eldest son Castello sat, combing through stacks of cash. Castello twitched, his eyes bright red from a very recent snuff of some sort of illicit substance. These people made me sick.

"So, Cain!" Lorenzo hums, "we are hot on the case for the

man who murdered your brother." He explains, scooping up a television remote and flipping the screen to a rough CCTV video of my younger brother's workshop.

On the screen, my brother was sitting there behind the counter with a book splayed open before him.

The video rolled on in silence.

I had seen it numerous times before.

I almost stopped breathing as I felt the approach of the static as the CCTV went fuzzy and the an intense whirring filled the room. In an instant, the picture resumed, and my brother was now slouched lifelessly across the workshop table.

I grimaced, feeling the blood pumping through my heart with thick heavy thuds as I bit my bottom lip. "That's the same as last time. Nothing's changed!"

Lorenzo's face brightened, "you think I am gonna be able to fix broken CCTV?" He booms in a boisterous laugh, "You idiot. I mean, we have more witnesses. But before I can give you any information, I need you to do me a quick job."

My eyes narrow. 'Quick job' was slang for Lorenzo wanting me to... clean up a situation for him.

"You see, our dear friend Kevin refused to give us the full payment for tonight's festivities. So, I need you to make a quick pit-stop to his on your way home. Your bestie is already there." His smirk reached his eyes with a fiery mischief.

I groaned in annoyance as I found myself pinching the bridge of my nose, "I thought I told you that I didn't want to do clean-up crew shit any more, Lorenzo."

"Yes, well if you want this from me, you have to do what I want as well." The sly man says with a dismissive wave. "Get on with it, the sun will be rising in three hours, so it needs to be done ASAP."

My feet seemed to move before my brain could comprehend and I was stepping toward the entrance from whence I came, my boots thudded heavily against the tile flooring before I was even aware that I was leaving.

By the time I arrived back at the stupid frat house, I saw a black two door Scion already parked in the grass out front. There was nobody else around, it was as if the world had emptied itself out and left nothing but the dregs of society… those being myself and my partner in this job.

I pushed through the thin wooden door that had been left ajar to find Cole standing menacingly over a frightened Kevin who was currently bound in a thick mass of bungee cords, a ball gag stuffed in his mouth. My friend turned to glance over his shoulder, a menacing expression displayed over his face. Rounded cheeks and a pointy smile. His brown hair was tied back into a messy man-bun at the back of his head, and he wore a pair of blue jeans with an oversized Hawaiian shirt.

"Ah! Look who it is!" Cole's voice chimes through the almost pertinent silence of the frat house, "it seems your worst nightmare has finally arrived."

One of my eyebrows arched, but my overall expression remains staunchly flat. I cracked my knuckles and rolled the sleeves of my leather jacket up to my elbows, revealing a full forearm that was covered from ligament to ligament, in ink.

Kevin stirred as I approached, a reaction that confused my senses as they balanced between the rush of adrenaline that was anticipated soon, and the overwhelming desire to just get the fuck outta here. But I couldn't. I needed to find the man who killed my brother.

I stepped toward Kevin, who now writhed in his seat, thrashing wildly against the slightly elastic hooked cables that bound him.

Coming closer, I became keenly aware that Cole had exacted his signature fate, the same one he uses on every asshole who doesn't pay us. The trail of freshly congealed blood sat at the corner of Kevin's lips, and streaked down from there to his jawline, and then to pattern the sweaty, beer soaked dress shirt that I had seen him in just an hour prior.

"You took his tongue?" I reel back to face Cole, who smiles at me innocently.

"Only the tip! Just enough so he knew we meant business." The brunet man gleefully stood in an intimidating stance.

I rolled my eyes in a huff and stood over Kevin, "Look, dude. We just need for you to give us our money and nobody gets... Well... any more hurt than they already are."

Kevin sneered, but he dared not speak. His eyes were locked on the man behind me, fear freezing him in place. But his silence was not submission, so I grabbed a clump of his black hair in my hands and ripped his head into my direction, staring into his soul.

"Look at me you sorry bastard!" I shouted, receiving only a pained whimper from the birthday boy.

I glanced down to see that his wrists were bound and his whole body was shaking aggressively against his restraints.

His trembling body filled me with glee, and I reached into my pocket to retrieve my knife. With a flick, I it shot open and I pressed the blade to his throat.

"You think I'm fucking playing with you, boy?" I snarled viciously into his ear, my other hand still clasping the tuft of hair atop his head. "You hurt one of my girls, and I don't take kindly to people hurting my girls." Though it was Sasha who had called out to me, it would be a lie if I said that she was the one whose pain embroiled my rage to this point. The flash of Val's terrified eyes filled my senses, and I pulled the knife along the man's skin before settling it just above his groin, poised and ready to puncture.

"One last chance, pretty boy. Pay up or I'll make sure you can never hurt another girl again." I applied a bit of pressure to the area where my knife lay, and Kevin began to squirm as tears pulled in rivulets down his dirty cheeks.

He ripped his head from my grasp, though I could see that I still held tight to a few strands of his hair. Kevin then thrusted his head in the direction of a tan leather bag in the center of the room, exacerbated cries emitting from behind the muffle of the ball gag. I glanced over my shoulder and nodded to the satchel.

Cole's smirk deepened in mischief as he stalked toward the bag, pulling it open to find bushels of wrapped cash.

"Count it!" I barked, adding pressure to my blade. Kevin let out another whine as he pleaded with us, clearly in pain.

My partner took his time counting out the stacks until he finally finished, turned over his shoulder and signaled me a soft nod, "it's all here."

"Fan-fucking-tastic." I recoiled my blade from the man's nether regions and ripped the ball gag from his mouth, "This is the property of one, Sasha Sins. And I'll have to invoice you for these additional services."

Kevin spat out clots of blood onto the floor, his breath hitching in sharp hyperventilation's as the cool air graced his lungs. He stared at us for a moment, terror still raging in his eyes as he spat out his next words clumsily, "My fa-er wi-no- we- you ge- away wi-h -is!"

Cole laughed, "Sorry, we can't understand you. It's like a

cat's got your tongue or something." He signaled to me and pushed through the door, allowing the cheap netted screen door to slam closed behind him. I heard the rumble of his Scion, which he aptly named The Batmobile, and then the blaring of Iron Maiden, before he peeled off in the direction of Lorenzo's house, leaving me and this disgusting wretch of a man behind.

I turned to face Kevin once more, a menacing shadow falling over him. "I'm not going to untie you until you give me some information."

His eyes widened, "Wha-? I gave you -he money!"

My shadow eclipses any shade of light as I hovered over him, then I pulled out the picture.

"Do you recognize this man?" showing Kevin the face of a man who looked almost identical to me, though younger and more out together. My little brother, Conor.

Kevin shook his head aggressively, "No ma-, I have- ever see- him i- my -ife." He struggled, still adjusting to the lack of percussive consonants that he could produce.

I narrowed my eyes and stared down at him for a moment. I could feel thestorm cloud rolling into my blue eyes.

"I swear, ma-!"

I leaned in closer and he whimpered in fear, only to be utterly confused as I unbind the bungee cords that secured him in place. I wind them around my thick, calloused hands, then shove them into the bag that Cole had abandoned behind me. "If you ever hurt one of my girls again, I won't just cut your dick off, I'll feed it to you. Watch you choke down the mass of fat and nerves."

Kevin stayed still in his chair, unmoving, and seemingly fearful of what would happen if he did try to follow.

35

I turned to leave the house, feeling the soft buzz of my phone in my jacket pocket. I rushed back to my car and and waiting until I had situated myself into the driver's seat before pulling out my phone. My face fell as I realized that it wasn't Val returning my call, but that it was my boss. My *normal life* boss.

A sigh escaped my lips as I saw the early crease of sunrise peeking from behind the skyscrapers. I slid the answer icon to the right.

"Good morning, Roy." I answered in the clearest possible voice that I could muster.

A gruff, joyous voice boomed from the speaker, "Good morning, Adam! You're up early again."

I rolled my thumb across my temple slowly and managed a wry chuckle, "Heh, yeah. Thought I'd get in a workout before I clock in."

"Ah, I see. I just wanted to talk to you, actually... I know today is your birthday." My recollection returns as I check the date. He was right... "A few of the guys and I are planning to go out tonight. We thought you may want to join us? You know, our special treat for being so helpful on the site recently?" His voice then softens, "I know life has been really hard on you since Conor passed..."

My heart thumped lightly in my chest as a warmth grew where bile usually churned. Roy had been like a father to me since I had started working as an apprentice under him, six years ago. If it weren't for him, I don't think I would be half the man I am today.

"Thanks Roy, that means a lot." I said with a gentleness to my tone.

"Does that mean you'll come?"

I brought my free hand to my lips and breathed out a soft sigh of deliberation as I glanced back to the frat house that was now seeing the first rays of sunlight.

"You know what... I'll come." I decided swiftly, throwing my knife down into the passenger seat. The slightest red outline could be seen peeking out from the back of the blade. No doubt, Kevin's.

A resounding cheer came from the other end of the call, and Roy's grin could be heard in his words. "Right then, I'll see you later!"

I nodded in a soft chuckle, "yes, sir!"

As the call ended, I stared down at my phone for a second.

The juxtaposition of the two lives that I lived during sunlight and then moonlight, was a shock on the system. By day I masquerade as a mid-level operations lead for a construction company that specialized in the manufacturing of prefabricated homes for impoverished families... By night, I drove around the queens of the Atlanta night-scene, provided them with protection, and then had to do some pretty fucked up shit.

I couldn't lie to myself, though, the idea of being appreciated by someone enough for them to remember my birthday, was a shock to the system. Not even my own mother could remember it now in this stage of her dementia ridden life... not that I can really blame her, that is.

I set my phone back down in the holder and turned on a gym playlist, pulled off from the college campus and headed toward my usual spot.

* * *

A cool breeze filled the stark white room of my shared office as I hunched over the load of paperwork before me. One would think that the boom in technological advancements would lead to an increased use of said technology for office work. But, unfortunately for me, thais is not the case.

Computers meant storage.

Storage meant data.

Data meant money.

Roy preferred to keep the costs low, and the cost of paper and printer toner was significantly more his speed than hard drives and servers.

The workday was now winding to a close, and despite the fatigue that was beginning to drill itself into my skull, I was excited for the monotony of paperwork to be finished for the day. Roy refused to tell me what we were doing that evening. In fact, I think his exact words were: "You'll find out when we get there, ya nosey little shit."

From behind me, the hallway grew loud with the rumble of approaching conversation, and then the door to the office swung open.

"Come on, you workhorse. Let's get this show on the road! We are going to the Varsity first… My wife will kill me if she finds out I am eating chili dogs without her." Roy roars and beckons me from my desk.

I laughed, and removed the reading glasses that sat lazily on my nose and I tucked them away for the day. I leaned back in my chair and crossed my arms, feigning a bit of birthday-boy defiance.

Roy's plaid shirt was tucked into a pair of dark wash blue jeans, a deep tan belt around his hips, and he had a pair of white tennis shoes on his larger-than-average feet.

A ring of cheers sounds as I stood and joined the group of men. These colleagues were hard, sweaty construction workers who then rallied around me, hooting and hollering as we made our way to the cars. I went to turn toward my work car, a simple Chevy Cobalt in silver, but Roy grabbed the sleeve of my thin navy-blue jacket.

"Ride with me. That way the surprise, stays a surprise!" He pulled me toward his Chevy Camaro with a big grin plastered across his stubbled face.

After the Varsity trip, the crew returned to their cars and peeled off in the direction of downtown. I raised an eyebrow as Roy began to follow wordlessly.

He continued to spout off stories from his childhood, talking about hunting and fishing and the lot, but then he parked outside of a shady looking nightclub... one that I was a bit too familiar with... The Midnight Raven.

When I glanced over at him, his grin spread ear to ear, "I know you would have protested, but everyone needs to experience the rush of a strip club once in their life. You're by far the most eligible bachelor in the company." Roy unclipped his seatbelt and ushered me inside.

The club entrance was dark, like always, with its quaint neon lights lining the walkways as the main entrance turned abruptly toward a large red pair of doors.

One of the other construction workers, a shorter black man named Warren, pushed the doors open and the sight of stripper poles, blazing neon, and crazy lighting came into view. It was busy, nearly full to bursting with the sleaziest men in the city...some of whom I recognized.

Roy guided our group of rowdy men to a large booth that had been reserved for us. It sat a decent distance from one of the central stages, a pole extending upwards from the center point of the stage. I stared at it for a moment before Roy nudged my shoulder and playfully tossed me into the booth.

"Hurry up, we're late! It's about to start!" He laughed.

I took a seat, watching as the lights shift from an electric blue to a deep crimson red, and then a heavy static of incoming music silenced the crowds.

"Ladies and Gentlemen," An announcer's voice rang loudly through the club, shaking the walls. "I proudly announce our star dancer in this hour. Please welcome to the stage: Miss Scarlett!"

The lights trained themselves on the center stage where we were sat front and center. A hush of excitement fell through the ground as the sound of grinding electric bass pulses through the speakers.

A rumble of enthusiasm courses through our group as the shadow of the stunning woman in a lace black suit sauntered onto the stage in time with the rhythm. She had these heels that had to have been at least eight inches tall, black platforms beneath the balls of her feet that were filled with glitter, and her long blonde hair was tied tightly into a high ponytail at the back of her head. On the first beat of the words, she began.

The rest of the room seemed captivated by her moves. Jaws dropped in awe as she struck her palm across her chest to pull out the beats of soft heartthrob sounds. But… I knew her. I knew this body. The curves than accentuated her in the most fan-fucking-tastic ways. The light obscured the features of her face, focusing on the lace suit-coat that she slowly undid to reveal her beautiful cleavage.

My eyes were locked on her as she sank into a deep split and then on queue with the music, she met Warren's eyes and then pulled the ponytail from her hair, launching the hair-tie in his direction.

Her golden locks fell graciously around her body, encasing her in strands of yellow that dropped with the down beat. The lights flashed off, plunging the world into darkness. I could feel my heart thudding hard against my ribcage as I searched the darkness. What was seconds, felt like millennia.

When the lights came back on, her face was plainly visible. There, climbing to the top of this pole, was Valentine.

I could feel my eyes widen as I stared at her, fixated. A protective instinct bubbled in my gut as I watched her dance.

It didn't matter how many times I had seen her, nor how many times I watched her dance. She took my breath away every time without fail.Roy smirked, jabbing me in the side with his elbow, "I told you. You've gotta experience the rush at least once in your life!" He cackles over the loud music... *If only he knew.*

My hands pitted into tight fists as I watched her every move.

The flutter of her eyes as she stared at other men, beaming her seductive smile. Her lips, those perfect fucking lips, I didn't think that I had ever really noticed how fucking perfect her lips were before.

Everything seemed to be going okay. The dance was stunning, and though I could feel my erection pushing lightly against the zipper of my denim jeans, I bit it back as I always have when I watched her dance. A man cannot help but react.

Then it happened, she scanned the crowd for a second, and then her eyes landed upon mine. Orbs of chocolate and honey... they darkened immediately as they fell on me and her face twisted.

I felt my heart practically stop, leaning forward slightly to catch the breath that her stare had just knocked out of me. I couldn't get the prongs that her gaze had sent meto release from my flesh.

She turned abruptly and focused her attention on the men who lined the opposite side of the stage, her smile now returning to its original brightness. With it, the warmth that her stare had offered me, faded into an icy cold silence. I sat back against the plush backing of the booth with a labored sigh.

Roy laughed, clapping a heavy hand on my shoulder, "I think she likes you."

"What? She almost just murdered me with her eyes!" I protested.

The lights come up again as Val's song faded and she vanished into the back. Once she was gone, I could feel the air rush back into the room and I let out a sigh of relief. Relief, that was, until I noticed that she hadn't left… she was standing just at the exit to the stage speaking with one of the other men from my group.

He jabbed one of his big fingers in our direction and then grinned widely. I saw him reach into his pocket and retrieve a wad of bills, which he slipped into her hand. Val… or rather… Scarlett accepted the bills and then accepted a hand from the man.

I narrowed my eyes in a half-menacing stare as he hoisted her down gracefully from the stage and approached our group.

Scarlett's brown eyes shone bright as she steps closer with a sultry wave of her hips. She knew exactly how to control her own body to get the exact rise she was looking for. The hornier the men, the more money they gave.

She shot a glance in my direction for half a millisecond, but I felt it like the sting of the whip on my cheeks as she then beamed at my boss. "Louis over here has requested a special dance for the birthday boy." She sang in a seductive tone, "so, which one of you is it?"

All eyes fell on me, and Roy grabbed both of my shoulders in his hands, pushing me from the booth to stand.

For a second, I thought she would turn away and outright refuse, but as if to save face, she smiled and turned to motion to a chair which faced my group of colleagues. "Please join me, Birthday Boy" To an untrained ear, that would have sounded like a plea… but I knew it was more of a warning.

I stepped anxiously toward the chair, and she placed her hands on my shoulders, pushing me to sit. One of Scarlett's hands lingered on my shoulder as she turned around to signal the DJ to start one of her songs, Kill of the Night by Gin Wigmore.

# The Birds and the Bees

# VALENTINE

What a sick and twisted joke.

At first, I couldn't believe my eyes when I saw Cain sitting in the audience at the Midnight Raven. I hardly recognized him in an outfit that didn't fully consist of black and leather. This was the place where I came to escape all of the fucking fiascos that Lorenzo Gonzalez put me through on a daily basis, and now my biggest thorn in my side was here in civilian clothing. His eyes stayed locked on me as I danced, and I was unable to escape them. I could feel them burning into the back of my head. And, I assume that this is all some ploy for him to be able to frisk me at a time that we have no business seeing one another.

I pushed Cain down into the chair, turning him to face this group of people who probably had no clue who or *what* he actually was…

With a hand rested tentatively on his shoulder, I turned to signal the DJ to start playing one of the most fitting songs for this particular dance.

As the beat picks up, I slipped further away from him and begin to step flirtatiously around the others, who in all fairness, seemed to really like Cain.

Eyes fluttering and hips swaying.

Then I double back to Cain and place my hands on his knees, bending to show his friends my ass while I stare menacingly into his eyes, "You asshole." I whispered curtly.

Something in his silence felt different, and his face held an expression that I had never seen on this wretched man's face before.

It was something almost kind. Though a disturbing level of alert protectiveness also hovered as it always seemed to in my presence. It was like he was on edge, waiting for shit to hit the fan…

I narrowed my eyes with the sound of Gin's raspy voice, and returned to the table of his friends behind me, crawling toward the older man who looked to be the boss. A seductive and saccharine smile on my face as I dipped, close enough to his face to feel his hitched breathing on my lips.

I smirked and pulled away, reaching up and tangling my hands in my hair as I stepped slowly back towards Cain. My gaze hunting and hungry as I searched his body.

Saying that he wasn't attractive would be a load of bullshit, I had danced on far worse looking men. But he… he had hurt me worse than any other man in my life had hurt me. It was his fault that I was so fucked up now. So, as I slipped my legs over his waist and rolled my hips into his very obvious erection, I found solace in the way he squirmed beneath me.

The helplessness in his eyes grew and he leaned his head back against the plush of the chair. It almost felt like he was pulling himself into it to escape my touch.

This only made me want to hunt him more.

I dipped my head low and placed my lips beneath his ear, "You're a fucking dick for hunting me down here. And then to have the nerve to claim it's your birthday"

He closed his eyes tight, his breath hitching as he whispered in return. "I-it is my birthday."

How fucking annoying.

I pulled my face from his soft tattooed skin and grabbed his brown hair, tangling my fingers in the small curls that I had seldom seen without the cover of his stupid beanie. I pressed his face into my chest as I rolled my hips against his, though I could feel his hands press against the flesh of my stomach, as if to hold me at bay.

I growl, "your friends are watching. They paid me. We better give them a show."

His head jolted lightly in a quick shake, "no. Rule number one-"

"Fuck the rules, Cain." I hissed, "We aren't Lorenzo's fucking pets right now. I told you to act like you fucking like this."

Cain's resolve wavered, and he allowed his hands to drop to his sides as I peeled away from him and turned myself in his lap. My ass was now perched against his erection as I leaned forward and pulled his large hands up to rest on my waist.

His skin against my own sent warm flutters into my chest.

As he grew more comfortable, I could feel his grip tighten... causing my own stutter as I watched the way his tight, ink covered hands were gripping at my skin.

I nearly missed my cue for the next move of my dance, because as I pulled away to release myself from his grip, they lingered for a few seconds longer.

The absence of his hands now felt irregular as I continued to dance for him. Despite all of the lust he had plastered on his face, that painful reminder of uncertainty lingered in his eyes, and I could tell he wasn't looking at me completely.

He never looked at me completely, not even when he was supposed to! *How could he see my need for him if he never even looked at me?*

*Need...?*

I couldn't even begin to think that I needed Cain... That I needed anyone...

Could it be the way his hands held so tightly to my hips?

Their lingering warmth as I pulled away?

Maybe it was the fact that I felt genuinely pissed that he only called me the once last night.

I glanced back at him.

His eyes still felt distant, almost as if his body coursed with exhaustion. *Had he even slept since last night?* I cupped his face in my hands and pulled him to look at me, the beading of a few sleep-hungry tears at the far corners of his eyes as he stared those dazzling blue's directly into my soul.

For a moment, the world stood still.

It took everything within me not to forgive him right there and then for what happened...

And I wanted to beam a smile at him...

But I didn't.

My smile was perpetually kept at bay by a raging anger that pulsed itself through my very veins.

My hands fell as the music slowly faded, and I turned from him without another word to toss some kisses at his friends, before slipping away towards backstage.

In that instant, when the stage door closed behind me, I had to press my burning flesh against the cool metal door, trying to slow my heart racing in my chest.

This wasn't fair.

Why did I have to feel this way, towards *him*??

Why did I want to see *him*?

I wanted to speak with him without anyone there watching us.

I pushed myself from the door and walked to the dressing area. I waved to Freya, the house matron, offering a soft smile.

"Hey Frey, I think I am gonna head home now. I'm not feeling too well." I said softly, dipping to undo the plastic clasp of my heels.

Freya pushed the side of her well-manicured afro with a soft smile, "No worries, gorgeous. Just make sure to put your house fees in the box when you go. Good job tonight." She snuffed a joint out in a bowl of ash before reeling me toward her for a hug.

She smelled of honeysuckle and weed.

"Thanks," I muttered, kicking off my heels and rubbing the skin of my ankles where they chaffed. I had left a black hoodie in my station along with matching sweatpants and a pair of simple black tennis shoes, so I pulled those on over the top of my lingerie and then packed everything else into my bag. I counted out my fee, and then stuffed it into the glass box by the door before slipping into the alleyway at the back of the club.

I slowly snuck around the side, mostly because I expected to see Cain's Charger parked out front, but there was no sign of it.

With a shrug, I began the swift walk home.

Once back in my apartment, I turned on a shower and reveled in the warmth of the water as it began to cascade down my skin…

At least for now… momentary warmth.

The faucet above me began to sputter and before I could react, ice cold water doused my whole body. I yelped and pushed through the cold to clear my hair of the soap.

I quickly shut off the tap and wrapped myself in a towel that definitely could have been more fluffy than it currently was, and then I slipped quietly to my bedroom.

As I closed the door, I saw both my phone and my charging smart watch alight with an incoming call.

I felt a surge of confusion as I saw Cain's name.

*This asshole just couldn't get enough of me.*

I rolled my eyes and slid the answer icon to the right, "What?"

There was an uncomfortable silence on the other end of the phone for a moment, but soon that familiar voice lifted through the speaker, "I wanted to say that I am sorry."

*Sorry?*

*Was he apologizing for ignoring me when I needed him?*

"Sorry for what?" I asked.

"You could have said no to the dance. Sorry if it made you uncomfortable."

I stared down at my phone with a disgruntled expression, pulling my arms into a cross pattern in front of my bare chest,

"Oh."

The silence resumed from his end for a moment before he mutters, "Lorenzo has a single client for you."

My eyes widened slightly, "is that the real reason you called me?"

"Um… yes?" He said with uncertainty.

I rolled my eyes, "Fine. What is the job?"

"Escort service." Cain mumbled, his voice hinting at annoyance.

"What?! I told him I wanted to be done with the escort service…", my lips pulling to a tight line as I listened further.

Cain pushed a soft sigh out, "I know, Val. I don't make the rules."

I frowned and tapped my screen, ending the call and immediately throwing my hands over my face. I felt the heat cross my cheeks as I pushed back the burning sensation of tears welling in my eyes.

I was so fucking fed up with this.

My phone rang again, and I answered it.

"Can you not take a hint, asshole?" I shouted into the mic, pushing back the scorching tears so they couldn't escape.

"Valentine…" Cain's voice was calm, soothing.

"What the fuck do you want, Cain? Can't you just leave me the fuck alone?" I whimpered.

He went silent for a few seconds.

It was a few seconds where the loudest noise I could hear was the heavy rapping of my heart against my ribcage.

"I will be outside your place in ten minutes. Don't worry, everything is going to be okay."

"That's so fucking easy for you to say. I'll be down in ten." I mashed the red button aggressively and threw my hands back over my face, allowing one soft scream of frustration to exit my lungs: to exit my heart.

I laid a few punches into my pillow and bit down hard on my tongue until I could taste a hint of iron.

Pain made it cogent.

I wrung my hands through my hair and sighed, wiping my tears away. No way in hell would I be able to get dressed and ready for an escort job in ten fucking minutes… but I guess I had to try.

I grabbed one of my long, especially elegant evening gowns that hung in my rickety closet. It was a dark forest green with sequins throughout. A deep v-neckline that brought special attention to my breasts, and a slit in the side that reached just above my mid-thigh.

Then for my hair, I decided to stick with a tight bun. It would be tidy and classy enough for most escort services.

I did a quick and easy makeup look with a smoky eye shadow and classic red lipstick, then searched for a matching underwear set to put on beneath my dress. The one I settled on was black leather with deep green lace. The leather straps encircled my thighs in cuffs and squeezed my skin lightly. I slipped the dress on over the top and then search for my black evening heels before making my way down the stairs.

Cain was precisely where I thought he would be, leaning against the hood of his slick black car. His usual black leather jacket was back, and his head was, of course, adorned by that stupid fucking beanie. I gave him a soft wave and then crawled into the back seat of the car silently.

Cain returned to the driver's seat and started the car, "You made good time today," He told me flatly, eyes still dead on the road.

"Thanks… I guess…" I returned, staring out the window.

"As I was trying to tell you, this is an older gentleman, about fifty. Just wants someone to go to dinner with him and talk." Cain explained this in a soft mutter that I could barely hear from my place behind him.

I nibble the soft flesh of my bottom lip as I opened the hidden email on my phone. Lorenzo's name was there in the unread messages section, glowing in bright white to show that I hadn't yet read it. The subject: Neil Flemings. I selected the email to open it completely and I began to read.

**Valentine,**

**Customer today has not paid for his tab with us for approximately three months. Normal service as usual, but spice up his drink enough for it to look like an accident. Use your brilliant skills as an actress.**

**Ciao!**

**Lorenzo**

I gritted my teeth and immediately deleted the message, eyes flicking up to see if Cain was paying any attention to what was going on.

Surprise, surprise… he wasn't.

Eyes facing clearly straight ahead and unmoving. Stoic and sharp as always. I opened my handbag and removed the small round compact from inside, popping it open to pretend I was checking the status of my lipstick, but I was truly more interested in the capsules that rested within the base of the compact.

I counted them.

Six thin white capsules with glittering silver dust within

them.

Content, I click the compact closed and return it to my bag.

"You never told me whether you were upset about earlier," Cain's voice ruptured through the painful silence like a cannon, pulling me back to reality despite a swelling of anxiety.

I turned my head to look at his rear-view mirror, and for once, his eyes fixated on mine. A warm sensation churned in my belly, but I quickly looked away. "I think it was a bit shitty of you to hunt me down when we weren't on shift."

Cain grunted and nodded understandingly, "I mean, it wasn't my choice. And I didn't know it was your night at the club."

Something in that statement made it feel a bit selfish that I was angry, but not enough to dissuade the anger. "When I saw Louis asking you questions, I knew something fishy was up…" he paused his words quickly and then suddenly pulled the car over to the side of the road.

Once we were stationary, he turned around in his seat to face me, "Listen, Val… those were my real-life people. My real-life colleagues… they know me when I am not being a broody asshole who's only personality trait is having a fancy four-door muscle car. I have tried my best to keep my identities separate. If Lorenzo finds out-"

"Don't worry." I cut through his panicked speech, "I am many things, but a snitch isn't one."

For a moment, he stayed in place. His cold blue eyes stared into mine as if pleading with me. But my eyes wandered from them and fixed for half a second on his lips.

Pursed.

Serious.

Unsure.

Then, he nodded slowly and returned to his previous position, his eyes soldered to the road as he focused on the journey.

The anxiety from Lorenzo's message reached a crescendo as Cain pulled up to the entrance of a fancy-looking five-star restaurant, stopping at the main entrance.

I crawled to the opposite door and then glanced back at Cain, "you didn't have to apologize, by the way. It is just my job." I assured, "Keep your fucking phone on. If this guy gets weird, I'm getting the fuck out of here."

Cain let out a soft chuckle and waved me away. "Right, Timer is set for an hour. I'll be in the area."

With a final, brief nod, I exited the car and plastered a saccharine smile on my face as I ascended the carpeted stairs to the host stand.

A young man with beautiful brown eyes and hazelnut-colored skin greeted me, "Hello! Have you got a reservation?"

The name from the subject header of the email flashes back to mind, "Yes! I am meeting a friend of mine here. Neil Flemings should be the name on the reservation."

The gentleman searched through their list that seemed to be about five pages long before his warm eyes finally brightened and he beamed back up at me, "Absolutely! Follow me this way, please!"

The host led me to the dining room.

Ceilings that reached heights I didn't quite expect with sparkling crystal-filled chandeliers with gold accents. I couldn't help but think of Lorenzo's gaudy Victorian mansion as I stepped over the red carpet with golden floral patterns toward a small circular table with a single unoccupied chair.

In the other, a man who didn't look anywhere close to the age that Cain had described, sat quietly over a glass of water reading a menu as it was propped against the long white tablecloth.

He looked to be about fifty… his salt and pepper hair fading to slightly more salt than pepper. His face was growing more wrinkles by the day, but only in the areas you'd expect: crow's feet from years of laughter and creases in his brow from decades of contemplation.

"Mr. Flemings," I called to him in a sweet voice.

His eyes shot in my direction, a kind, generous smile covering his deeply dark skin as he stood. He smoothed down his light tan tuxedo and extended a hand to me.

The host bowed his head and took his leave as I gracefully accepted the handshake. They felt strong, and sturdy, with a slight oil from a nicely perfumed cream. A perfume that lingered on my fingertips as I pulled from his grasp.

"Please! Call me Neil!" He sang, moving to pull the chair out for me.

This man was on par with most of the men who requested personal escort services.

A lot of the time, they just wanted a pretty girl to sit with them and just talk.

I graciously accepted the gesture, sitting down in the chair as he pushed it back beneath me and then returned to his own chair.

"It is lovely to meet you, I have heard that you are one of the most sought-after girls that Lorenzo has to offer." Neil spoke excitedly as he looked me up and down.

A feigned blush rose to my cheeks, and I giggled lightly. "I don't even know where to begin with that. I would say that we have a fair few girls that are just as competent as I am."

A smile broke apart Neil's full lips, flashing the sight of his perfectly white teeth, "I think it lies in more than just competence. You're a stunning woman."

"Thank you, Neil. That is very kind of you." I said sweetly, a dash of uncertainty peaking in my chest.

Neil waved down one of the servers, beckoning them over to the table. "Would you like something to drink, Miss Valentine?" A woman with dark brown hair approached us.

"Oh, yes! A glass of soda water with lemonade!" I cheer brightly, the server nods, writing this on her notepad.

"Soda water with lemonade?" Neil asks with a soft chuckle.

I grin wider, "Yes! I visited England a few years ago and their lemonade is different to ours. It's carbonated. I learned that I prefer it that way."

Intrigue pipes up in Neil's eyes and he nods, "I think I would like to try that as well, actually. Two of those, please."

The server added a note and then smiled kindly, "I will have those out for you in about five minutes. The bar is slightly backed up at the moment." I nod with a contented smile and place my hands in my lap.

Everything was going according to plan.

"So! Tell me about yourself, Neil." I mused, placing an elbow on the table and leaning my chin to rest on my palm in an intrigued poise, my brown eyes fluttering.

As most people do when you give them space to discuss their favorite topic: Themselves.

Neil straightened and crossed his legs, leaning back lightly in his chair. "I am an ornithologist. I am head of the research division for the Atlanta Ornithology Association. I have been working towards a Nobel Prize."

I widen my eyes, "So you get to study birds all day, for fun?" I asked, a superficial look of awe growing on my cheeks as I peeked up at a sparkling chandelier above us, "maybe I should quit my day job."

I catch a glimpse of the server approaching with our drinks and I quickly return my attention back to Neil.

"Have you decided what you'd like to eat?" I asked, pulling my own menu open to have a look.

Neil nodded, "I am quite interested in the carbonara."

A soft hum escaped my lips as I nod, my eyes falling upon the pasta section, "I do love a good carbonara…"

He grinned, "Go for it! You look like you have never seen a carb in your life. My treat." I smiled.

The waitress returned to our table, placing two glasses of sparkling lemonade in front of us. "I squeezed some extra lemons in as well so that you didn't lose any of the flavor because of the dilution!" She beamed, "Are we ready to order?"

Neil piped up, "Yes, absolutely! We have both decided on the chicken carbonara. Please let the chef know that I am severely allergic to shrimp."

An alibi.

Their conversation continued as I reached into my purse and retrieved the hidden compact.

I pulled out one of the silver capsules, and just as Neil's attention returned to me, I cracked the capsule open and emptied the contents into my drink.

"What are you doing?" he asked, an eyebrow raised.

I glanced up at him and put a grin on my face, "I know it is a bit silly, but I think anything that looks like a magical potion tastes better."

I pull the paper sheath from over the straw and plunge it

into the drink, swirling it around. The liquid slowly begins to sparkle, a glittering sheen throughout.

"My mom used to make my drinks like this. Said it was the only way she could get me to drink anything other than chocolate milk. It's tasteless, but it makes your tongue all glittery. Wanna try?" I took a quick sip through the straw, enough for the liquid in the cup to visibly decrease, and opened my mouth, allowed my long, slender tongue to roll from side to side inside my mouth. My eyes locked with Neil's knowingly, as he took a very brief moment to examine the sparkles on my tongue, now visibly shifting in his seat.

Neil's eyes gleamed for a moment in curiosity, and he shrugged, "Why not?" He returns, grinning.

I opened a second compartment in my compact and re-trieved a capsule with a slightly darker shade of glitter, "This one has gold shimmer mixed in. It'll look cooler in the lemonade." I giggled innocently and then cracked the seal of the capsule along the rim of his glass. I focused my eyes onto his and smiled seductively as I empty the contents into his drink. I removed the paper from his straw and kissed the side where he would be drinking from before plunging it into the drink, mixing and until it had the same effect as my own.

Neil watched me in silence, the dark skin of his cheeks reddened slightly, and he cleared his throat. Beneath the table, he adjusted his position again.

He was under my spell.

Right where I wanted him.

"Tell me about birds, Mr. Nobel Prize Candidate." I mused, leaning back in my chair and pressing my triceps against the sides of my breasts to push them out to make them slightly more obvious. The crease of my cleavage was accentuated by the motion.

He cleared his throat and reached for the glass of sparkling lemonade, taking a quick swig before his face changed to one of delight, "You know, Miss Valentine, I think you are onto something here. Maybe I'll mix glitter into all of my drinks from now on." He chuckles as he tried to compose himself.

"Um… right… birds." He hummed, pulling at the lapel of his jacket to smooth it out.

"I am actually incredibly interested in tits…" His eyes widened, "The- the bird! Paridae's!" He corrected. The previous richness in his cheeks deepened as the blush crept down to his neck. "You know, chickadees?"

I allow a subtle laugh to fall from my lips and I nodded slowly.

"Yes… a lot of my work is currently surrounding Carolina Chickadees and their mating routes. In Atlanta in particular, we have noticed a steep decline in their numbers in the past few years." He cleared his throat again, glancing around. "S-s-sorry, I must be nervous. I have a tickle in my throat."

He reached to take another sip before sighing with relief. "We have some pretty groundbreaking research that is coming out soon."

My smile softened at his words, and I nodded along, "You know, Neil. There is no shame in being interested in tits." I leaned forward with my elbows once more on the table, a brandishing that made him stutter once more.

"No! No. You're right… and you sure have lovely… tits." He ran a hand through his hair nervously.

"What would you say if I told you I had something that may… prepare you for what happens after this dinner?"

I reached to remove a small pink box from my bag and place

it on the table.

Neil looked down at the box, then his eyes flashed back up at me.

"Open it," I laugh in a sultry tone, pushing the tiny box toward him.

The man looked at the table in contemplation for a moment before lifting the cardboard lid.

Inside, resting on a bed of pink silk, was a small purple silicon remote with two buttons.

One plus.

One minus.

His brown eyes widened and deepened with something akin to lust as he stared at the remote. He removed it from the box and stared at it as it rested in the palm of his hand.

Watching him squirm like this filled my void with adrenaline as I felt it being pumped inside of me.

I grinned and leaned back.

"Go ahead, Neil. Nobody will know but you…"

His lips parted once more; a smile now displayed on his face that would have melted any normal woman. His thumb hovered for a second over the plus, rubbing at the edge of the soft silicon button before pressing down.

"Hmmph," I laughed, "you'll need more power than that to get a reaction from me." I placed a hand over my lower belly and lifted one of my feet to graze his leg beneath the table.

Neil's face twisted into one of desire and he pressed it three more times.

The vibrator on the lace panties began to pick up speed slightly, sending pleasant vibrations directly to my clit. I signaled to him that it was working by biting down on my lip and allowing my eyes to gloss over.

Before we could speak again, the server approached us with our food, ready to eat.

Neil took this opportunity to increase the vibrator's speed once more, and I shuddered in pleasure.

This pleasure was real, but it felt wrong.

It always felt wrong.

Vacant.

I ran the heel of my shoe along the seam of his lower pants leg, nodding gratefully to the waitress as she vanished.

Neil smirked, "you handle these things well. I like an experienced woman." He hummed in a low tone.

I grin, my teeth poised against my bottom lip in a sultry bite as I lean forward to grab my fork. "It takes skill to really show a woman what pleasure is." I hummed lightly, but I pressed the front of my pelvis against the chair to position the vibrator a bit closer. I pulled a forkful of the pasta to my lips and began to suck a dangling noodle from my plate, eyes still locked on Neil's as I let the white sauce spatter all over my lips.

He gritted his teeth and increased the speed on the bullet between my legs and I let out a whimper of a moan, just loud enough for him to hear.

"You should eat. The faster this is done, the faster you can get what you want." I reminded him, my eyes pointing down to his waist.

This seemed to encourage him to eat, and he lowered the level of the vibrator by three, but I could still feel it.

It still sent me jolts of occasional pleasure.

Soon though, that tickle in his throat became a stabbing sensation that burned throughout his throat.

My date began to struggle and looking around with wide, panicked eyes.

My own eyes widened at the first sign of his struggle, "Neil?" I ask, putting on my best concerned tone. "What is it? What's wrong?"

His face began to break out in hives.

Bumps rising over his cheeks with quick succession.

He stared into my eyes, clutching at his throat, the other hand clutching the remote tightly.

He started to choke.

"Help!" I called, tears brimming around my eyes. "Somebody help! I think he is having an allergic reaction!"

Neil tried to stand, but his weight was too much for his weak knees to bare and he collapsed… with his thumb pressed tightly to the plus button. The vibrator surged, jolting to the highest vibration that sent coursing electricity through my body.

I yelped, partially out of pain between the bursts of pleasure as my cheeks flooded with tears.

I scrambled to the floor and pulled him into my lap as the concerned patrons and staff huddled around us.

I managed to retrieve the remote, turned it off and shoved it deep into my bag. I sat there with Neil in my lap, trembling both from the adrenaline, and the overwhelming sensation that the vibrations had caused.

Before I knew what was happening, an ambulance had arrived and the paramedics were seeing to Neil.

Servers and patrons doted over me.

The server for our table looked quite distraught, "I must have given you the allergen free one…" She muttered morosely, tears highlighting her own delicately painted features.

I clasped a hand over her shoulder, now standing free of Neil's weight, "you cannot blame yourself. Things like this happen." I pulled her into a tight hug.

"He's dead!" One of the managers suddenly shouted, and I turned to let out a pained wail.

Suddenly, two arms encircled me, clutching me tightly against a very large chest.

This smell.

I recognized this smell.

Earthy and smooth.

It was Cain.

He shushed me and slipped me effortlessly out through the front door. The rest of the guests seemed to not notice as the commotion continued to grow within the bar.

"What are you doing? You could have fucked this all up?" I ask sharply, snapping out of the act that I had just put on.

Cain's arms dropped from around me and he stared at me for a second, "time was up. Get in the car, blondie." He said gruffly. I frowned and opened the front door of his Charger, first throwing my bag to the floor and then myself getting in.

Cain grumbled something under his breath before slamming the door shut.

The echoes of Neil's helpless gags now filled my mind, facing me constantly.

That heat that coated my body as he collapsed to the ground was unreal.

I could feel the need to climax buzzing on every single nerve ending as I sat there in Cain's front seat.

Frustrated in all of the worst possible ways I could have possibly been frustrated.

Cain got into the car and slammed his own door shut, "Fucking pain in my ass. You should have messaged me; I would have gotten you out of there sooner." He griped.

I sat, silent.

I wasn't supposed to talk about my real purpose behind this particular job… nor the other jobs that Cain believed to be *just* escort jobs.

I folded my arms tightly against my chest as the sound of Neil's choking and sputtering continued to fill the vacant space in time.

Cain looked over at me, his eyes narrowing, "Why the fuck are you sitting there like *I've* just ruined your day? Do you even want me to do my job?"

Genuine tears began building up behind my burning eyes, but I looked away from him.

These tears were real.

They were so…*so* fucking real.

I clenched my fists so tightly that I swear I felt the skin split beneath my manicured nails.

I didn't care anymore.

I did not give a fuck anymore.

"Fucking speak to me, Valentine." He said, his words tipped with a poison of their own.

I shook my head, turning my body away and toward the door of the car.

He extended a hand, placing it on my shoulder and then pulling. He turned my body back to face him and then pinned me aggressively to the seat.

Waves of confusion washed over me as a whimper escaped my lips. I stared up at him, eyes the size of headlights as I was fully unaware that my forced-away tears had begun to streak slowly down my cheeks.

Cain's eyes were thin, and his face was stern, but as he noticed how heavily my chest rose and fell, and as he saw those genuine tears rolling down my face, he relaxed.

He removed his hand from my shoulder, and he sank back.

The softness that overcame his figure was overwhelming, and I wanted nothing more than to dive into his arms and soak in whatever comfort he could provide me with.

"He… he overloaded my-my vibrator." I whimpered in a low whisper, placing a hand between my legs where the warmth still glowed in a slowly fading buzz. My cheeks burned a crimson blush that spread over my skin and painted me in blotchy pink speckles.

A blush joined Cain's face, and he cleared his throat, but as the tears fell continuously from my face, I curled back into myself, "I hate this." I mutter. "I hate this. I hate this. I hate this."

Sobbing with no end in sight.

Burning rivulets of pain, tortured anguish, and loss.

"I want to die, Cain. I want to die." I began to hyperventilate, "Please," I turned to look into his eyes, "Please kill me, Cain. You're the only person I trust to do it right. Please… please" The words poured out of me like water as I felt the desire to go on waning faster than one could be expected to cope.

His blue eyes softened and a pain flashed into the pupil at the center of his eye. He reached out to me and cupped my cheek, flicking his thumb with some sort of snake tattooed on it across the damp skin to collect tears and then push them away.

I wanted him to do it.

To grab my other cheek and snap my neck.

End it right there.

But he didn't.

# Pinned

# CAIN

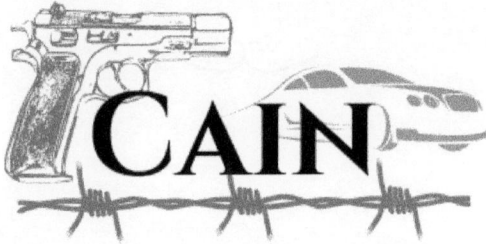

"Fuck... why don't you just tell Lorenzo you're fed up and you want to leave?" I almost choked on the words as they left my mouth. Anger soaked onto the point of each word as I looked away from her face.

Her cheek was damp against my palm.

Valentine shook her head quickly, letting a heavy sob roll from her chest. "He'll hunt me down like he always has... I can't escape him."

Her face was red, streaks of black mascara carving chasms in the painting of foundation that she had applied.

This fucking asshole. All he ever did was take... but as far as I was aware, Lorenzo was no slave trader...

He wouldn't hold anyone against their will unless they wanted something from him.

Behind the car, blue and red lights began to flash as police arrived on the scene. I glanced at Val, only to see that panic swarmed in her eyes and her hyperventilation had transformed into quick, labored gasps for breath.

The heavy thud of a thick knuckle crashed against my window, and I angrily turned to see an officer with a large metal flashlight pointed into the car. I narrowed my eyes and pulled my hands from Valentine's face before pressing the button to roll down the window.

"You're parked in front of the building. We need the access point," A big greasy man shouted at me, his face obscured from view by the bright light of the flashlight.

"Alright, alright! Get that fucking light out of my face." I raised a hand to block thebeam from my eyes as I turned the ignition and began to pull forward away from the restaurant.

Val's panic seemed to slowly subside as we gained distance, and she grew extremely quiet in the passenger seat next to me.

The pressure of annoyance and frustration bellowed out of my chest in a sigh as I ripped off my beanie and tossed it into the back seat, running a hand through my hair to fluff it and remove some of the trapped heat.

"Why can't you escape him?" I asked, placing my left elbow against the door of my car and leaning my chin on the palm of my hand, eyes still forward.

She was silent for a moment, her own eyes staring straight ahead wordlessly.

"Well there must be a reason-" she cut me off.

"Someone killed my best friend." She muttered softly, I could perceive her moving slightly, facing away from me again to stare out her window to watch the scene around us changing.

A nod, I understood that wholly and completely.

"My brother." I said in a silent bond that we now shared. "I have been trying to find who killed him... Lorenzo is the best private detective in the state... so I signed away my life."

She turned her head slowly back to me, those beautiful honey-brown eyes settling on the side of my face as she tried to read my expression. I turned my own head slightly in response and gave her a kind nod.

"Same... I want to find the person who pushed her in front of a train two weeks before her baby was born." Valentine closed her eyes in a slow, labored blink and then faced her head straight to the road again

She seemed exhausted, "Lorenzo makes me..." Her voice caught in her throat, like there was something she wanted to say but her body told her not to.

I allow her the space to think, but I couldn't help but wonder what the hell Lorenzo had made her do. If it was anything like what he made ME do... it was sick and twisted.

She shifted in her seat again as she saw familiar surroundings growing nearer, "We are going to Lorenzo's house?"

"Yeah, he said he had something for you," I said plainly.

Val became quiet once again.

I loathed the silence that always managed to confine us to our separate worlds. This force that pushed us so far from one another.

The air smelled salty, like the scent of sweat and tears. My mind flashed back to earlier when I had pinned her against the seat. The way she looked at me like I had never seen before. *Fear? Hatred?*

And yet, as much as I loathed the silence, I think that I also reveled in it.

I craved it.

This space where we didn't have to speak, we could simply exist.

People make such a habit of filling up empty space with pointless chatter. I liked that we didn't have to persist with pointless chatter. That we could simply be.

That silence persisted as we entered the driveway to Lorenzo's home, and then continued as we walked through his front door. An energy radiated off of Val like the way steam rolled off of a hot coal.

Something exciting yet reserved.

Halted.

I approached Lorenzo with a blank expression as Val slipped away from us and toward the dining room where Mags and Sasha were perched in expressive discussion.

"She looks fucking terrible," Lorenzo commented gruffly, jabbing his meaty thumb in Valentine's direction.

Annoyance punctured a crease in my brow, and I rolled my eyes, "Well, she might be slightly traumatized. The client she was escorting tonight went into anaphylactic shock right in front of her. I don't blame her for being a bit of a mess right now."

A sparkle of something menacing grew on Lorenzo's face, and he smirked. "Neil Flemings is dead?" He inquired.

I shrugged, "not sure. The ambulance rushed him away, but Val has been fucking beside herself."

I lifted one of my dark tattoo covered hands to tousle my

hair, realizing that I had abandoned my beanie in the car during my frustration.

"Heh." Lorenzo glanced over his shoulder, "she looks like she is haggard for another reason," his slimy lips peeled apart to tighten into an equally slimy grin. "If you have tried to soothe her in any... special way... you've done it wrong."

Valentine turned around to face us, her arms crossed over her breasts as she stared at me as if I were the one to say something so vulgar.

Her honey-brown eyes ate me alive.

"He never touched me. I had given my remote to Neil, and when he fell, he mashed the button of the remote to the highest setting."

I found my eyes glancing at the fabric of her velvet green dress as it rested in a perfect triangle form above where her vibrator would have been attached, feeling a lump grow in my throat as I thought things that I definitely shouldn't have been thinking.

When I reached her eyes again, she was staring into my soul. Daggers shooting deep into my pupils... like she wanted to stab me from the inside out.

Lorenzo laughed, a booming sound that ricocheted about the room in a cacophonous round before settling into our ears, "HA!" He shouted, throwing a hand over his eyes, "I thought you smelled like desire. I was thinking Cain had finally fucked you!"

I could feel the heat of her gaze explode into flames as I pinched the bridge of my nose, attempting to call my senses to return. *Thank fucking God that Mags and Sasha were there.*

"I think she'd be glowing if Cain finally got the nerve to fuck her." Mags pipes up. She threw a handful of her braids over

74

her shoulder as she grinned at me.

Okay.

Maybe not.

Valentine growled and turned away from us, sitting down in the chair next to Sasha in a huff.

"Why not make yourselves useful and help her get off?" Lorenzo called to the group of women, "Sasha knows how to make *anyone* cum."

"Could you not be so vulgar?" I snapped, gritting my teeth.

Lorenzo turned to me with an eyebrow raised, "they are quite literally sex workers, Cain. If they can't cope with the vulgarity, then maybe they are in the wrong business."

The door behind me opened and another set of women entered the house, their driver following swiftly behind. Cole and his band of troublemakers.

These girls had clearly just returned from a show. Their faces blush laden and satisfied. The overwhelming sensation of eyes upon my visage was crushing as one of the girls approached me with a pouty look on her face.

"Cainy!" Her high-pitched, childishly sweet voice rang out. She wrapped her arms around my bicep and pressed her breasts against my arm enough to expose the majority of her skin. She smelled of a familiar chemical smell akin to something that wanted to be a strawberry, but missed the mark by a few hundred notes of scent.

I glanced down at her, a hot pink bob of hair framing her chubby face. "Hello Callie," I hummed at her softly.

Her face brightened, "I missed you so much! You should drive *us* more often." She cooed, pushing herself to stand on her toes to gain access to my ear, "you'd have a lot more fun with *us*."

The sound of her purr as she breathed into my ear filled me with a world of conflicting feelings. Against all of my faculties, I still had to adjust myself to avoid any sign of the erection I had taken up.

"Thank you, Callie. I am sure Cole thoroughly enjoys your brand of fun." I hum, glancing back at my friend. Today's Hawaiian shirt had rainbow-colored cats on it.

I turned my glance to see my usual patrons at the dining room table. Each of them stared me down with their arms crossed as they watched the College Park Canaries surround me. The bouncing of silicon-filled breasts pushed harshly against the thin strings of their lingerie.

Cole stepped a bit closer, "come on now, girls. Let's leave them to their discussions. We can have a debrief in the lounge."

Callie's eyes sparkled and she seemed to go rabid at the sound of this. Something told me that a debrief wasn't exactly a debrief in the traditional sense... Maybe it was the way Callie and Sophonie rushed to clutch at Cole's unbuttoned black and rainbow-colored shirt, or the way he lustfully gazed at them as they slipped into the next room... but most definitely, it was the sound of their moans mere seconds later as Cole managed to already slip his cock into Callie.

"Record timing," Sasha grunted, rolling her eyes. "When I see girls like that, I remember that I am not here for the same reasons."

Lorenzo snorts. "You prude bitches," he rolls his eyes, "I've watched you finger fuck Mags until she squirted so hard that we had to pay to clean the client's carpets."

Sasha frowns and leans bashfully against Val's chest.

"It's performance art. We aren't meant to actually enjoy it. We just have to put up with it while the crowd enjoys it,"

Valentine posited.

Mags nodded quickly, "wait till those girls have to escape the clutches of a meth-fueled dickhead with a shit-smearing kink. I'm sure that bubbly shine will leave them just as it has left us."

"All that matters is that the clients are pleased." Sasha mumbled.

Lorenzo rolled his eyes, "Man, you really need a fucking vacation." He snorts, "speaking of which... I have a job for you that is going to require a bit of beach time."

In an instant, all three of the girls seem to brighten, sitting up straight as they listen to Lorenzo's next words.

"One of my buddies is having a bachelor party. He is willing to pay for your travel in exchange for one of the usual shows as well as a private foursome." Lorenzo smirks, "I assume your contraception is fully up to date?"

Val's eyes darken, but the other two stand up quickly, cheering excitedly.

"I thought we agreed that the Vixens didn't do private foursomes." Val spat, her brown eyes darting to the side.

She was uncomfortable. I could feel it. Not because of any disdain for sex in general. It was clear that she liked to fuck. It seemed she was less so concerned with the act and more so the purpose. Her eyes lifted from the table, and they searched for me, as if hoping I would step in and stop Lorenzo from making her go through with it.

But I couldn't do that.

She knew better than to wish that of me.

"You are to do as your told, Valentine. Your insubordination recently is absolutely appalling." Lorenzo's nose turned up in an annoyed grimace. "If you do anything to risk this job's completion, you will be restricted for two months."

"Two months?" She shouts, pushing herself up, palms flat on the table.

"My word is final. You will let him do, as he pleases, to whomever in the party, that he pleases to do it to." Lorenzo frowns, "you are a *sex* worker. Not an exotic dancer. Not a stripper. a SEX worker."

Valentine's lips pursed, pulling her plump pink lips into a thin line as she closed her eyes and drew in a deep breath through her nose. "Fine." She grumbled behind clenched teeth.

Sasha placed a kind hand on the small of her back and smiled at her, "it is gonna be okay, Val. We will all be there."

I glanced at Lorenzo, a rage bubbling in my core from the way he spoke to these girls as though they were just shit on his highly polished shoes. He seemed to catch my thought and grinned at me.

"Don't you worry your pretty little head, Cain." Lorenzo sneered, "you have a ticket as well. My best girls have to have the best protection."

I narrowed my eyes, "I do have a life outside of your fucked-in-the-head jobs, you know."

"Yes. And if you would like to keep it that way, you'll listen to what I tell you to do." He snorted, stepping out toward the lounge as Cole's moans became perceptible once more.

A resigned sigh left my lips and I glanced at the girls. The energy which I had used in the past 36 hours was fading faster than I was happy to admit, and I could feel my eyes grow heavy.

"Shall we go?" I queried to the three women who most frequently inhabited my car.

Val was the first to stand.

She walked quickly past me, her shoulder knocking lightly against mine as she went by. She then ducked straight out the front door. Mags and Sasha were kinder, smiling at me as they joined.

The girls crawled into the back of the car and Sasha rejoiced as she found my askew beanie resting on her seat, "Oh goodness! Is this a present from our dear Cain himself?" she giggled, pulling the knit cap over her head, sitting on the edge of her seat, legs dangling out of the door.

"I'm Cain. I'm all big and bad and covered in tattoos. I like to complain about everything and make people uncomfortable." She mocks in a comically low voice. An action that summoned forth from me a small smile. Respite from the annoyance we had encountered already this evening.

I decided to get a bit of revenge, stooping my head below the ceiling of the back seat, a hand pressed firmly against her chest as I pin her to the seat. Her head rested in Mags' lap as I smirked down at her and plucked my beanie from her head.

She mutters, a flustered blush growing on her cheeks as she sits up and rushes to adjust herself in the seat, "Stop. You'll make Val angry," she whined.

The smirk deepened, and I ripped the door to the passenger side open, dipping inside and placing a hand onto the shoulder-rest on either side of Valentine's head, staring into her eyes in what could be mistaken for lust.

Val's surprised stare shifted mysteriously between my arms as I locked my eyes on her. The streaks of black still caked into her makeup plainly visible as I lean in close to her and growled into her ear, "did that make you angry?"

Mags and Sasha squealed, flapping their hands about mischievously as they watched in wonder.

I expected Val to push me away, to chastise me as she always had. To frown and cross her arms. To call me a dickhead or an asshole. But she just stared. She stared right at me with a dazed look. For a second, I thought I had hurt her.

Suddenly, the blank, doe-eyed look on her face melted away and the Val that I knew returned to the surface. She growled, pressing her palm to my chest pushing me away, "Fuck off, Dickhead!"

I obeyed her order, pulling back with a nervous chuckle.

I shut her door slowly and walked around to my side of the car.

I stood there for a second before finally slipping into my own seat.

Val's vacant expression that had lingered throughout the night, was gone now. A mix of frustration and annoyance now poised on her face, but the energy in the car was much brighter.

In the backseat, Mags and Sasha were giggling like children. A welcome change from the severity we had just been through in the outrageously opulent den of our master.

I cranked the engine and set off toward home.

# Get Your Roommate to Do It

# VALENTINE

Rattled was an understatement.

I sat in abject silence for the majority of the ride back into the city.

Cain had been thoughtful enough to turn on music for us, allowing Mags to control the playlist. It was a cycle of show tunes and early R&B. Bouncing from one extreme to the other.

As the end to Defying Gravity was punctuated by Sasha's songbird voice, the gentle synth piano of Boyz II Men began to strum. Mags took over with her stunning voice that was destined to sing along to songs like this.

I could feel the strong thud of my heart in my chest as I

nibbled the back of my lip. As the car pulled to a slow stop in front of Sasha and Mags' apartment, I leaned forward to pull my hair free of the bun that had grown quite messy by now. My long blonde hair fell behind me, and I sighed from the relief. I clutched the bobby pins tightly in my hand as I removed them, running my thumb over each as I listened to the crescendo of "I'll Make Love To You".

The car again began to move, and I had hardly even noticed that the other girls had got out.

I pulled myself back to reality from that place inside of my mind where I had disappeared to. Peace and tranquility juxtaposed by the low decrease in volume as Cain clicked the steering wheel's volume control down.

"I wanted to apologize, if I upset you earlier." He mumbled in his usual deep voice.

He never tells me what he is apologizing for.

*Is it the way he didn't stand up for me in front of Lorenzo?*

Even though he knows that I hate actually participating in the act of giving my body to a person.

*Was it that he didn't push the Canaries away as they fawned over him?*

"Why?" I asked flatly.

He glanced over at me for a small elapse of time, his eyebrows furling, "You make it seem like I have to apologize for existing."

*Well, THAT would be nice.*

I crossed my arms and exhaled sharply through my nose.

He rolled his eyes, "I'm sorry for pinning you to the chair. You looked terrified of me for a minute. I didn't mean to scare you, I just wanted to tease Sasha and Mags."

My face flushed lightly, a pink dust covering my cheeks.

"Oh." This response triggers something in Cain… Something between frustration and anger, and he leaned his head back against the headrest behind him.

"You're such a pain in the ass," he reminds me, "why can you never be pleased with anything I say or do?"

"Have you thought about the fact that everything you say and do is annoying?" I shot back, turning away from him, if only to conceal the fact that my blush had spread to my neck.

Cain was silent, his foot growing heavier on the accelerator as the Charger roared a bit louder. I glanced at him in the reflection of my window and groaned loudly.

"Fuck!" I threw my head back against my own headrest. "I can't fucking think straight!"

His eyes flash to me briefly in intrigue, but he didn't speak. My apartment was approaching fast, and I couldn't help but squirm. The discomfort from being blue balled by a dead guy was wrecking my brain.

I snatched my handbag from the floorboard and pulled the little silicon controller from within it, staring at it as Cain pulled into a parking space near the entrance to my building.

I nibbled the back of my lip for a moment before I gathered every bit of courage within me.

"Cain," I started plainly.

He looked over at me, disengaging the ignition.

"Will you-" my voice cut off as I begin to feel panic surging within me, "I- um…"

Cain sighed but didn't speak.

I groaned, "I can't do it myself." I muttered, the blush now heating the flesh of my chest, "I just… can you please help me?" I handed him the remote.

The man beside me sat silently, holding the remote in the

palm of his hand.

His eyebrows raised in confusion as he ran his thumb along the silicon body.

After a moment, he looked at me... like really *really* looked at me.

His thumb hovered over the button.

"Why do you want *me* to help you?" Cain asked, his words felt different. I don't think I had ever heard this tone from him.

*Was it confusion?*

*Embarrassment?*

I clasped my hands together in my lap and stared into the velvet on my evening gown, "I- I don't really know..." I muttered truthfully.

He frowned, reaching over to grab the cuff of my wrist.

My heart leapt in anticipation... but as he turned my palm to face the sky, he placed the remote in my hand and folded my fingers around it.

"Get your roommate to do it."

I don't know what came over me, but I snatched my bag from the floor and shoved the remote into it. Without another word I was out of the car and halfway across the walkway to my building, bounding up the stairs. By the time I could bring myself to glance over my shoulder to where Cain had parked, he was gone. Like a ghost.

I hadn't even heard the motherfucker leave!

*Get your roommate to do it???*

*What the actual fuck?*

Most men would leap at the opportunity to have a girl cum in the passenger seat of their car. I narrowed my eyes, rummaging through my bag to find my keys.

They weren't there.

I groaned, feeling the heat of annoyance replace the blush as I pounded heavily on the door to my unit.

Finn ripped the door open.

"Fucking hell, Becca!" Finn shouted, rubbing his forehead. His brown hair covered his ears. He looked like an extra from The Walking Dead. Sunken eyes and pale skin with obvious blisters from picking.

I grimaced, shaking my head, "Sorry. I forgot my keys."

"Don't do it again. I was just about to go to bed." He grumbled, walking away from the door and then stalking his way through the house to his bedroom.

The sound of his door finally slamming was somewhat of a relief.

I softly pushed the front door to the unit closed and secured the latch, then finally stepped through to my bedroom.

I locked my door and placed my handbag on the vanity chair.

I sat down on my bed with a huff, throwing my hands over my face in despair.

A brief reflection in the handheld mirror reminded me of how disgusting I looked at this moment, so I grabbed a pack of makeup wipes and returned to my place on the bed.

*Why was Cain such a dick?*

*Why would he pin me to the car seat when he knew I was sexually frustrated?*

All I could think about was the way his jacket sleeves covered the tattoos that I had seen so clearly earlier in the day.

*The sound of his voice as he growled into my ear...*

He had no idea what he did to me. And he had no idea how much I hated him for it.

I dragged a wet wipe across my face, feeling the cake of products peel away with each swipe. Eventually, the majority of it was off, but I felt exhausted with the idea of cleaning my face completely, so I tossed the pack of wipes on top of the the cluttered vanity beside me. Then I grabbed my smart watch from where I had placed, pulling it once again over my wrist.

The velvet of the dress was beginning to itch.

I stood, pulling it off over my head and staring at myself in the small circular reflection of the mirror. The leather and lace lingerie set complemented my body, and despite the darkness of residual eyeliner around my eyes, I felt pretty.

An image flashed to my mind of earlier at the Midnight Raven.

The way that Cain's hands held me at a distance.

Pushing me away... but I still felt the sting of his hands on my hips. How he gripped at my flesh until I ripped myself from his grasp. The hunger in his eyes as I danced for him.

My core grew warm, and I glanced back at the remote that peeked out from within my bag. I plucked it up and stared at it.

"Will you help me?" I whispered into thin air.

*Yes*

I heard his voice mutter in the recesses of my mind. A smile arose on my face as I closed my eyes.

"I'll strip for you," I mutter, placing the remote on the plush top of my bed and grabbing my phone.

I scrolled through Spotify for a minute before finally selecting a song. As I set my phone down on the dresser, a soft thumping beat began to emit from the speakers. I swayed to the tune of the song, imagining Cain sat at the edge of my bed. His steely blue eyes examined me... His hands caressing

87

my skin...

I removed the bralette, allowing for my boobs to fall.

I grabbed at them, squeezing their soft fat and twisting at my nipples.

Before long, I was slipping off my panties.

As I did, I removed the vibrator from the pouch where it lived and tossed the clump of lace and leather to the floor.

A towel was at the end of my bed.

I grabbed it just in case, laying it out across the blankets. I crawled on top and spread my legs, pressing the plus on the vibrator at the same time.

I imagined Cain holding it in his palm.

His thumb brushing over the soft silicone.

I pressed the lightly buzzing vibe to my throbbing clit.

The music swelled lightly as it grew to a crux.

My chest rose and fell and sweat began to bead in tiny droplets across my skin.

I bit my lip, imagining Cain between my legs. I increased the vibrations by three.

Toes curling, I imagined reaching my hand down to tangle in Cain's brown hair... *without that stupid beanie.*

I reached that hand down, circling the soaking wet entrance to my pussy as I spread my lips with my fingers and plunged them deep inside myself, curling to search for the clump of nerves to which I was so accustomed..

The vibrator felt amazing, but I couldn't help but pretend that my fingers were Cain's.

Reaching inside of me.

Searching me.

I added a third finger and felt a moan raise to my lips as I hooked my fingers within me, scooping them as I pulled them in and out.

I imagined the way that Cain's shirt would tighten against his broad shoulders as he fingered me, my heart leaping as I swore, and I could almost see him there for a moment…

My eyes rolled back in a lull of bliss as I placed the vibrator on my pelvis and reached for the remote, quickly increasing the speed to the max as it had been earlier in the evening. As it crashed in an unbearably strong vibration against my clit, all I could think of was Cain's voice.

A deep growl sprung to memory.

*Did that make you angry?*

"Yes!" I called out in a hushed, breathless tone. I could feel his smirk against my skin, the pressure from his touch.

I could *smell* him.

I plunged my fingers deep inside of myself as I could sense the impending release of an orgasm. The music on my phone beside me stopped as my phone began to ring, the watch on my wrist began to hum.

I glanced over at it, cheeks hot and red as I fingered myself aggressively.

It was him.

It was fucking Cain!

Ecstasy flooded my body as I locked my eyes on his name. The slowly pulsing white letters of the call went unanswered. I let out a harsh moan, feeling my walls tighten quickly around my fingers.

The climax took hold of my entire body, and before I could move enough to switch the vibrator off, the call had declined.

I yearned for his touch. His voice.

But as the orgasm faded, I felt the weight of the world fall down upon me. I cleaned myself up, pulling on a pair of fluffy pajamas and crawling underneath my covers.

Cain hadn't tried to call me again.

The frustration and pressure had been released, and I felt the eaves of sleep fall upon me.

\* \* \*

The rays of early morning sun shone through the thin glass of my bedroom window, but the brilliant display of daylight wouldn't be the cause for my waking. Instead, it was the rapturous noise of shattering glass from the living room.

I shot straight up in bed, my heart thumping against my ribcage as I threw the blanket off of me.

A moment of silence was followed by the sound of angry shouting.

I clutched my hand over my chest as I pushed the door open to my room just in time to see Finn with one of the kitchen chairs over his head. Glass covered the floor from the coffee table I had bought not even a month before.

Finn saw me, turned, and launched the chair in my direction.

"What the fuck!" I shouted, dodging the chair as it smashed into the wall beside me, partially embedding itself into the plaster, partially disintegrating.

Finn rushed, and a wave of panic coursed through me.

I pressed the screen of my watch repeatedly, just barely managing to press the shortcut I had programmed into it that would send out a message to my emergency contact as Finn tackled me to the ground.

"You little shit!" Finn shouted, his face red in a blackout

rage, "How fucking DARE YOU touch MY phone! It is ruined because of you!"

Confusion poured through me as my watch began to vibrate, but Finn ripped it from my arm, throwing it across the room.

I screamed from both fear and adrenaline, and I noticed the taste of blood in my mouth; I must have bitten my tongue as I collided with the ground.

"I-I didn't touch anything! You fucking PSYCHO!" I screamed in return, clawing at his chest to get him off of me.

I managed to get him good in the face with one of my acrylic nails, and he reached up to grab his face, peeling away his attention from me.

Finn reeled back and grabbed a lamp from the end table beside the couch, lifting it above his head before bringing it crashing down against the back of my skull as I tried to crawl away.

I felt the sudden explosion of pain, a warm wetness growing, and saw the shards of broken glass fall around me...

and then I saw nothing...

*Her Laugh...*

# CAIN

The office was abuzz this morning at my day job.

Preparations for a massive overhaul of the company and an upcoming exposition to get our names on the map were underway, and I was running damage control with the internals.

You see, the thing about working in a company full of blue-collar men with skin so tanned that it is essentially leather is that they are extremely *EXTREMELY* hard-headed.

And this was coming from a man who drove around three of the most hard-headed, hot-blooded women that he has ever had the pleasure of meeting. Days like today made me wish I was in their company. They would at least pretend to like what I had to say.

As the operations assistant, I had to facilitate everything that these men did.

That is, a whole buttload of bullshit work that they genuinely had no desire of accomplishing. These men came to this company to get away from the physical labor and normal mindset of construction sites.

Less time roasting in the sun, sitting in a nice cushy warehouse that paid far too much for the air conditioning bill. And here I was, about to tell them that they have to give up their nice cool air-conditioned workspace and build these homes directly onsite.

I had already received a fair amount of abuse this morning alone, so I decided to sit in my quiet little cubicle to nurse the biggest possible mug of coffee that I could find, that didn't entail taking the pot straight off the drip machine.

Bitter.

Old Beans.

Watery.

Weak.

I choked it down alongside a simple blueberry old-fashioned cake doughnut, my favorite.

Roy was off for the day. Convenient, as I had multiple things to discuss with him. For one, I didn't think he would be too pleased that I would be needing Friday off to accommodate the whims of my psycho, self-obsessed nighttime boss.

On the other hand, I had put in more work for this company than any of these other fuckers who tried to claim that they pulled their weight. The very least that he could do was give me a day off.

As I brought the final bite of my doughnut to my lips and clamped my jaws shut around the fluffy dough, I heard a commotion out on the warehouse floor. I pushed myself away from my desk and stepped toward the door to peek out and see the issue.

A few men were getting ornery about the way a fixture had been fitted. I grinned and rolled my eyes, but then felt my pocket buzz.

I retrieved my phone from my pocket and froze immediately, eyes fixing to the single word that scrolled across the screen beneath the name tag for Valentine.

*Focus*

*Her safe-word?*

*What kind of fucking joke was this?*

I narrowed my eyes, feeling a crease form above my brows as I swiped through my contacts to find the Vixens, each of their numbers was starred. I selected Val's and waited.

It rang… and rang…nothing.

"The person who you are calling had a voicemail box that has not been set up yet. Please try and call again later. Goodbye." A robotic voice spoke.

I rolled my eyes, my annoyance growing. *What was she playing at?* She never messaged me first. She hardly even answered my calls.

The more I deliberated, the more anxious I became.

Something *must* be wrong.

I dipped back into the office and approached my supervisor. A tall man with a white cowboy hat, strong southern features indicative of his heritage. A real 'John Wayne' of a man.

"Lionel," I said, dipping down to his height as he sat leaning back lazily in his chair

Lionel turned to me slowly, his eyebrows raised in a silent question.

"Would it be possible to take my break early today? I got a message from my mother's nurses, and they need my help with something."

I pulled the excuse out of thin air, hoping he would understand.

The grey-haired man hummed, "You best be back before One" he pronounced it: wuhn. "I have shit to do today." Lionel tipped his hat, "give yer mawma a good long hug."

Relief cascaded over my face, and I nodded quickly, turning to grab my denim jacket from the back of my chair and raced out to my Cobalt which sat vacant in the parking lot.

Val lived about a twenty-minute drive from here. I knew all the roads in the Metro-Atlanta area like they were the back of my hand, so all I had to do was get in the car and go.

By the time I arrived, I was struggling.

She hadn't called me back and she hadn't messaged to say that she was okay, or that it was a mistake message…

I didn't know which unit was hers, only which building… but even that could have been a facade that she kept up to keep her unknown identity intact.

I climbed up four floors, and then the instant I arrived at the top floor I became keenly aware of exactly where I needed to be. The first door on the right was ajar, the doorframe cracked as if someone had burst through it already.

The scene within was carnage: A large glass coffee table had been absolutely demolished, only the legs of it remained unscathed. There were several holes in the wall, a chair that had been launched was stuck halfway into the wall, legs now protruded into the hallway.

There she was...

She was in the hallway, face down with blood oozing from a grotesque wound at the back of her head.

My jaw dropped as I looked at her for a moment, eyes wide. Nobody prepares you for this type of situation. I had cleaned up full-scale murder scenes and I was still so incredibly unprepared to see Valentine unconscious on the floor in her pajamas.

"Val!" I shouted, rushing to her side.

She was breathing and had a pulse, but she had been knocked clean out.

Around her head, shards of glass were strewn. Most likely the weapon used to attack her.

I gathered her in my arms, pulling her close to my chest. As I lifted her, glass fell from her bloodstained blonde hair.

I grimaced as I noticed her eyes beginning to open. Val looked at me through a glassy film, whimpering.

"Cain?" she mutters, hardly perceptible.

"I'm here, Val. Don't worry. I'm gonna clean you up and then get you out of here."

I pressed my palm to her cheek. "I'm going to get your things. Where is your bedroom?"

She coughed weakly, lifting a hand to point to the first bedroom. I hoisted her up and placed her gently on the edge of the bed for a moment.

"You've gotta stay with me, Valentine. Okay? I'm right here, but I need you to stay awake." I urged, ensuring that she was secure before grabbing one of her duffels and throwing clothing into it. I didn't even look to see what I was grabbing, I just packed.

When I turned back to her, she had pushed herself to stand

and was able to grab her phone, clutching it closely to her chest.

"Is there anything else you need?" I asked, hooking my hand under her arm for support. She pointed to a lockbox that was just out of direct line of sight. I grabbed it, stuffed it into the bag, and then stepped back to her tosupport her wobbly steps.

"We need to call an ambulance... Who did this to you?"

"No... I'll take care of everything myself," she told me, a pained look on her face. "I just need the dizziness to subside. He didn't hurt me too badly."

"Valentine there is a gaping hole in the back of your head," I reminded her.

As we approached the stairs, I held the duffel over the railing and dropped it into the grass below.

"What the fuck, Cain?" She mutters, annoyance flooding her face.

I ignored her protests and scooped her into my arms, carrying her down the three flights of stairs, finally placing her back on her feet once we hit bottom.

"I could have walked. You didn't have to throw my shit." She complained.

The desire to roll my eyes was immediate. I scoffed and walked to the duffel of clothes, "It is literally 90% fabric, Princess." I sigh, scooping up the bag from the ground. I motioned her towards my car. "I swear to god if you get blood on my white seats, I'll never forgive you."

Her face twisted into a grimace, and she narrowed her eyes, "Why did I think you were going to be anything other than a dick about this?" She grumbled.

It brought a soft smirk to my face, "I'm joking. My seats are black. I'm not an idiot."

She rolled her eyes as she sank into the passenger side.

I threw her things into the back of my car and joined her in the front. A massive exhale escaped my lungs as I soaked in what had actually just happened. To think I was literally at work half an hour ago, thinking that life couldn't get worse than asking your boss for Friday off.

Valentine was quiet, a pained wince displayed on her face as she leaned against the passenger side door.

"I'm taking you to a hospital," I said plainly, throwing the car into reverse.

Her eyes opened wide, and she shook her head "No, Cain. I don't have any insurance."

"Nobody has insurance. You also don't have a real name, so how the hell are they gonna find you?" I laugh, driving toward Emory University Hospital. "I only have twenty minutes left on my break or else I would stitch you up myself."

She glanced at me for a moment.

Something new was in her eyes.

Shame.

"You left work to come check on me?"

I narrowed my eyes, "Of course, I left work to check on you. Off duty or not, I still have to protect you. You message me your safe-word without any context, and I figure that something has gone very wrong. Obviously, I was fucking right." My voice took on a tone it hadn't taken on since I had spoken to my little brother Conor.

It had now been four years since his death.

Val sank into herself, no longer bothered by the prospect of seeing a doctor. "Thank you," she said softly.

I felt a smile find my face, and was slightly relieved that she could do anything other than bully me. I reached across with my right hand and gently squeezed her knee. "Don't worry about it. It's my job."

"Just your job?" She asked.

I thought for a moment, then looked at her. I hadn't quite had the time to think about the request she made of me last night when she was getting out of the car. All of this felt like some sort of evil mind game she was playing.

"I would have come to check on you regardless of whether it was my job or not. You are a priority to me."

She remained silent, though something in her silence told me that she felt content.

As we approached the emergency room at Emory University Hospital, she glanced at me before getting out. This time a soft, thankful smile on her face.

"Hey," I gently grabbed her wrist. She turned to me once more. "I will be here as soon as I finish work. Don't you dare leave with anyone other than me. Capisce?"

She smiled lightly and nodded, "Capisce…"

My hand squeezed lightly around her wrist, "Please call me if anything comes up. I will try to check in with you, but I do have a massive meeting."

A genuine, beautiful laugh escaped the woman standing in front of me, and her smile brightened. I almost forgot that I was talking as the sound made my heart leap. She nodded, "I got it, I'm a big girl. Remember?" She rolled her hand lightly, placing her fingers around my wrist as well, "Thank you, Cain."

I didn't even have the ability to hide the blush that had encroached upon my face, staring blankly at her as I nodded slowly.

She slipped from my grip and walked slowly toward the

urgent care department. I watched until she disappeared inside, then began my drive back to work. I don't know what changed with her just now, but the way that she smiled at me. The warmth in her hands as she touched my skin… the way that she smiled at me.

AT me!

*I don't know what I did to transform that stubborn, brazen, bratty woman into that gorgeous, friendly goddess… but I will be DAMNED if I don't do my absolute best to do it again and again for however long she graces me with her presence.*

# Bachelor's Paradise

# VALENTINE

Hartsfield-Jackson's domestic terminal was abuzz with the everyday chatter of people who were ready to vacation. To get away from their everyday monotonous lives of waking up at eight a.m. and coming back at five p.m.

Smiling families bound for Florida, heading to Disney, or to the beaches. Rolling sands and the opportunity for a nice day of reading by the surf.

I sat waiting at the gate for the incredibly tiny plane that would take us from Atlanta to Savannah in an hour and five.

Beside me, a disgruntled Sasha combed through her fire-engine-colored hair with her fingers. She was restless and agitated by the bustle around us. She was wearing a hoodie from Pinewood Studios, cut lazily directly across her diaphragm and showing the pink band of her sports bra beneath it. A pair of grey knee length leggings hugged tightly to her curves, even now as she sat with one knee up, leaning into Mags' lap.

Mags wore nothing more than a lime green tube top that matched her eyeliner and lipstick, and a pair of black booty shorts with lime green sandals. Her hair was done differently now; box braids changed for a new weave with gold strands sprinkled throughout.

It suited her... *everything* suited her.

I stared out at the large glass wall that overlooked our tiny plane. *Was it so hard to fuel and clean such a small vessel?* A tin-can for us sardines.

There were about twelve other people here for the same flight. I could genuinely taste the claustrophobia now. An hour of complaints from absolutely everyone that they crammed into that thing.

The smell of feet.

The desire to gag snatched the air from my lungs just thinking about it.

Cain sat beside me, one leg crossed over the other as he clutched a Kindle in his hand, reading over something that he didn't want to discuss. Even my persistent fawning over the subject granted me no closure.

Ever since the morning that he came to my aid, I felt the world between us becoming brighter. Lighter. Not that I had sought out his presence, but I also didn't push him away when he was near like I usually would.

I had stayed the past few nights on Mags' couch. A comfy enough situation, but not a permanent one. Finn had tried to call me, but I dared not answer with any of these three within earshot. He was usually nasty when coming down from highs, and I didn't feel like putting myself into that situation.

I stood, smoothing the white, floral-patterned fabric of my sundress as I stepped along the miles of window. My hands clutched tightly behind me as I hummed the tune of a song that I probably couldn't even recite the words for.

To think that we were literally being flown to where we could have driven in four hours. Rich people spend pointless money on pointless things... like three horny sex workers and their bodyguard.

"Boarding flight Three-Seven-Eight now. Please make your way to the gate." A robotically muffled voice rang out.

I turned on my heels and returned to where I had just been seated. I stooped to grab my carry-on, but Cain snatched it from the ground first with a childish smirk.

"Hey!" Sasha whined, "You could at least carry ours, too!"

His face brightened and he walked to where Sasha sat, dipping to grab her and Mags' bags by their handles, "come along, pillow princess."

She gasped dramatically, throwing her hand over her chest, "ME? A pill- Mags, can you even believe what he is saying?"

"If anything, you're the pillow *Empress*," Mags teases, pushing Sasha off so that she could stand for boarding. My giggle lifted my spirits, looking up just in time to make eye contact with Cain.

In an instant, both of us looked away as if to pretend as though we hadn't just stared into each other's souls.

Sasha raced towards the gate, leading us down the tunnel and toward the plane. She sat at the window on one side, then Mags in the aisle seat, Cain took the next aisle, and I was positioned at the window.

Sandwiched between Cain and the plastic, or fiberglass, or whatever-the-fuck material, was enough to make any woman swoon, but I tried my best to relax and not think about how comically large he was compared to me and the other two ladies in the row.

"I like the wig you choose," Cain mutters softly, dipping to a whispered tone. He didn't look at me, just stared straight ahead.

The blonde wig I wore contained streaks of red and brown throughout, and though it looked like a natural color, it definitely wasn't my natural color, but it was necessary for now to hide the scarring on the back of my head.

I smiled lightly, turning slightly to face him, "Thank you… it is odd to see you in anything other than long sleeves."

I glanced down at his forearm. Plainly visible from the unbuttoned short-sleeved Hawaiian top that he must have borrowed from Cole. He wore a white tank top underneath it and a pair of blue capris.

For the first time, I was able to start to study the artwork that he'd had done on his arms. The one nearest to me showed a stunning red koi fish that was swimming amongst cherry blossom petals and lily pads. Around it, artistic renditions of samurai swords, katanas, and various eastern-inspired art pieces.

The other, however, was different. His left arm was covered in various things, from pieces that made little sense, to those that seemed to be quite impactful. Sprinkled amongst the artwork were the kind of things that you'd expect an impulsive or inebriated teenager to have done. A melting smiley face. Various knives. Swear words.

But his hands intrigued me the most. He had intricate pieces done on his hands that depicted them as being metal within; mechanical parts that were broken up by wires. He also wore two silver rings on his right hand, but none on his left.

"They were expensive," he said softly, turning his arms over and outstretching his hands, "But I like them."

I smiled slightly, but as I gleamed a view at the girls across the aisle, I sighed. They were sitting close together, talking, seemingly having a good time. Mags had an iPod with a pair of headphones split between the two of them. They were having fun.

A man walked down through the center of the aisle and stopped directly in front of our row. He wore a red tracksuit with white piping down the sides. He had fluffy blonde hair and a very handsome face.

He couldn't have been more than twenty-five.

His hands slap down on the chairs on either side of the aisle as he beams.

"Ah! The Vixens!" He cheered, "Glad you could make it. My name in Ronny."

I waved sweetly, and the other girls cooed at him in a sexily. Sasha had a large red lollipop in her mouth that she pulled slowly from her mouth as she fluttered her eyelashes at him.

Ronny seems to waver slightly as he blushed like a child. He offered a small wave at Sasha specifically.

"Anyways," he cleared his throat, glancing at Cain by my side, "it was lovely to meet you all. I am sure we will see each other again very soon." Ronny winked at me, his long eyelashes catching some of the residual sunlight from the windows of the plane. The wink forced me to blush, so I settled back into my seat.

Maybe… just maybe, Lorenzo is right. Perhaps I need a vacation to sort out my head and get me back to enjoying what we do.

In two hours' time, we had landed in Savannah and it was now Cain's turn to take over as the driving once more. Ronny handed him the keys to a rental car and gave us directions to the hotel on St. Simons Island.

As we pulled into the villa's property, the smell of salt water and sulfur was pungent in the air. Spanish moss hung from the branches of threes that must have been centuries old.

Sasha began to squeal excitedly as she saw a massive pool full of young, attractive men of various shapes, sizes, and colors. It was no surprise that the pair of girls from the back of our car, now darted out to the poolside to fully immerse themselves in the party.

I giggled lightly at my friends, "you're going to leave us to carry all these bags to the room?" I called behind them. But it was a call that fell on deaf ears as I turned my eyes back to Cain.

He had already started to unload our luggage.

A serious expression fell upon my face, "Hey, you're a driver. Not a servant." I said, reaching to grab my own bag from the top of his pile. I plunged my hand into the trunk and retrieved Mags' rolling suitcase that held our gear.

Cain's expression softened and he gave me a wordless nod in appreciation.

It was so weird. Ever since the other day, I noticed Cain's silence so much more. I kind of *wanted* him to speak to me…

So, this walk that we took from the car's trunk toward the hotel bedroom, felt awkward in a way that I couldn't express. I found myself brainstorming topics of conversation, but anytime I'd try to speak, my throat would clench and I would end up just shrugging it away.

When we arrived, Cain pushed the room door open. There were two rooms in this suite. One contained a king-sized bed and the other contained two queen-sized mattresses. A communal section of the suite offered a large, beautiful bathroom equipped with a tub and shower. There was even a kitchenette, and a small sectional which would comfortably host the four of us around a small flat screen TV.

Cain hummed, "Awkward sleeping situation." He chuckled.

I shrugged lightly, feeling the reins of a migraine pulling at my temples. The doctor said that these kinds of migraines were normal following a concussion. They could persist for months.

"I think that us girls are more than content to share beds with one another, you can have the master bedroom."

When I glanced up at him, his blue eyes were drinking in my appearance. Narrowed slightly in concern.

"You doing okay?" he asked, placing one of Sasha's bags on a table near the door.

I thought for a moment, debating whether or not to tell him the truth.

He stepped closer, placing the painted skin of his knuckles against my forehead, "I think you're a little warm. Is the travel getting to you?"

His touch…

This was the first time that he had intentionally touched me where I didn't feel the sting of disinterest.

I had felt a soft heat radiate around my wrist when he grabbed me as I went to leave his car for the emergency room. That heat now flickered upon my cheeks.

"I think I am just a bit exhausted. We have been travelling all day and I have a bit of a headache."

Cain nodded one time, very slowly. "I will keep an eye on the others. You take a shower and a nap. I will come wake you up an hour or so before you need to be ready for the show."

I nibbled the flesh of my lip lightly and nodded graciously, "Thanks." I raised my hand to rub lightly across my blush as if to conceal it.

He watched me for a moment.

Wordless and contemplative.

I felt embarrassment surge within me as I tingled between my legs.

"Why are you staring?"

He seems to reconnect. Like he was a program that had gone offline. "Are you wearing makeup?"

I narrowed my eyes and shook my head, "N-no. I'm not."

Something sparkled in his eyes, "I love your freckles," He admitted, a grin appearing on his face as he winked, "maybe you should leave them showing tonight."

"Cain!" I threw my hands over my face to hide the fact that I had turned bright, beet color.

He laughed softly and placed a hand on my shoulder, "I'm slowly proving to myself that the delusion of you not hating me, might just be true. Get some rest, Val."

He pulled away from me, walking toward the door.

*What did he mean?*

*Of course I hated him... Right?*

*When you hate someone, do you get butterflies in your stomach when you catch them looking at you?*

*Do you wreck your brain trying to find topics to talk to them about just so their voice breaks through silence?*

*Does their touch... or even the idea of it... send you absolutely crazy?*

I absolutely hated Cain. With every fiber of my being.

*Right?...*

The throbbing of my migraine pulled me from my existential crisis, and I decided (for once and ONLY once in my entire life) to do as Cain said. Starting with a shower. One that's warmth persisted throughout the entirety of the act. It soothed the ache at my temples, but hardly touched the ache further within.

Then I crawled into one of the two queen-sized beds with nothing on but a loosely wrapped towel. The balcony door was slightly ajar, and I was lulled into a peaceful nap by the soft wave of warm summer air through sheer curtains that captured their heat, and then displayed it in a gorgeous orange shadow throughout the room.

\* \* \*


Just as he had promised, Cain woke me an hour and a half before the show started. His hand rested across my bare shoulder blade as he rubbed gentle circles into it.

I blinked, my eyelashes fluttering as I stared up at him.

Part of me felt happy to see him, another part not so much. "Fuck, why is it that you only bring me bad news?" I groan, pulling a pillow from the top of the bed to cover my face.

A chuckle left his lips, but it was obvious that even he wasn't entirely sure what I meant. He shrugged, "The other girls are getting ready. You should too." He moved to push himself off the bed, but as he did, his hand grazed the exposed skin of my upper thigh.

I sit up quickly, "Hey! Watch it, Buster!"

"Sorry!" He threw his hands up in a show of innocence. His eyes instantly locked onto the chair seated in the corner of the room, his eyes now shadowed by his hair.

I looked down to see that my towel had succumb to gravity and was now pooled around my waist, leaving my breasts fully exposed.

I narrowed my eyes and crossed my arms, "You act like you haven't seen Sasha eating out my pussy! Now you can't even look at my tits?"

"Do you want him to?" Sasha piped up, "Look at your tits, I mean." Her smile was mischievous.

My face grew bright crimson, and I shook my head, "N-no! That's not what I meant."

"I think that is exactly what you meant, girl." Mags adds, "You want him to ogle, you dirty bitch." She smirks.

Cain took this chance to escape out room, closing the door quickly behind him. I frowned as the door closed and Sash grinned.

"Oh my god." She coughs out an evil laugh.

I shoot her a daring glance. "What, Sasha?" I asked.

Her and Mags exchange a glance, "are you actually fucking him? You look like you're literally dripping wet right now just thinking about him checking you out!" Mags said, and Sasha grabbed my knees, forcing them apart to check for herself.

"Oh my god, you are!" She roared with laughter.

"What?" I throw my towel between my legs, "No. No, we aren't fucking." I muttered, but these girls knew me far too well.

"Well duh. That's why you're still so wet," Sasha explained matter-of-factly.

Mags grinned and tossed me my outfit for the evening, "Do us all a favor, Val. Use this to our advantage. We need to rock this Ronny guy's world tonight, and if you fuck him with the level of frustration you've got pent up right now… I think you may get us extra pay."

I frowned, "Mags, I hate the sex part."

"Well, honey. It's a bit too late for that. You're already a sex worker. You've gotta work your sex like the boss ass bitch that you know you are, now. And then tonight when you're horny as fuck because we didn't let you finish, you can slink into that King-sized bed of his and rock Cain's world."

I fanned myself, feeling hotter with each moment… and more wet.

I looked down at the outfit for tonight. We were all dressed as Playboy bunnies, but our one-pieces were sparkly and red like Jessica Rabbit. There was even a little slit in it which is where the next thing Mags gave me would come in. It was a butt plug with a fluffy white bunny tail on the end. It would poke through the slit in the ass of our one-pieces.

Sasha giggled, moving to straddle my waist as she covers my face in makeup.

She then offered Mags the same treatment.

I slapped her ass as she crawled away from me, finally pouncing upon Magnolia.

This was the happiest that I had seen everyone in a long time, and I couldn't help but think that something was going to go very wrong… but, as the night progressed it seemed that I was mistaken.

We paraded ourselves onto the stage; Cain announcing our general rules. We made it through most of our sets like a breeze. But I felt like things were going too smoothly… Maybe

Cain was watching me too closely?

No... anytime I glanced his way, his protective stare was all-encompassing. He watched each of us for any sign of distress, but it just never came.

And as the time grew closer for us to disappear into Ronny's room, I felt a tether lodge deeply into my chest.

I stopped at the entrance to Ronny's bedroom. The giggles of my friends could be heard amongst the gentle smack of occasional kisses. I glanced back from the doorway to see Cain standing at the end of the hall.

Protective.

Defensive.

Like always.

I felt the string pull tight around my chest; the thuds of my heart's beats were so loud in my ears that it was almost painful. I wanted him to call to me, to ask me to stay...

But as I met his eyes, they settled upon me with a gentle nod, as if he was sending me away. I nibbled my lip and turned back into the room, closing the door behind me.

Ronny sat on a mountain of pillows, watching Mags as she fingered Sasha while sucking at her clit. He smiled, and beckoned me over to sit on his knee. I did, perching there like a dainty fairy. He reached up to grope one of my breasts and I felt a swell of anger building in my chest...

But then Sasha's words echoed in the aching chasm that was my mind. She was right. I needed to fuck Ronny within an inch of his life tonight.

I sank to the floor beside him, placing a trail of pecks along his legs as I slipped my hand beneath his loose cotton trousers. His cock was hard, and thick. I began to move my hand along the shaft, squeezing lightly to add sensible pressure.

He tensed beneath me, shuddering out a moan.

Sasha pulled away from Mags and crawled seductively towards me. She grabbed my hips and flipped me to face Ronny, between his knees now. Sasha between mine.

As Sasha started to slip her fingers into my wet pussy, I removed his dick from his trousers and began to suck lightly at the tip, making use of my own pleasure as I moaned against his erection. I matched Sasha's rhythm.

Then just when I thought Ronny was fed up with my mouth, I pulled away and pushed him back against his throne of pillows, angling his tip at my entrance and then crashing down on him with full force.

Mags sat on Ronny's face, rolling her pussy against his licks, and Sasha grabbed his hand, making him rub at her clit.

I closed my eyes, allowing my moans to roll out of me.

I imagined that this was Cain's cock.

Cain's cock throbbing deep inside of me, and filling my soul.

I was nearing my release, but Sasha knew me too well. She pulled me away from him and took her own seat on his cock, bouncing with far more agility due to her smaller frame.

I stepped away, my pussy absolutely dripping. Ronny was no longer aware of my existence, so I grabbed one of our smaller dildos and positioned it at the entrance to his ass. With a bit of help from my juices that remained on Ronny's skin and a bit of lube, I pushed the dildo inside of him until he began to moan in pleasure.

It wasn't much longer before he bucked his hips, crying out loudly against Mags' clit as she ground away. I thrusted the dildo against his prostate as Mags traded places with Sasha to finish him off. She clenched her walls tight around his cock, and Ronny moaned even louder, though it was muffled beneath the soaking wet pussy of Sasha that now rolled over his mouth.

With one more final thrust into his prostate, he let out a wail and grabbed onto Mags' hips, holding her in place as he filled her to the brim with his cum.

She pulled herself off of him and allowed his cum to drip out of her, splashing onto his stomach.

That's where we left him, sitting there, completely covered in his cum and our juices.

Our job here was done.

We wrapped ourselves in dressing gowns and exited the room. Cain stood waiting outside as we returned, though his gaze was heaviest on me. He walked us back to the bedroom and waited for each of us to shower before escorting us to dinner.

Surprisingly enough, the other girls managed to scurry away.

It was like they planned this.

# Cain's Valentine

# CAIN

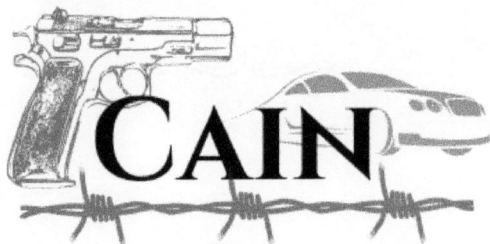

The dining area was busy tonight. Some of the more inebriated guests for the bachelor party seemed to be really
interested in the girls. Sasha and Mags had vanished into
the sea of eligible rich bachelors as soon as we entered the
dining hall, but Val stayed close. She seemed to hover in my
shadow like a duckling, seeking the safety of my gaze. This
wasn't natural for her. If anything, Valentine was usually
the ringleader of shenanigans. To see her so timid was
concerning... but I know that she had a migraine earlier. If the
session with Ronny was rougher than she expected, maybe
she was suffering more than she let on.

She was sitting on the opposite side of a small round table, a glass of deep red wine in front of her and she nibbled on a piece of a cookie. Her eyes stared beyond the crowd to where the ocean was visible. The pale grey rumbling against a deep blackish-blue backdrop speckled with colorful blinking stars.

"Hey," I dipped my head low enough for my words to carry through to her ears, "I was walking around earlier during your nap. There is a nice terrace that steps down onto the beach. Maybe it's quieter over there."

Her brown eyes met mine for a second, flecks of gold floating amongst the ocean of deep amber. She shoved the rest of her cookie into her mouth and nodded sweetly.

I grinned and stood up, leading her toward the quiet terraced area. A dark, isolated corner of the resort that held little attention from the partygoers. Far too distant from the music and merrymaking… but perfect for a bit of a private chat.

"Would you like me to stay with you or did you want to be alone?"

Val turned to me, her eyes communicating a subtle panic. She glances at a pair of lounge chairs packed closely together in the far corner of the terrace, then back to me, "please stay."

A hint of desperation seemed to cling to her words as she walked to sit in the closer chair. Her thin skirt that reached her knees blew lightly in the wind against her steps. I watched the outline of her hips as it glowed within her skirt. She sank to the chair, curling her legs behind her and patting the other seat with a soft smile.

I joined her, sitting in the furthest chair from the entrance to the terrace. It was peaceful out here. Quiet.

Before us, waves crashed lightly on the shore in tiny ringlets that pulled at the sand. The moonlight cast a gentle glow below the deck. The soft, lulling sound of distant birds and the faint sound of music from the party rang through the night.

Valentine closed her eyes, pulling a deep breath in through her nose and holding it in her chest for a few seconds before exhaling through her mouth. Her perfect body leaned back against the lounger, and she closed her eyes, absorbing the numerous sensational stimulus.

This silence felt new.

Content.

It felt as though nothing must be said.

Nothing *needed* to be said.

I soon allowed myself to relax, but I kept my eyes open. I stared directly above us at the stars. They were never this bright in Atlanta. The last time I saw a sky full of stars like this, I was deep in the Blue Ridge Mountains, camping with Conor.

Valentine's gentle, soothing breaths called to me. She looked peaceful. I allowed my eyes to fixate on her features highlighted by the moonlight. Her beautiful pink lips pursed lightly as she breathed in the salty air.

"I'd love to live somewhere far away from Atlanta." She muttered, whispering as though the very air would wisk her deepest darkest secrets from within her.

I smiled, my eyes finally settling upon hers. They were slightly open, staring back at me with the same intensity.

"Yeah?" I ask, shifting to lie on my side.

She closed her eyes again and nodded once.

I felt my cheeks warm, despite the beautifully cool night breeze.

"Val..."

Her eyelids fluttered open and she again looked to me.

"If you didn't ever have to do anything for Lorenzo, ever... what would your dream be?"

Her features shifted and her brown eyes joined the constellations above us. Deepening in their richness. She pulled her knees to her chest and thought for a few brief seconds.

"I've always wanted to open a school to teach pole dancing," she giggled, shaking her head, "it was my dream. I mean, I enjoy what I do. I like the rush it gives me. But I adore the art of pole dancing." A contented smile fell over her soft features, and she placed a hand against her face.

That suited her. She had the personality, and the talent.

"Why didn't you seek out a normal private investigator?" I laid my head across my arm as I stared at her.

She shrugged, "I thought Lorenzo would solve it faster... I guess hindsight *is* 20/20" She muttered. Sadness eclipsed the once calm expression and her eyes dropped from the starlight to the ocean, "I regretted the choice to work with Lorenzo as soon as I signed the papers. Always felt like he played me, and this gnawing thought in the back of my head is that he has no fucking clue... and that he just keeps sending me to do his bidding without recompense."

I understood *that* part more than she probably realized.

The thought of hopelessness. Being trapped like a bird in a cage. Lorenzo didn't care about us. He didn't want us to be okay. He only wanted us to work. For me that meant driving around his most precious cargo and cleaning up his fucking messes. I was a lucky man when the day didn't end up in murder... but now those days were few and far between.

The blood on my hands was fresh, ripe, and though I was

able to put a solid wall up between my professional day life and my professional night life.

This week that wall has been crumbling slowly.

Chipping away.

I only wondered if Lorenzo would come smashing through it with his big fucking nose, or even something equally as grotesque and annoying.

"Is there a difference between pole dancing as an art and pole dancing as a stripper?"

She beamed at me, "Absolutely!" her soft tone felt brighter, "Pole dancing doesn't have to just be sexy.

It can be beautiful.

It can be thrilling.

When I strip, I spin a few times around the pole and shake my ass. Men want to see me crawl across the floor, begging them for their money." Val pauses to push herself to sit up, "But when I *really* dance… when I feel the music and let my body lead me" Her eyes lock onto the moon, drinking in the pale blue light, "I feel so free." She finished in almost a whisper.

Valentine was stunning. A cloud of apprehension grew upon my shoulders as I stared at her up and down.

I wanted to save her.

I wanted to pull her free of Lorenzo's clutches.

I wanted to see the Valentine that felt this free.

I wanted to be able to encurage the version of this woman that didn't have to put up with any shit that she didn't enjoy.

While I was lost in thought, Val slipped from her chair to stand, leaning against the wooden railing between us and the sandy beach below.

The hair of her wig swept lightly in the air, casting ringlets of golden curls through the atmosphere behind her. The floral print of her sheer skirt followed suit.

She looked like a figment of my dreams.

"Cain," she muttered, flattening her forearms against the banister and resting her cheek against the skin. I pulled myself to the end of my lounger, sitting closest to her at the end with my legs hanging off. A silent motion that told her I was listening. "The other day when you dropped me off at Emory…"

A flutter of nerves gathered in my chest, I nodded slowly, "I thought you were behaving differently," I commented, following it up with a gentle tease: "Usually you slam the door in my face."

Val glanced back at me for a moment, a grin pulling at the edges of her lips, "Well, can you blame me?" She giggled, then turned away from me again. The world in the absence of her gaze felt cold and empty.

I craved her eyes on me, but the realist within me stood steadfast in the belief that I had let her down in an unforgivable way. Any chance of… anything with her was lost.

She shook her head lightly and sighed, "I have been guarded against everyone other than the girls. I have a hard time believing that anyone is a genuine person at all." She hummed, "I mean, Sasha has cried into my arms after shows before, and I've had to physically pull Mags off of a man who was nasty to her. I've seen them both when they were at their lower places. They've lifted me up when I was in my own… But you have always been equally as guarded as I have. In fact, I thought you were an asshole who hated me."

Guilt began crushing down on me.

A weight lowered onto my head, pulling my eyes from her. I sighed, allowing it to slip out of my chest. It burned at the edges of my lungs as if to punish me, "No, you're right, I was absolutely an asshole."

"So was I," Valentine turned to me, "but that day, you came for me. You picked me up in your work clothes. Your normal car. You took your break early for me and kept tabs."

The resounding sound of her laugh echoed in my mind as she spoke, and it gave me the sensation of flying. I smiled bashfully at her words.

"Do you remember what you said to me?" She asked.

Reality pulled me back in at lightning speed, and suddenly I was searching through all of our conversations, mindlessly forgetting everything that I had ever said in my entire life.

This, probably accompanied by the dopey look on my face, triggered a giggle from Valentine. "You told me you would have come for me whether it was your job or not." She turned around and leaned backwards against the banister.

"That made me feel…" Her words halted. Honey-brown eyes searching the distant skies for the correct thing to say.

My heart throbbed in my chest; I wanted her to finish speaking.

I wanted her to tell me what she felt.

I wanted to know that she too felt the electricity in the air.

"…human." She simply concluded.

*Was thatwhat I was expecting?*

No, probably not, but I didn't even really know what I expected to begin with.

Valentine bent down, unfastening the straps of her sandals and then removing them. She placed the shoes on her lounger and started toward the opening of the banister which carried her two small steps down to the sandy beach below.

The soft percussion of the pads of her feet against soft

golden sand was beautiful music, and as she glanced over her shoulder to beckon me to join her, I felt her presence squeezing tight around my heart, pulling me from the lounger and down to her place in the sand.

My own shoes were placed beside hers as I joined.

Val smiled at me, "Would you do something for me?" She asked. A flash of the last time she had asked me to help her rushed to my mind. I could still practically feel the silicone in my palm as I pictured her face that night. She was exhausted, practically in pain from need. A need that I myself hadn't created.

I pursed my lips tighter together as I felt my apprehension grow. *Would it be wrong of me to hope that she wanted me to help her do that again?*

But my silence didn't entertain her. She stared up at me with a soft, beautiful patience.

Shaky breath escaped me as I spoke, "I think it depends on what you want me to do." I admit earnestly.

"Would you hold me?" she asked simply.

"Hold you?"

Val closed her eyes and nodded, "This is the perfect night with the perfect temperature. I feel at peace. I just want to be held."

I stood for a moment in contemplation, looking down at the woman who reached just below my shoulder height. Before I allowed myself to screw this up too, I closed the distance between us and draped an arm awkwardly around her shoulders.

She giggled and leaned into me, placing her head against my chest.

She was warm.

Her presence felt *nice…*

I could only hope that she couldn't hear the absolute cannon fire in my chest as my heart thudded aggressively against my lungs. She then reached for my other arm, pulling it around herself.

"You're a big lout. Have you never held a woman in your life?" she teased.

A pout pressed to my lips, and I adjusted my arms to hold her like I would have held a girlfriend, "I obviously have. Just not for a few months." I stated.

She laughed.

That laugh sent electricity through my bones.

"Riiiight," she shook her head, a nuzzle of her cheek across my skin, "as if any woman would want to be held by you."

"That's a bit pointed, coming from you." I fired back, resting my chin on the top of her head, careful to avoid the wounded patch at the back. Mostly to conceal the blush that now covered my cheeks.

Valentine sank into my arms, a muffled giggle coming from the space between us.

Most people would dream of this experience. Holding a gorgeous woman on a beautiful beach. But a part of me remembered that this was a simple flash of fantasy that would most likely fade from our realities in an hour.

We would return to the suite, say our goodbyes, and then disappear behind the closed doors of our respective bedrooms.

And then, in the morning, as we returned to the hellhole of Metro-Atlanta, she would remember all of the things that pushed us apart to begin with.

Life would resume.

I would be stuck watching her as she forces herself to parade around with the men of the night to appease a beast that would never truly let her go.

"Your heartbeat has changed," Val mutters, her head moving so that her chin rested on my sternum.I could feel her eyes staring up at me.

Her words summoned me back from the other world I had gone to and I looked down to meet her eyes.

"What's wrong?" She asked in a whisper, "Is this, okay?"

Words raced around in my head, but all were finding an impasse at my vocal cords. *Was* this, okay? I bit down lightly on my tongue as I examined her honey-brown orbs.

She began to recoil from me, pulling herself slowly from my grasp. It felt like my heart was being ripped out of my ribcage as she pushed away. "Sorry, I didn't mean to upset you."

I looked down, the cold night air eclipsing the warmth that had once glowed between us.

"No," I muttered, "I just... I don't know how I feel." I admitted.

"About me?" She asked.

My eyes widened, my head shaking quickly, "No... No, I am fairly confident with how I feel about you. I just don't quite understand how I feel about everything else."

Valentine stood before me, the moonlight casting a glittering light through her eyes, lacing its fingers through her hair. Her mouth was poised, lips slightly parted. "Well... how *do* you feel about me?"

That familiar apprehension grew again inside of my chest, and I felt the burning desire to run in the back of my mind. I lifted a hand to my ear, tugging lightly at the lobe as I searched for the right words.

"I... I think you're beautiful," I said anxiously, "You're hard-working and committed. You experience your emotions in all of the rawest, and genuine of ways."

I thought I would stop there, but the words kept tumbling out.

An avalanche of admittance.

"When I am not around you, I long *to* be. When I hear your voice, no matter how annoyed or angry you are, I want to hear nothing else but your voice...

And your laugh!

Fuck me... your laugh makes me feel alive. I want to do the stupidest shit just in the hopes of making you laugh."

I pulled my hand from my ear to pinch the bridge of my nose.

Her eyes widened slowly, head tipping to one side as she listened. "But... if you feel this way then... why do you resist my advances?"

My eyes drop to the water just meters from us, sighing once more. I was becoming keenly more aware of just how much I fucking sigh.

"Because when you ask me for things like that, a part of me knows that you only ask out of need. Not want. Not desire. You don't desire my touch; you need *a* touch. And you couldn't possibly want my touch. I know that no matter how much I make you laugh, or how much I make you smile... you still have that pain from what happened at the frat party. The way you called to me. You made direct eye contact, and I fucking let you down. I thought you were being a dick, and I let you fucking go into that room alone with him. I should have saved you..."

"Yes," she said flatly, "You should have."

I felt a blade of ice stab directly into my soul, a cold chill rushing over my skin. Absolutely covered in goosebumps as a wave of complete and utter shame. But she didn't stop there, she stepped closer.

"You should have put the argument that we had that night, behind you. You should have burst through the door and picked me up off the floor before he held that knife to my throat and forced me to submit to him."

Shame. Shame. Shame.

My skin began to flush, and a pressure built behind my eyes. "You *should* have been there for me."

She turned away from, now facing directly into the moonlight. It enveloped her, highlighting the signs of morose on her face. But there was something more there, something longing.

"But I have definitely been a bitch. I have been nasty and spiteful. Aggressive, and mean. Even before that night, I was nastier to you than you have ever been to me." Her hand extended upwards, fingers pressing against her chin as her eyes dropped to the sand.

"We have both been horrible to one another, but we aren't horrible. We are just hurt. We don't trust each other... but you unlocked a level of trust with me the other day that has now completely changed how I see you." Val turned her head, eyes lingering on mine. "When you say that I don't want you... you have no fucking clue how wrong you are."

Val stepped toward me slowly, her eyes welded to mine, a spark of electricity shooting into my pupils, electrifying my brain. The shard of ice that had sapped my energy and chilled my nerves vanished, replaced by the steady hum of her buzzing energy.

Something felt so wrong.

So unbelievably unreal.

*This woman whom I had dreamed of in all of my nightmares and all of my daydreams, standing in front of me telling me that she had, what? Forgiven me? That she liked me?*

Perhaps my confusion displayed plainly on my face, because Valentine's face shifted to a kind glance, and she reached to place a hand on my bicep.

"What do *you* want?" I asked, my eyes moving to her hand on my arm.

Val's brown eyes sparkle, "I don't know what I want. I don't know what I am allowed... but whatever the hell it is... I want it with you."

Tidal waves.

Fireworks.

Meteor strikes.

Tsunamis.

Hurricanes.

Nothing that this fucking world threw at me would be able to tear me down from this high. I stared at Val with a soft, uncertain look in my eyes. She began to pull away again, just as she had before. Without thinking, my opposite hand grabbed hers, pressing it back against my skin. Her face flickered with a smile, and she stepped closer.

"What is it that *you* want, Cain?" She asked.

The question bounced around in the racing thoughts behind my eyes, and I *really* thought about it for a moment.

"I want you..."

I felt the words fall from my lips before I could even think. Before I even understood what I was saying. My hand squeezed hers against my bicep, but my breath hitched in my chest and my eyes wavered.

Her face fell as if she understood my reaction. "It is because of my job… isn't it?" She asked.

I glanced at her, the taste of bile now entering my throat as I shook my head slightly. "It isn't the job that you do… it's the way that you have to put up with being treated. The way I would have to put up with you being treated."

Val's eyes brimmed with a soft line of tears, and she nodded slowly, eyes cast down to avoid mine. The sight of her hurting was enough to tear any man to pieces.

"What if this version of us stayed the way we are." I mutter, hooking a finger under her chin to guide her eyes back to me. "What if Valentine and Cain are simply that. Valentine and Cain. Escort and her driver."

She seemed confused by this, her head tilting to the side.

"Let's try that again." I held her in front of me, "When we get back tomorrow, I'm going to take you out for a date. But not as Cain. Not as this asshole who hurt you. The one who let you down. I'll show you who I am behind all of this."

The electricity in her eyes zapped me again, but this time my defenses were strong enough. I smiled and let go of her completely, watching as her hand dropped from my bicep. A smile burned at the edges of her lips, and she nodded quickly.

"That sounds nice."

My heart leapt in my chest and my eyes softened, "Cool."

She giggled, "Cool."

We stood for a few minutes, staring at one another. Val then turned toward the water and stepped through the sand until the ocean water tickled her toes.

She stood there for a moment before turning to me, "Would you mind if I stayed out here alone for a while?" She asked.

My eyes fixed on her for the final time that night as I nodded slowly, "Do you have your phone on you?"

She nodded, pulling the slit in her skirt aside to show a pocket with her phone securely tucked away.

"If you need me, I'm a message away," I said, allowing my eyes to savor her figure for a moment, then I left her there at the waterside and went to find Sasha and Mags.

*  *  *

It was an easy enough task. They sat beneath a thatched straw canopy sitting on the laps of some excited men who were just happy to have such gorgeous girls in their vicinity. When they saw me, their eyes lit up and they rushed from the group of men to stand in front of me.

"Soooooo?" Sasha sang, standing on her toes as she stared into my soul.

Mags grinned, biting down on her bottom lip.

I raised an eyebrow, "Soooo?"

The redhead's eyes narrow and she crosses her arms, "So?! How did it go with Val?"

Confusion knitted a stitch between my brows, "Why would anything *go* with Val?" I asked.

Sasha stared into my eyes for a minute, searching my face for the smallest hint of what happened, "You know for a fact that she totally has the hots for you."

"You've been trying to score her for months. Don't think we don't see the way you look at her. The way not even she sees." Mags smirked, her brown eyes connecting with a soft blush that dusted my cheeks.

I crossed my arms, "She wanted to be alone for the rest of

the night, so she is out there by the ocean."

The red-headed woman before me frowns, her eyes widening, "You left a girl who is HORNY as FUCK for YOU alone by the water instead of taking her back to the bedroom and fucking her?" She emphasized, probably louder than she should have.

I tossed a hand over her mouth and growled, "Sasha, shut it." I mumbled,

Mags laughed, "You're the one making stupid decisions."

I sighed and pulled both girls to a quieter area, "Listen, you better not tell anyone about this… but I've asked her on a date… a real date."

Sasha's eyes fill with the shine of glitter and confetti as she grinned widely, "Like… with Not-Cain?" she asked boisterously.

I chuckled, nodding softly.

Both girls exchanged glances, excitement rolling in their eyes, then they turned to face me as one.

"We swear to God, Cain. If you ever hurt her, we will absolutely kill your ass." Mags said, crossing her arms in front of her, "She may be *your* girl, but she was our girl first, long before *you* came along."

I laughed, nodding softly and raised my hands as a shield.

"I got it! I understand."

# Shatter Me

# BECCA

My name is Rebecca Cassidy, but I go by Becca. I am twenty-seven years old, and I work as a dancer by the name of Scarlett in a club called the Midnight Raven. I enjoy listening to music, dancing, and long walks on the beach...

Am I selling it to you yet?

Honestly, I don't think I'm even selling it to myself. Valentine had become my life, and anything in between Becca and Valentine was simply sleep and a bit of club dancing.

I don't really know who Becca is anymore.

But this is what Cain asked for. He wanted to meet me as

me… and I guess that means he wants to meet Becca.

I sat on the floor of Sasha's living room. My hair was a mess of curls that I wasn't too pleased with and Sasha herself was doting over me like a precious gem.

She was employing her fantastic skills of makeup on my face, but as she approached my face with foundation, I bit my lip.

"Erm, Sash… can you let my freckles shine through a little bit?" I asked bashfully.

She smirked, "Oh, does Cain like your freckles?" She teased, delicately painting a thin layer of foundation on my face.

I turned my eyes away from hers, "He told me that I should show them off more often…"

"What a dick! That's so fucking cute." Sasha grinned, and then I watched as her expression dimmed as she looked deeper into my eyes, "Are you sure about this, Val?" She asked softly, placing the makeup brush on a towel laid out beside us, "You can always tell him you don't want to go, and we can watch movies here instead."

My eyes softened and I pulled her into a gentle hug, careful not to cover her shirt in the freshly applied makeup, "I would be a liar if I said I wasn't absolutely mortified… I haven't been in a relationship since…"

"Yeah, since Finn was a shithead and decided to start doing heroin." She interrupted and shook her head softly; she reached for a wet wipe and fixed a mistake she'd made. "But I am more worried now because Cain isn't gonna just move into another room and call you his roommate while he gets high off his face. I mean… are you going to sleep with him?"

All of these were questions that I didn't have answers to, and all of these possibilities scared the shit out of me. *Is it wrong to sleep with him on the first night?* I didn't even know. These past few years where sex is a skill to be sold for profit… I didn't know what it meant anymore. Was it *actually,* okay?

I sighed heavily and looked at the compact mirror that Sasha held in her hands. She was so good at this. My black and gold eye shadow matched perfectly with the deep red lipstick… and she left the constellation of freckles around my nose just visible enough.

Sasha brought over my dress.

It was a simple black dress with a deep V-neck that plunged nearly to my belly, and it had lace trim around the skirt. I pulled off my dressing gown to reveal a pair of lace undergarments. Nothing incredibly fancy, but pretty, nonetheless. Sasha helped me pull the dress on over my head and then squealed.

"Well, if he is stupid, you let me know. I'll take you on a date and treat you right." She laughed.

I walked to the hallway where a floor-length mirror leaned against the wall. I *did* look pretty. Sasha came over and giggled, pulling me toward the couch.

"He isn't going to have a clue who you are. Ready for a date two fucking hours early. You can't even get ready for work on time!" She laughed, her green eyes locked with mine, "Come sit and have a minute to chill."

She was right.

I was chronically late to everything…

A nightmare to deal with. And here I was two hours early to a date with a man I didn't know… or at least, a version of the man I didn't know.

Now all that I can do is wait.

# CAIN

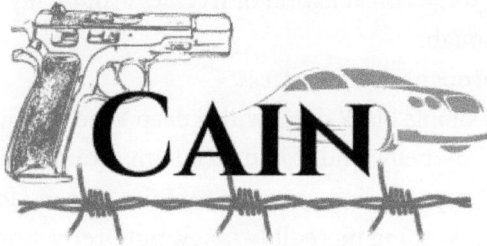

My whole body buzzed with anticipation as I pulled my car into the driveway of my megalomaniac boss's Victorian mansion. I'd already gotten ready in one of my nicer black pairs of jeans, with a tan leather belt and a deep, crimson-colored flannel. My hair was left untouched by anything but nature, just the way I liked it.

I strode up to Lorenzo's front door with a clear plan in mind. I had even rehearsed my words numerous times in my head, over and over ever since last night when I told Valentine that

I couldn't cope with her job.

I was going to pay her debt.

I was going to free her soul… no matter what it took.

And everything seemed to be going to plan… at first.

The way I sauntered up to his front door with the suave of a man on a mission.

The way I turned back to my car to click her lock and make sure the doors were fully sealed.

I cannot say, however, that turning to see Lorenzo's greasy face staring at me from an open door to be part of my plan.

There he was though, all five-foot-seven of him. Standing at the entrance to his home with a massive shit-eating grin.

"Cain!" He hissed in a sickeningly friendly tone, "How nice of you to drop by!" I narrowed my eyes, warily staring him down. He was far too happy for anything good to have come of it.

"Come in, Come in!" He beckons me through the door, "I have some amazing news for you."

I sighed, "I can't stay long, Lorenzo. I just have something really important to discuss with you."

His nose bounced on his face as he nodded quickly, "Yes, of course you do. And I have something that is probably equally as important to you."

I stepped inside and allowed him to pull the door closed behind me. The usually brightly lit home was now cast in shadows as Lorenzo lured me toward his lounge, where the only source of artificial light was stuttering from a still frame on the television on the wall.

Lorenzo sat with his legs crossed before himself, now facing me. "Go on, Cain. I imagine you want to get this off of your chest quite urgently, or else you wouldn't have shown up unannounced."

Suspicion coated the hair of my eyebrows as I stared at him, drinking in that disgusting, greasy grin, "I want to make a transaction."

His eyes shined in genuine intrigue, "A transaction? What could you possibly want to purchase from me…" His lips point upward into a sneer, "Wait, are you asking me for a private night with Valentine?" A howling laugh escaped Lorenzo, echoing menacingly throughout the halls.

"No… I want you to release her from her contract. I will pay for any financial losses. You will continue your work on helping her find her friend's killer. I will work double if I need to and pay you in cash."

I expected Lorenzo to laugh again, but he didn't.

In fact, his face fell into some silent… contemplative stare as he looked me up and down, "You want to take over the financials for Valentine's contract?" He queried.

I nodded once, stern and steadfast.

Lorenzo chuckled, a deep malevolent roll of his gravelly voice, "Cain. I think that you had better think long and hard about this one… I have a feeling that what I have to show you today, just might change your mind entirely."

*What the fuck was this bastard getting at?*

The way his body language shifted proved to me that my offer was not falling favorably on his mind.

"After all, what I have to show you has actually bought you your own freedom." Lorenzo's voice boomed in the chamber as he reached for the slender black remote control and pressed play.

My eyes sealed to the video as it began to roll the familiar CCTV footage of my brother's workshop…

But this time it was different.

This time there was more.

I stepped closer to the TV to watch, eyes narrowed to focus on any detail. I watched all of the movements that my brother had made, the ones that I had recognized, memorized. Then he changed. In the seconds where I expected the whirr of static and silence… it continued.

Conor was still seated at the desk, the book splayed out before him. But this time something triggers his attention to the door.

*A customer?*

Conor didn't seem fearful. He actually seemed delighted. His face brightened as he smiles at a woman who approaches his counter.

*It was Valentine.*

I turned back to look at Lorenzo, "Why *the fuck* is Val there?"

He didn't speak, only motioned for me to continue watching.

Valentine leaned over the counter, the leather of her cropped jacket pulling tight against her shoulders and her blonde hair curled to perfection. She smiled, flashing that horrible… fake seduction at my brother as a siren would to lure sailors to their rocky deaths .

Rage burned in my chest as she pulled a piece of chocolate from her purse and began to nibble.

Conor obviously teases her a little, and she giggled in response, then reaching into a separate compartment of her purse for another before placing the chocolate between my brother's lips.

Then she stood on her toes and kissed him.

The blood in my body began to boil as I felt utter betrayal coarse through me.

And then, Val pulled away from him, flashing a saccharine smile and a flirty wave before saying a few words that left Conor giddy.

Valentine exited and Conor returned to reading, though it seemed his eyes fixed themselves on her form long after she had disappeared through the glass.

Lorenzo pushed the button on the remote to speed through a passage of time before he switched it back to normal speed.

Conor now looked breathless.

His eyes darted around as he clutched at his throat.

This part was all *too* familiar.

I wanted to reach through the screen and save him, to have been there for him...

And then he collapsed against his desk, dead.

Waves of nausea rushed over me as I felt whatever infatuation I once held for Valentine, shatter, crushed to dust in an instant. I growled and turned to Lorenzo with a fire burning in my eyes.

"What the fuck was that? Is that fucking real?" I snarl, my eyes fixed on his beady brown eyes.

Lorenzo smirked, his shoulders raising lightly in a huff of satisfaction. "My price for Valentine's freedom is five bricks," he said flatly, a long scraggly finger digging into his bulbous nose, "Though, I am sure you can see that your contract has been fulfilled. Your brother's killer has been found." He removed a wad of congealed snot and flicked it to the floor.

It landed with a sickening thwack on the tile.

I growled, looking down between my feet. "I need to speak to her. I need time."

Lorenzo grinned widely, "Sure. But unfortunately, I cannot have retired employees on my premises unless they are inquiring about my business. So, Adam Hunt, you should be leaving immediately."

An alarm on my phone began to sound, the sinister chimes of a call toward a fate that I wasn't exactly sure I still wanted. I retrieved the singing device from my pocket and slid the alarm for silence.

Finally, I shot Lorenzo a deadly glare, and then proceeded to walk straight through the doors and out of the mansion.

My Charger sat there in the driveway, sparkling in the evening light.

An intense, morphing stare tethered my gaze to the shiny black coat of polish and tinted windows. That fucking car had served me no purposes other than speed and annoyance.

At this present moment, all I wanted was to pack up my life and hightail it out of this fucking place.

But something pulled deep inside my gut that told me not to. I told me that I had to keep myself afloat, and that I had to at least speak to Valentine first.

# BECCA

I was curled up on Sasha's couch, listening to her rambling on about this new show she was really enjoying, but I couldn't help but keep my eyes fixated on the window just beyond my red-haired friend's face.

The sunlight was beginning to recede into the horizon, and I felt my heart leap with joy as I waited anxiously for my phone to ring. To ding. To do fucking anything.

Cain was never late.

And he never failed.

As the clock flipped from 6:59 to 7:00 a message finally

popped up from Cain.

**Cain: Here.**

This was odd… he never messaged when he was here. He *always* called. I typed a quick message to let him know I was on my way down and then gave Sasha a big hug before rushing out the door and down the stairs to where Cain was usually parked.

There, in his usual spot, the Charger sat idling. Cain was seated in the driver's seat, his head leaned back against the headrest with his eyes closed as though he was in stasis.

I felt a pang of worry in my chest as I pulled the handle of the passenger side door open.

A rush of cold, stagnant, suffocating energy rolled out like smoke from a hotbox. Cain didn't move, his eyes opening only enough for him to be able to peer through the slits at me.

"Um… hey!" I muttered, unsure now if I should even get into the car.

*What was wrong?*

*Had something happened?*

He nodded to me. It was a kind of silent rejection that stung me to my core. Even when he was annoyed with me, he always shook his head and called me a pain in his ass.

*What the fuck is going on?*

A rush of anxiety coated my nerves, and I drew my right hand to grip onto my left forearm. I couldn't help it but stand there and stare at him.

"Can you please get in the car?" Cain mumbled, motioning to the passenger side seat with a breath of ennui.

That feeling that I had before every single show that Lorenzo forced me to do began to crawl over my shoulders.

I choked back this morose fear that felt suffocating, and I slipped into the car. My sight blurred as a thin glassy film overcame them, my eyes instinctively locking to the floor.

The car hummed as Cain adjusted his position.

A heavy, frustrated sigh left him as he turned to me. He pinched the bridge of his nose, "I need to speak to you about something incredibly important."

My heart thumped in my chest, but I nodded, "Yes… yeah of course." I mumbled.

Cain turned off the car, and as the key pulled from the ignition, I felt my heart sink. The idea of the joy this night would bring shattered in his hands. The 6'2" man beside me, covered in tattoos and radiating this energy that snuffed any and every sense of who I thought he was, removed his phone from his pocket. For a moment, silence hung in the air like thick smog.

Then he turned his phone so the screen would face me.

Displayed on the pristinely cared-for screen was the face of a man that I absolutely knew.

I *absolutely* recognized him.

A well of bile began to build in my stomach and I glanced past the phone to see that Cain's blue orbs had soldered to me in intense examination. His face rested against his fist, propped up against the doorframe by his elbow as he searched for my expression.

"I-I know him," I muttered.

Cain's eyes fell, almost as if he wanted me to lie and say that I didn't.

*Why would I lie to him?*

"Can- Can you just fucking speak to me?" I coughed out, holding back my own frustrations that burned at the base of my eyelids.

"What is his name?" His tone was venomous, but shaky.

*How could this man be so fucking terrifying and so fucking broken at the same time?*

I racked my brain, searching for the name, "I- I don't remember... Cain, I haven't spoken to him for years, I-"

"WHY haven't you spoken to him for years, Valentine?" Cain spat at me.

"Um... I think... I think he might have died?" I muttered, feeling my words catch up to me.

I *knew* he died.

I knew *I* was the one to kill him.

*Why did Cain know?*

*How did Cain know?*

"His fucking name was Conor. Conor Hunt!" Cain yelled, throwing his phone into the backseat. It bounced a few times and then fell to the floorboard.

"Y-yes..." My chest burned, "I remember now."

Cain balled his hands into tight fists and slammed them against the steering wheel, "Fuck!"

I couldn't tell if he was angry or dejected, but when Cain turned back to look at me, his thoughts were displayed directly upon his face.

Hatred.

Betrayal.

Anger.

Grief.

Through clentched teeth he finally managed, "My name is Adam Hunt...

You. Killed. My. Fucking. Brother."

The thud of my heart against my ribs seemed to stop in an

instant.

I was removed from this place of fear and anger and ascended the ranks into being downright destroyed.

I stared wordlessly at Cain; our eyes sealed together in some sort of shared agony. I had only been following orders.

Conor was just another customer... it was ages before Cain even started as my driver!

His eyes narrowed, sending shockwaves of torment throughout my soul before they closed completely, and then Cain's body slumped back against his seat. His hands reached forward, gripping the wheel with all of his might and channeling himself into one final, broken sob.

"Cain," I muttered, though my voice fell into the void of silence, never to reach his ears. I extended my hand to touch his bicep. I wanted to explain, but he ripped himself from my touch.

"Don't fucking touch me, Valentine."

I peeled back quickly, completely shoving myself back against the door behind me. Swells of panic opened fire throughout my body as I felt this rapturous pain envelop me.

And then he fucking did it...

He turned to me and delivered the most fucking devastating blow that I have ever felt in my life.

Cain turned to look at me, his blue eyes now stained red from the tears he was forcing from demanding release. He gritted his teeth, "I loved you, Valentine. I-" he shook his head quickly and faced away, staring out the window, "I fucking loved you."

That was it.

That was all I needed.

The tears began to streak down my face as this delusion

of peace that I had built in my mind finally came crashing down at swift speeds. My hand launched to clasp over my mouth, sealing within my palm the sobs that threatened to escape. I turned, searching for the handle. As I pulled, my weight against the door pushed it open and I practically fell from the car.

Cain's hand shot out and he grabbed my wrist in perfect timing to prevent me from falling.

Eternities passed as the tight grip of his hand held me in place.

Then with all of his strength, he ripped me from where I dangled and then crashed our lips together.

A final seal.

The sparks from his lips sent waves of anguish through me and all I wanted was to fall into his arms and sob.

He was the first to pull away, and as he did… I knew it was over. He looked me directly in the eyes and said with complete and total conviction: "Focus."

My heart ached, the tears morphed to those of sadness, and I nodded slowly.

Focus.

It was my safe-word.

It meant that whatever was going on, no matter the passion, no matter the feelings, it was shut down.

Halted.

Silenced.

Snuffed.

A million other fucking synonyms that meant that this was over.

My cheeks were soaked and warm as the heat from his kiss radiated at my lips.

I yearned for him... not just sexually, but wholly, and completely.

I nodded and scooted myself to the open door.

For a moment, I stood there.

This delusion of hope that he would beckon me back. That we could go on like this had never happened. That we could go on and have dinner like we were meant to... but he didn't. As I closed the door, the ignition turned over and he drove away, leaving me and all of my broken pieces on the curb.

# To Love You More...

＊ ＊

Looking up at the stars, I know quite well
That, for all they care, I can go to hell,
But on earth indifference is the least
We have to dread from man or beast.
How should we like it were stars to burn
With a passion for us we could not return?
If equal affection cannot be,
Let the more loving one be me.
Admirer as I think I am
Of stars that do not give a damn,
I cannot, now I see them, say
I missed one terribly all day.
Were all stars to disappear or die,
I should learn to look at an empty sky
And feel its total dark sublime,
Though this might take me a little time.

**W. H. Auden**

# Two Glasses of Grape Juice, Please!

# ADAM

Nursing homes are sterile at the best of times.

Medication, hydrogen peroxide, and the sickening stench of after-market lemon-scented sanitization wipes, always hung heavily in the air. I stood at the front desk; eyes downcast as I filled in the paperwork that I had seen every single time that I came to check in on my mother.

You would think that after visiting every Monday for the past three years, they may start to recognize or remember me, but the jury is still out on that. After all, my mother *is* in a dementia ward. Who's to say that the staff aren't a bit memory-challenged, as well?

I scratched my signature across the dotted line at the bottom of the page, then stowed the pen securely on the top of the clipboard.

A quick glance around the tiny reception area told me that I was completely alone. Even the receptionist had slipped away to abandon me in this place that held far too many bad memories. I put the clipboard on the reception desk for when she returned and sat back down in the uncomfortable black chair.

My eyes wandered the room, drinking in the sober reality of my whole life right now. I remembered vividly standing behind my brother as he held Mom's hand. Waiting for the word to guide her to her new bedroom.

She had been far better then. It had worried us that she had been forgetting our birthdays or even Conor's son's name... but she'd declined so severely since she first enrolled in the program.

"Mr. Hunt," the receptionist beckoned, ripping me forth from the sober memory of who my mother used to be. My eyes fell on the woman in her bright green pastel smock, with her brown hair tied back.

She offered me a reassuring smile and nodded slowly, "You can go on through now." Her tone was kind.

My heart lurched in my chest, and I nodded slowly, pushing myself to standing. On shaky legs, I stepped quietly through the doorway towards my mother's bedroom. A steady thrum of my heart met the downbeat of each step.

I pushed the door open with a gentle knock and peered inside. She was there, sat in a comfy recliner chair with her big fat cat pillow resting in her lap. Wispy white curls clung to her pale scalp, and a pair of thick glasses rested on the bridge of her nose. The large lenses magnified the size of her eyes, and as I entered, her sweet head turned to me and those massive lenses put her dark blue eyes on showcase.

My eyes soften, "Hey, mama." I muttered. Though heartbreak tugged through my soul as her eyes searched me, as though she was trying to place me in her mind. I took a step toward her and sat down in the spare wooden chair next to her bed.

Her eyebrows furl like tiny fluffy white caterpillars as she looked me up and down, face scrunching into a disapproving grimace as she settled upon my tattoos.

"Oh, Adam!" She snorted, "You know I hate those blasted tattoos!"

She didn't. My mother and I got matching tattoos on my 18th birthday. She always encouraged me to get more art done... but that didn't matter.

At least today she knew my name.

A soft blush rose to my cheeks, and I tugged at the cloth of my sleeves, "Sorry, mama. I should have known better."

Mom's eyes darken and she nodded once, exaggerated and stern, "You absolutely should have."

I grinned lightly; it was rare to see the fight in her eyes like I did today. It was refreshing. My eyes settled on the plush cat in her lap and I extended my hand to stroke its fur, "How is Muffin doing today, Mama?"

"Oh, Muffin is always good. I think I'd die without his comfort." She prattled, then led on into a disjointed story about how she used to raise cats when she was growing up on the farm in Spokane.

This also wasn't true. My mother had been born in a rich family south of the Okefenokee River basin, just above the Florida-Georgia line. She had worked all her life as an assistant teacher and actually hated cats until she found companionship in this plush toy... a gift from Conor.

"I had never heard that story, mama. Where is Spokane?" I asked, taking in the time of genuine conversation where she was lucid enough to at least remember me.

She sucked at her teeth, "Spokane is in Kansas!" Her tone told me that I absolutely should have known this fact, so I acted out an animated *DUH*, throwing my hand over my forehead.

"When is Conor coming?" She asked suddenly.

I glanced up to meet those brilliant blue eyes.

She was serious, wholly and completely.

The guilt that grew in my heart faltered and I felt the crawl of sadness as it encroached. I remembered Valentine's face. But as I tried to pull myself back together, the idea faded and I smiled, "He should be coming tomorrow."

This was the cruelest lie I could ever tell. Yet I told it to my mother every time I saw her since he had died three years prior.

It was actually only a week after she was admitted here.

It was best for her... that she didn't have to worry about her son. She would never grieve his loss, and he would never grieve hers....

But me...

I would grieve them *both*.

And I think that I already grieve them both every day.

"Oh," Her eyes drifted towards the window beside her, searching out into the maintained courtyard. This answer never satisfied her, but it was just enough to push back concerns or questions. Mom then turned to me again and said with a serious look on her face: "You are upset."

A spark of confusion sizzled between my eyebrows as I turned my own eyes from my mother. "I am fine,"

"You're not fine." She said in full lucid stare, straight at me. I could feel the cool kindness of her eyes on my skin.

I sighed and shook my head, reaching up to tousle the curls of my brown hair, "It is far too complicated to really explain right now, mama."

Her face sank into an annoyed humph as she stared me down, but after a moment I noticed the gaze change. The care and concern in her eyes drifting back into the vacancy of an unknowing stare.

My heart broke again as the feeling of loss, for the few moments of her that I had that were fully real, returned.

"Are you, my nurse?" Mama asked.

And though the lie was painful, I choked back my pride and nodded slowly, "Yes, Louise. I am your nurse. I was just about to bring you some grape juice."

A pleased smile teased at the edges of her lips and she nodded happily, "Oh, that would be wonderful! My son Conor will be coming today. Could you bring him some juice too?"

Tears forced their way to the rims of my eyelids, but I nodded, "Yes ma'am."

I pushed myself to standing and placed a final squeeze on her shoulder before finding my way out of her room and then asking the first nurse to bring her a glass of grape juice.

As I staggered out into the parking lot, I felt the pain lessen. Once I was through the doors it didn't feel so real.

It didn't feel like she was actually gone. Just staying somewhere else, where she would be taken care of.

My phone buzzed as the alarm I had set for the end of my

lunch break went off. I pulled a sigh from the depths of my chest and silence it, sinking into the front seat of my Cobalt and then driving towards the site.

Today marks three months.

Three months since I had that awful discussion with Valentine.

Three months since Lorenzo had thrown me off the team without a second thought.

Three months since I lost track of who the hell I actually was.

I often find myself driving circles around the city at night, circling the route I used to take to drop off Val and the girls. I would drive to the Midnight Raven just to see if I could ever spot her walking home, but I never did.

Probably for the best. If it was up to her, I would just go jump off a fucking bridge.

She was a mess.

She was a liar.

A manipulator.

She was a Killer…

But I still yearned for that laugh…

I still craved the sensation that my body cried out with when she turned to me and smiled, like I was the only person who existed in the entire world. And I still felt the electricity behind that fucking kiss.

I had told her… that I loved her.

I had said it in past tense…

*What a fucking dickhead, right?*

As if I could have actually known that I loved the woman whose smile only fell upon me twice in the entire two years that I had worked with her.

*Who the hell did I think I was?*

The road towards the site grew heavy with traffic and I felt annoyance creep in over my shoulders, enveloping me in a disdain for other people. I felt like that a lot in the past few years.

My phone rang, and after a quick glance at the clock on my dash, I realized that I was already late. I sighed and swiped the answer key without actually looking down. "I'm so sorry, Roy. The traffic is terrible, I'll be about twenty minutes."

"Roy?" A familiar voice spoke. A thick southern drawl with hints of sass that were strong enough to tell me *exactly* who was on the other end of the phone.

I glanced down at the screen to confirm my suspicions. "You can't have deleted my number already, Cain." Mags' voice called out.

I felt the annoyance fade slightly and a wave of confusion replaced its ebbing wave, "Magnolia? Are you okay?" I asked, searching the road around me for a break in the traffic. Hopeless. It was a standstill.

A scoff bounced from the other end of the phone, "I didn't think you'd care how any of us were. Considering you dipped off the face of the earth after ripping Val's heart out and kicking her to the curb."

My eyes rolled as I sat back in my seat, groaning, "Did you call me to lecture me?"

She laughs. It was the kind of laugh that made you instantly feel like not only the biggest asshole, but also the biggest fucking idiot in the world. "No, actually. I called you to tell you something important."

"Oh, yeah?" I pried, staring anxiously out the window, the annoyance of the traffic beginning to override my confusion for hearing Mags' voice again.

"Yeah. You see, your girl is in a bit of trouble." She said, an inflexion of seriousness dancing over her bouncy tone.

I sighed, "Mags, I don't have a girl."

"Yeah. I fucking know. I scraped her off the pavement after you drove away. But listen to me for a minute, you shitface." Mags took in a deep breath through her nose before returning to the serious tone, "We have a new driver."

"That's usually what happens when someone retires," I glanced out the window to my left at the drivers in different lanes who were shouting, annoyed at the others.

Mags returned to me with a sigh that was comparable to my own, "Can you shut the fuck up and let me talk?"

Silence.

After a moment, I heard her draw a shaky breath. "Listen, Lorenzo has been putting V up to some real shady shit, but this new driver guy... he seems to be *real* touchy. I mean REAL touchy on your girl!" She paused, as if debating on giving me room to speak, but then continued, "And I really don't like the way she acts around him. It is like she is starstruck."

I narrowed my eyes slightly in annoyance, "Why are you telling me this, Mags?"

It must have been a ploy. Something to make me jealous. Something to anger me... and I can't lie, the more I think about the situation, the more I realize how heartbroken I am to have lost the friendship I had gained with Valentine. I missed being able to trust that she was going to be a pain in my ass no matter what happened that day.

Mags hummed, "She is self-destructing."

"And why do you think I am the best person to speak to about this? She literally murdered my brother." I sighed, rubbing my temples. The sound of car horns began to pepper the distant soundscape.

The woman on the other end seemed to shift, a sigh escaping her lips, "Lorenzo told her that you left because of her. She's been drinking nonstop since that night."

I frowned, shaking my head lightly and leaning my head back in my seat, "That isn't true..."

"It doesn't matter what you think is true, Cain. What matters is that it hurt her, and now she is doing everything in her power to hurt herself without doing the actual damage, herself." Mags said sternly, "She is being nasty, and aggressive, and sometimes just plain mean."

I wanted to know more, but I didn't want *her* to know that. I wanted to understand why Mags was so worried, but this shadow within me eclipsed the desire to grow close to Val again. "Have you thought, maybe this new version of her is actually who she has been the whole time?"

Mags was silent for a moment, but I felt the sting of her eyes as if she was there with me, "I cannot fucking believe you." She uttered in a low growl, "You really are a fucking dick, aren't you?"

A response chewed at the back of my lips. Suddenly, my phone began to buzz lightly as a second call was coming through. This time from Roy. I sighed, "Right, Magnolia. I have to take this call."

Before I could even finish speaking, the sound of the call-ending tone droned loudly throughout the cab on my car, and the next call immediately connected.

"Adam?" Roy asked, his voice was cheerful. Grating. The worst possible tone to nurse the throb that began to grow in my head. "Where are ya, kid? Lunch ended ten minutes ago."

It was impossible for me not to soften at his words. The traffic before me still stood at an impasse and I groaned, "I am so sorry, I am stuck in traffic right outside my mom's clinic."

He laughed, a bolt of light that shot through the darkness that was beginning to encircle me. "You can probably just head home, then. I have sent the rest of the crew home for Memorial Day weekend any ways."

I glanced at the clock on the dashboard, feeling a thrum of impatience in my chest, "Are you sure?"

"Yes!" He chuckled, "That's probably why you're stuck in traffic in the first place, to be honest."

"Right… thank you," I said flatly.

Roy paused for a few seconds, "You alright?"

*Was I?*

"I'll be fine. I just finished talking to my mom. She doesn't seem to be really changed from last time." I stared out the window to the miles of cars, shutting my engine off to save its life.

He hummed, "The week of your birthday, you seemed really energetic and happy. But for a few months, you have gone back to being broody and depressed." Roy cleared his throat, "Why don't you meet me at that nice steakhouse on Jeff Davis?" He asked. "I'll make sure you don't spend Memorial Day alone. I'll bring Ashley and the girls."

The annoyance that chipped away at my faculties began to wane and I could feel a smile tugging at the corners of my lips.

"Well?"

I coughed out a laugh, "Yeah… that would be nice. Thank you."

"Great!" The smile on Roy's face was audible, "I'll see you there at seven! Don't be late! Ashley hates tardiness."

"Yeah, yeah. I'm never late." I grinned.

Roy howls laughter, "Ha! Yeah. Sure, you aren't." He laughed in an animated way that mimed out his movements in my mind. The way he threw a hand over his slightly chubby belly, wiping a fake tear from his face. "I'll see ya at seven!"

The line dropped, sending me back into a cacophony of silence within the cab of my car.

I could feel annoyance as it chewed at my thoughts, spitting them out into worthless globs of dead ideas.

Roy was great, and I needed this.

I really *really* did.

# My Bitch? Ew.

# VALENTINE

A steady thrum of music and heavy bass sent vibrations through the club.

The smell of sweat, musk, and alcohol hung heavily in the air as I threw myself back against the thick body of King.

He grabbed my hips, clasping his large dark-toned fingers on my flesh and slipping one of those hands down the front of my mini skirt to teasingly touch me. An electric thrill ran through me, and I moaned aloud, leaning back to rest my head in the space where his collarbone met his neck.

Nobody could hear us; the music was too loud. Nobody could see us, the lights flashed far too quickly in their flickering neon to alert anyone to the fact that King was now full-on fingering me in the middle of this club.

I swelled, rubbing my ass in circles against his hard-on that was tucked right up against me. King's luscious lips crashed hungrily against my neck, and he swirled a slick finger around my clit.

The world around was disolving into flashing, pulsing, and gyrating, when suddenly King grabbed me by my hair. He pulled his hand from my skirt, then tugged at my blonde hair to lead me toward a bathroom.

He practically kicked the door to the bathroom open, revealing a group of startled inhabitants who were huddled around a pile of white powder on the bathroom counter.

"Get the fuck out," King demanded in a gruff, cruel voice. A voice that I feared just as much as I craved.

I watched as he stepped toward them, striking a hand through the powder and sending them running. He was massive, he had to duck through doorways... and when a man that size tells you to get out, you had better listen.

With the two of us left in the room, King points to the edge of the counter. A silent demand... one that I obey. He snatched me by the throat, the other hand guiding my waist as he placed me on the countertop.

"You aren't wearing underwear."

I nod, my eyes meeting his in the dim lighting. My heart ached... but my pussy craved more.

A smirk crawls across his face in a menacing fashion, and he nodded, "You knew I'd want to fuck you brainless. Especially after watching those guys have their way with you, earlier today."

A flash of annoyance. *Why did he have to bring up work?*

167

He unhooked his belt and yanked out his massive cock.

He presented it at my entrance, no need for additional lubrication as I was already wet enough. He pushed inside of me, and I swear, I could see stars! He was just that perfect size that made you feel completely and utterly full of cock… which, I might add, is significantly better than being completely devoid of cock.

He grabbed my hair and pulled it roughly to one side, sucking the pigment from my lips as he thrust into me. I could feel myself trembling lightly…

But it was all over too soon, and within two more thrusts, King pulled himself from inside of me and emptied his load all over the front of my black leather mini skirt.

*That annoyance from before? Oh… it's back.*

He smirked as he stood back, "You were shaking then! Must have felt great!"

"Yeah," I mumbled, feeling my pussy begging for more, but knowing it would have to settle for nothing else.

King grinned and turned to wash his hands. "I'm gonna go for a smoke. Meet me at the car when you're ready."

"No need," I pushed myself off the counter, "Let's go. I'll wait in the car for you to smoke."

His eyes narrowed, "Don't be a bitch, Valentine. I'll make sure Lorenzo teaches you how to behave."

A callous laugh escaped my lips, and I step toward the door, my ass shaking intentionally as I push through, leaving him in there on his own.

I continued out through the front door that led to the exit on South Jeff Davis and started the walk through the mostly quiet streets toward the shiny black Range Rover that King had parked outside of a nice steakhouse up the road.

"Hey!" King called after me, "What the fuck is your problem?"

I ignored him, acting as though I couldn't hear him over the sound of occasionally passing cars. The cool night air was enough to sober anyone up... even from a full night of debauchery and disappointment.

King continued to yell at me, getting closer to me by the second. His legs were so long that one of his strides matched three of my own. But as I grew closer to the slick black automobile, I noticed a familiar silhouette leaning against the wrought metal wall of the steakhouse, a cigarette in hand. My heart lurched in my chest as I immediately fell back a few steps.

It was Cain.

I couldn't let him see me like this...

Covered in cum...

Well...

I guess he has probably seen me in worse conditions.

He hadn't seen me yet, and for a millisecond, I hoped it would stay that way. That he wouldn't glance at me with those blue eyes... those fucking... Ugh!

It doesn't matter.

It never mattered.

I will never find peace.

King grabbed me by my wrist and turned me abruptly to pin me to the car. That feeling of exhilaration that I had once felt with his presence, instantly faded to black and I stared at the towering man above me with fear locked away behind my brown eyes, trembling.

Cain...

I wanted help.

169

I wanted to escape.

I wanted to leave.

"You little bitch! Why can't you just act right?" King shouted, a bead of saliva crashing against my eyebrows as he did. His hand pinned mine above my head with brute force, enough to leave the imprint of my knuckles on the door of his luxury rental car.

I gritted my teeth, feeling anger bubbling from within me, "Why can't you fuck a woman right?" I shouted through my clenched jaw.

That was it.

That one did it…

King lifted his other hand and crashed the heel of his palm against my cheek with a loud enough sound to echo in the block of city buildings.

"Hey! Fuck off!" Cain's voice boomed.

Fuck. Fuck

Fuck.

FUCK.

"Who the hell is you?" King snaps back. His grip tightened on my wrist.

I felt a whimper escape from between my teeth, "Focus!" I managed in a pained shout.

In an instant, Cain stiffened and stepped back.

King looked at him, then at me. His eyes narrowed, deepening with a haunting anger. "How the fuck does he know that word?"

"You should really fucking listen when she says it, dude." Cain interjected, a deadly serious tone coating each word.

"Oh yeah?" King scoffed, letting go of my wrist to face him, unknowingly biding me a bit of time. "Why do you think you get to tell me what the fuck to do?"

Cain laughs, "I don't, I am only offering you some advice."

I stepped back, heart racing as I watched King tower over Cain, but this didn't seem to faze Cain.

My mind raced and anger pulled its way through my veins, sapping every ounce of gratitude I had from my conscience and a blind, unabated rage buzzed through me. I watched with balled-fists as these two fucking dickheads stared each other down.

"King," I growled, eyes narrowed angrily.

His head snapped in my direction, an eyebrow raised.

"Take me home," I demanded, arms crossed in front of my chest.

I could feel his gaze on me… confused. He stepped away from Cain and threw himself into the driver's seat, slamming the door closed.

Now alone on the street with the man who caused my entire world to crash and burn around me not too long ago, I stepped lightly toward the passenger side door and slipped inside.

Cain's eyes never moved from the wall to his left. Shaded by his brown hair. He flicked the cigarette down and snuffed it with a crunch of his boot, and then slipped back inside.

He never once fucking looked my way.

"Who the hell is he, Valentine?" King grumbled, pulling off from the curb with a loud rev of his engine.

My own eyes cast downward, and I sighed softly, "Nobody you need to worry about, King. Just take me home please."

"Motherfucker should know better than to fucking speak to me when I am taking care of my bitch," he growled, eyes bulging as he gripped the steering wheel tight enough for his dark skin to lighten.

That fucking title…

I was *nobody's* bitch.

I was nobody's fucking property!

"Maybe you shouldn't call me your bitch. I don't remember being anyone's possession," I fired back with angst on my tongue.

King looked over at me, "Yeah?" He chuckled, shaking his head, "I bet you were *his* bitch. Weren't ya? No other reason he'd get all stiff and shit when you-"

"Can you shut the fuck up and do your job? Just drive the fucking car." My eyes locked on the road with a burning pain seeping from behind my sockets.

King hated being spoken to like this, but for some reason he was letting me off. He seemed angrier to have been challenged by another man than to be disrespected by the whore he toted around in his luxury rental car.

He pulled the car to a sudden stop when his phone rang and turned it on speaker as Lorenzo's voice peeled over the stereo system, "Hello King, how was the show?"

King's eyes darted to me, "The show was fucking fine, boss man. But your little princess, ain't been so fine."

"What is she doing?" Lorenzo's voice sounded enthused.

Bleh.

"Aw, man. She wasn't fucking listening to me, so I grabbed her and this random ass motherfucker tried to square up. I swear to you, Zo, I would have beat his ass, but then little Valentine over here said her safe-word and his ass froze like the pussy he is and backed away." King laughed, triumphant in the non-existent fight that he couldn't have won to begin with.

Lorenzo chuckled, "Some random man responding to

Valentine's safe-word?" He asked, mischief hinting in his voice as he laughs in response, "What did he look like."

I felt panic rise to my chest and shouted to the stereo, "just some random person, Lorenzo. Bug off."

But King was persistent, "Nah, nah. Zo he was massive, man. I mean, not bigger than me but he was huge, bro! Covered in tattoos and shit."

"Cain?" Lorenzo's words shot straight through me, a blade of ice that impaled me, pinning me to the seat. I felt the interior of the car around me beginning to lessen, like the walls were closing in.

King looked over at me, "What? THAT was Cain?" He snapped, "And you didn't fucking tell me? I would have ended him!"

"Stop," I demanded, throwing my hands over my face in frustration. My heart thumped hard against my chest.

"What was Cain doing there, Valentine?" Lorenzo pushed.

It felt like the gremlin was crawling through the phone to nibble at the last shred of sanity I had left from this bullshit night. And he didn't seem to enjoy the long pause of frustrated silence that I allowed to permeate in the car.

He growled, "Valentine?"

I threw my hands up in defeat, ripping my seatbelt from the clip and forcing the door open to the car.

Before King could stop me, I took off running back in the opposite direction.

I searched for an open door, a busy restaurant, somewhere that I could slip into and disappear.

My heart pounded in my chest, and I could almost feel King's breath on my neck.

Suddenly, a hand reached from around a corner and pulled

me into an alleyway. A second hand clasped tight across my mouth as a heavy weight pushed my body against a sharp brick wall.

Terror surged through my nerves as I reached up to grasp at the hand that covered my mouth. The heat of the air increased sharply with each nauseating breath and less oxygen entered my lungs than necessary. I scratched at the hand, feet writhing against the wall.

All I could think is that if King caught me, I'd be as good as dead.

Darkness began to creep in at the edges of my vision as burning tears fell down my cheeks, but a face lowered and let out a long "hush," then the hand peeled from my mouth and cupped my cheek.

It felt so familiar.

So warm.

The heavy, clumsy sound of footsteps clambered down the sidewalk, and just as they nearly reached us, the weight shifted, blocking me from the view of the street. The sound of heavy footsteps continued for a moment, but the panic in my body still returned briefly as the footsteps once again returned, but with a barrage of curses and shouting as I heard the car in the distance start up and skid quickly away.

I finally felt a breath release, and as the squeal of luxury tires and an expensive rental fee faded into the distance, the weight that held me still against the wall pulled away and streetlight illuminated the soft brown curls of the man that had held me.

Cain stared down… well… *around* me, I guess. His gaze never actually locked onto me. My own gaze, however, locked directly onto him.

This welling of extreme emotions swirled in my mind, and

I felt dizzy. It was far too much, so any semblance of direct emotion drained rapidly from my face, and I stared directly at Cain with eyes that probably could have killed him a few too many times for his own comfort.

"Thanks," I muttered under my breath, dropping the gaze which I had afforded him to my feet.

Cain pulled in a quick breath of air through his nose and held it in his chest. It seemed to hang there in his lungs forever before he finally let out a long, steady stream of air. The silence hung over us just like it always used to, but Cain seemed so much more accustomed to it now. He reveled in it.

"Adam?" A man's voice called from the front door of the steakhouse. A man who I recognized, but not quite sure where I recognized him from, peeked his head around the corner. His big, green, fatherly eyes danced between us in confusion.

Cain's gaze lifted to meet the new man's face, and his entire demeanor changed. His stiff shoulders relaxed and fell into an at eased position. His blue eyes sparkled and he adjusted his hair so that it no longer eclipsed his face. He beamed at this man with a kind smile, "Thank you for the invite tonight, Roy. It was really lovely to get out of the house."

The man... Roy... nodded with a bright smile, "An old friend of yours?" He nodded to me.

Cain didn't turn to look back in my direction, "Yeah. I guess you could say that. We were colleagues once upon a time." He explained.

Roy smiled, "It is good to see you socializing, kid. I'll see you at work on Tuesday?"

Cain nodded, his eyes never losing that consistent, bright connection with the older man. He waved lightly to him as Roy disappeared back around the corner.

But as Roy faded into the distance, so too did the easy-going, bright expression on Cain's face. He turned his body back to face me, hands tucked into the pockets of his dark-wash denim jeans, with his gaze moving about his boots.

"Are you safe?" he asked, his voice hardly reaching more than a whisper.

I don't think a single ounce of me wanted to answer his question affirmatively. My eyes softened, but I turned to face away from him, looking further into the alley now, "He knows everything… He knows where I live."

"Are you safe?" He repeated.

As if I didn't fucking hear him the first time.

I groaned and rubbed my temples, "Fuck off Cain,"

"Adam…".

I glanced back and he was looking into the alley beyond our position as well. "I prefer Cain."

"I won't answer to it."

I scrunched my nose up, "Well, that's fine. I don't plan to fucking use it." I grumbled, bringing my hand to cup my neck anxiously.

Silence.

When I turned back in his direction, I half expected him to be gone, but he wasn't. He was there. Motionless. Once more, he asked that fucking question. "Are you safe?"

He really pissed me off.

He made me want to break things.

I clenched my fists tight, searching for a way to tell him to fuck off once and for all. The more I searched, the more hopeless I felt, and the more the reality of my situation hit me.

My shoulders fell and I hung my head.

"Come on," Cain turned from me, pausing at the entrance

of the alleyway. He did this when he wanted me to follow him. He always did. Like when I was late and he showed up at the apartment I shared with Finn. When I was the last to leave the dressing room. When I was the last to leave the car. He *always* waited for me.

Self-absorbed dickhead.

He MUST have a savior complex. He *has* to!

I swallowed my pride and stepped toward him. He led me down the road to where his Cobalt was parked, and he then slipped into the driver's side door.

I deliberated for a moment. Should I turn and run? A part of me wanted him to drive away and leave me here, but he didn't. He waited.

Soon, I persuaded myself to pull open the passenger side door and sit down inside the vehicle. His smell hit me immediately; an intoxicating slap in the face of nostalgia that caused a burning ache in my chest. The scent of my own destruction.

Cain waited until I was buckled, then cranked the car and drove in the direction of my old apartment. I narrowed my eyes skeptically until he took a turn towards College Park.

Just before he exited Metro Central, he pulled into an apartment complex with a gate around it. The car slowed as it approached the gate, and then as if by magic, it opened and allowed the Cobalt to enter.

He pulled the car through a small winding road until he reached a duplex with a two-car garage underneath it. He pushed a button clipped to the visor above him and half of the garage began to open. With a final maneuver, the car pulled to its stop inside of the garage, right beside a vacant, slick-black Dodge Charger.

"Please don't hit the Charger with your door." He asked softly, removing his keys from the ignition and pressing the button above him to close the garage door. He then stepped out of the car and started to walk toward a set of stairs that would lead to the duplex's entrance.

I pushed the door open carefully and stepped slowly behind him.

Now it was my turn to be silent.

As Cain pushed through to the entrance of his home, he removed his shoes and placed them on a small mat that held two other pairs of shoes. One pair of boots that were similar to those that he had just removed, and a pair of normal tennis shoes that looked well worn.

I nervously slipped my stilettos off my feet and then placed them on the edge of the mat.

The sudden chime of Cain's phone went off and he answered it, walking through the white hallway to a carpeted lounge that was deep grey plush, and held an L-shaped sectional couch with a decently decorated interior.

"Hi Mags," he says into the phone, the speaker pressed to his ear. That smile grew on his face again, along with a burning in my belly. He crashed into the couch with his cell phone in hand, "No, no. I have no clue what you're talking about."

I could hear Mags' muffled arguing on the other end, and Cain's face brightened with a bit of delight.

"No, Mags. Tell this King guy that if he wanted to know where *his bitch* was, maybe he should start by checking under his left fucking testicle." Cain glanced in my direction, seeing that I was still was standing by the entrance.

He motioned to the couch, and I reluctantly approached to sit down at the far end.

"Do you really think that Val would trust me? Of all the people in this world? You're literally her best friend. Maybe you should call her yourself." He paused to listen, his eyes glistening in mischief. "You know, Mags, maybe you should tell His Royal Highness to step off his fucking high horse and actually do his fucking job and look for *his bitch,* and not rely on other people for help." He removed the phone from his ear and ended the call, but I watched him type something furiously into a text message. He then placed his phone on the couch and leaned back into his spot.

For a few minutes, we stayed silent. I didn't know what to say or do, and he didn't say or do anything. Eventually though, I became keenly aware that my clothing was absolutely disgusting. I had actually managed to forget about the massive cum stain that had now dried on the front of my mini-skirt, and I gritted my teeth in annoyance.

Cain's eyes landed on my figure for a few seconds, then he stood and disappeared down a corridor that I hadn't travelled yet. When he returned, he had a towel in his hands alongside a pair of boxer shorts and a long, oversized T-shirt. He placed them on the couch beside me, then returned to his spot on the other end of the couch. "Bathroom is down the hall. First door on the left. You may use my products." He motioned down the hall from whence he came.

My eyes looked to the pile of fabric, then down the hall. I released the hem of my skirt and stood, retrieving the items from my side and slinking toward where he had directed me.

The bathroom itself was very clean, as was the rest of Cain's house. It didn't feel lived in at all, really. Like he just decided to appear in the showroom lot of this complex at the edge of Atlanta.

I set the clothes down on the counter and pulled myself free from the annoyingly tight outfit I was wearing. It was only now that I noticed the various dried substances all over my body.

I shuddered in disgust and turned on the water for the shower.

Steam slowly filled the room, surrounding me in soft flowing clouds of translucent white. I stepped in and pulled the curtain closed, sinking beneath the warmth of the water.

As it touched my face, I felt myself beginning to crumble.

It had been about a month since I had access to a hot shower. I'd been using the showers at a gym recently... As, I fucked the manager, and in return he would let me use the facilities on occasion. But the hot water never worked.

The soft embrace of heat enveloped me, and I felt this intense relief, a few stupid tears falling down my cheeks. I felt so safe here... *Why the fuck do I feel so safe here?*

Cain is literally in the next room, and I can feel this rush of emotions that I had managed to keep at bay for so long, suddenly crashing through me... but at least he couldn't see me cry. At least I could pretend to be stronger than I was.

I grabbed the soap from a shower caddy and coated my body in it, scrubbing as if I wanted to remove the skin itself. I lathered the soap onto my face to remove my makeup, even though I knew for a fact it would dry my face out. I wanted to scrub hard enough to mask the redness from crying.

After I felt sufficiently clean, I shut the water off and took a deep breath as I stepped onto the soft white bathmat that lays in front of the tub.

Once I dressed myself and wrapped the towel around my long, blonde, sopping-wet hair, I stared at the doorknob anxiously.

*How the fuck did I end up here?*

I glanced into the mirror beside me, and despite the fog I could see my outline. The swirl of a towel on top of my head, blue t-shirt that would have been oversized on anyone, and a pair of boxer shorts that were also slightly too big for me. With a final breath, I pulled the door open and emerged into the crisp, cool air of the hallway.

Cain was seated in the living room wearing a pair of black pajama trousers and a white t-shirt. Lounged back with a bottle of some sort of craft beer clasped to his hands. Something was different though, perched on his nose was a pair of glasses.

"I didn't know you wore glasses," I said softly as I returned to the lounge. In my spot, Cain had placed a folded blanket, a bar of chocolate, and a bottle of the same beer. My heart fluttered slightly.

Cain didn't respond.

I sat down, pulling the blanket over my knees as I glanced at the television to see what he was watching. It was a rerun of the Big Bang Theory.

Cain eventually sat forward and placed the empty bottle of beer on the coffee table in front of him. Then he clenched his fist and squinted, before dipping to grab it again and standing up. He entered the kitchen which was visible from where I stood to throw the bottle in the garbage.

*Why did he do that?*

He returned to the edge of the lounge, staring at the TV with his arms crossed in front of him. I took this opportunity to look at him. His biceps seemed larger than they used to be. Thick chorded muscles bulged beneath his sleeves.

Covered in tattoos, including one piece that I didn't think I quite recognized. A sketched piece on his bicep just below the cuff of his sleeve, the imprint of a lipstick mark.

Cain seemed to catch my gaze and turned his attention back to me.

For the first time in our lives, he actually looked at me…

Not through me…

Not towards me…

*At* me.

His expression was flat, as if he wasn't thinking of anything. And then after a few seconds of sharing eye contact, he returned his glance to the TV.

I pulled the blanket closer around myself, then looked down at the bottle of beer, "Cain…"

He turned his head to me.

"May I have a bottle opener, please?" I muttered.

Cain turned to grab it from the kitchen counter and then walked back towards me. At first, he extended it out, but then snatched it away from me at the last second as I went to grab it.

"Adam," He corrects softly.

I stared at the bottle opener, then glanced up at him. His brown curls shadowed his eyes lightly, but not enough to block them from view.

I nibbled the inside of my lip, "Adam." I echoed.

He nodded once, allowing me to now retrieve the bottle opener. But as I took it, he stayed in place, staring down at the bottle with an obsessive amount of attention. I popped the cap, and he instantly extended his hand to retrieve both the cap and the opener, before then returned it to the kitchen and tossing the cap into his trash can.

*Why was he being so obsessive?*

After this, he sat down in his place again and the episode ended, leaving us sitting awkwardly in silence as we waited for the next to start.

"Um... Thank you for tonight," I said softly.

Cain... *Adam* glanced over to me and nodded slowly with a shrug, "I mean, I told you before."

"Told me what?" I asked.

An eyebrow lifted from its normal place, and he chuckled, shaking his head. "I told you that I would protect you whether it was my job or not."

My heart beat heavily in my chest, but he wasn't finished.

"Of course, that was before I found out about Conor..."

The air fell cold between us, and he ensured his eyes were glued to the television, "But a promise is a promise."

I looked down at the blanket that covered my lap, my eyes welling as I studied the pattern. Guilt bubbled, and I placed the beer on the coffee table.

His eyes shot to the bottle, but I quickly grabbed a coaster to quell his anxieties.

"I need to tell you something," I said softly.

His eyes moved from the condensation dripping down the glass of the bottle to my hands that now rested in my lap, then they finally flicked up to zero in on my eyes. A silent act of encouragement.

I felt a lump growing in my throat and I drew in a deep breath, throwing my hands over my face, "I wasn't entirely forthcoming when you asked me about your brother." I admitted, feeling the anxiety tingling in my chest. His eyes narrowed inquisitively, and I felt like I may explode. "And... Lorenzo wasn't truthful with you either."

183

He seemed to reel back, rolling his eyes, "Listen… I know you might be trying to manipulate this into it not being your fault, but I literally watched you put poison into my brother's mouth."

I frowned, "Okay, first of all, I'm not trying to manipulate anything…"

Adam sighed and shook his head, "Look, Valentine. I have done enough already, giving you a place to stay. I could have left you out there on the street."

Tears welled in my eyes from frustration, and I groaned, "Please let me explain."

He exhaled mockingly as he leaned back against the back rest of the sofa, arms crossed in a clear defensive position over his chest.

Choking down a gulp, I continued.

"Lorenzo uses me a bit differently than the other girls. He always has. About five years ago, he forced me to kill my first victim." I stared into the knit pattern of the blanket to avoid his eyes, "Since then, I have killed about fifteen men… all under the guise of an escort service. All ordered by Lorenzo for one reason or another." I choked back my words, "Conor was apparently a regular user of Lorenzo's services… and hadn't paid him in over a year."

I could feel the heat of his gaze, but a part of me was terrified to lift my head to meet his eyes.

"The last man I killed… I was with you… Neil. He was a bird scientist. Shrimp allergy." I felt a weight lift off of my shoulders from all of the pent-up thoughts.

"When you asked me about Conor, I wanted to tell you, but you were so hurt. So angry… I couldn't speak. I couldn't bring myself to admit, that to you, I was a murderer." A single tear slipped down my cheek.

Adam was silent, but I could feel the atmosphere cool as he turned his gaze away from me, fixing it on the far wall where a door sat untouched. I assume it was the door to Conor's bedroom.

"Valentine," he said coldly, but this time I stood my ground. This time I didn't waver under the weight of my emotions.

"Becca," I corrected, my eyes lifting to search for his. I nearly lost it when I saw that he was staring directly at me, peering deep into my eyes as if to search for a hint of a lie.

His eyes softened and he nodded, "Becca."

*He said my name.* Tasting it like it had some semblance of texture that he would have to get used to.

"Are you telling me that this whole time, I have been blaming you for something that wasn't your fault?"

My heart ached, and I shook my head, "No. I did kill him." I muttered, "I killed all of those men…"

Adam pushed himself to the edge of his seat and sighed, "You didn't want to kill those men any more than you wanted to fuck those degenerate assholes who request your services from Lorenzo." He rolled a hand through his hair with yet another sigh.

"For Fucks-sake." He muttered breathlessly, pulling his hands to cover his face, "Fuck!"

Adam stood and slammed his hand into the arm of the couch. The whole room rattled under his sheer force.

I looked down at my hands, clasping them together in my lap, one more tear slipping out.

I didn't fear him the way that I feared other men. With him, anger was personal. He kept it to himself and treated those whom he treasured as obsessively as he treated his home.

185

He turned around to face me again, but for the first time, I truly and wholly felt the veil between us finally lift.

His eyes narrowed in a fiery acknowledgement of my pain and struggle. But he softened at the sight of my tears.

Adam stepped closer and knelt down before me on the floor. Somehow, he was *still* taller than me. His hands reached up and cupped my cheeks, thumbs swiping the residual wetness from my cheeks as his blue eyes stared softly into mine.

"Becca, I meant what I said to you that night," he admitted, "I hope you know that I want to work towards making sure that I can rewrite those words and put them into the present tense."

My eyes fluttered as the pink warmth of a blush began to climb over my cheeks. I remembered that night so vividly, the pain and devastation that I had felt. But I knew exactly what he meant. The words that hurt me more than anything else.

Adam gently leaned his forehead against mine, "I promise I want to fix this. I want to fix everything…"

I felt my arms begin to tremble and tears began to slip down my cheeks as something that was broken deep inside of me started to heal. He continued to swipe away the tears gently with his thumbs and pulled his face away from mine, "I'm so sorry for not giving you the space to explain…"

I shook my head, "Even if you had, I wouldn't have… I was too scared of Lorenzo." I muttered.

His eyes softened and he pulled his hands away, wiping the tear-soaked skin on the soft black fabric of his trousers, "What changed?"

My eyes widened and I froze, a soft, almost imperceptible shake of my head.

Adam reached a hand to circle around my wrist and his

thumb rubbed soothingly along my forearm.

A sob left my lips as I melted in his grip, "I…" I tried to speak, but coughed out a sob instead, "I think the thought of dying was more welcoming than the thought of continuing on in this world without you to hold my wrist like this when I needed it."

The blue of his eyes melted into a storm of raging ocean, and he tugged me forward from the couch.

I thought for sure that he would kiss me again like he had that night… in fact, I craved that, but instead he pulled me into his lap and encircled me in the tightest hug he could muster without hurting me. His hand braced my lower back and the other gripping at the towel that now very loosely clung to my wet hair.

I grasped at him, my hands gripping around the fabric of his shirt as I fell into his warmth. He held me there until the rapture of emotions inside of me had calmed and I was finally able to breathe clearly for the first time in a long while.

He pressed his chin lightly to my hair, "Remember when we were on the beach. You asked me to hold you."

I nodded.

"I dream of that day every night. I miss you, especially when I smell salty-air, vanilla and coconut…" He rubbed my back soothingly, pressing his own back against his coffee table. "I'm so sorry for the way that I treated you."

I shook my head lightly, "It isn't your fault." I muttered.

He sighed and nodded softly, resting his chin on my head again. His arms embraced me as though I would slip away from him. As if he was worried that I would try to flee.

*I wouldn't lie…*

I felt an extreme urge to ask him to have sex with me. A

drive to make him happy in the only way I knew how...

But I wanted this to be different.

I wanted to *feel* different.

I can't believe that I *ever* hated this man.

I could't believe that I was unable see the heartbreak staring me straight in the face as Mags and Sasha peeled me off of the tarmac that night. Then the following slow decline into madness as I allowed it to eat away.

I can't believe that anyone like *him* could want somebody like *me*...

A big part of me wanted to run. To ask him to save himself... Save himself from a life full of lies and a heart full of pain and sorrow.

I was sick, and I worried that he would never understand my sickness. The paths I take *never* seem to go well; failure follows behind all of my choices like a shadow.

I feel my head sink into his chest with morose submission, but rather than let go, Adam tightened his grip. He held me tighter than before, cementing me right there in place, surrounded by the protective spell that he cast.

*Maybe I could get used to this.*

# Who Hit You?

# ADAM

My alarm buzzed at 6:00 a.m., a symphony of morning chimes that mixed delicately with a throbbing migraine. I pushed myself up in bed and searched around my room for some way to get relief from the annoying noise.

I had left my phone by the door. Typical.

After pushing myself out of bed and dragging my knuckles across the floor to silence my alarm, I peered through my door to the living room. There, asleep on the couch, was the girl who I had thrashed from my life three months prior.

A soft smile warmed me, and I pulled the door closed again, moving to search for my gym clothes.

After getting dressed, I stepped through to the lounge and placed a gentle hand on Becca's back. She roused instantly, flinching away from my touch in genuine panic.

I pulled my hand from her respectfully, "Hey you," I said in a hushed tone. "I am going to the gym, and then I have to go see my mom. Would you like me to drop you off somewhere?"

For a second, confusion and fear flashed in her eyes, "You want me to leave?" she asked softly.

Her question sent a buzz of concern through me, and I quickly shook my head, "No, no. I just thought you may want to grab clothes from somewhere. And I don't want you here alone... just in case."

Becca pushed herself to sit up, her pout turning into a soft frown. "Could you take me to Mags's?" She asked.

I nodded softly, "Will you be okay?" I asked.

She narrowed her eyes, but nodded, "I got a message from Lorenzo. He wants us to do a job today."

My chest ached, but I tried to keep my displeasure from showing, "is *he* going to be driving you?" I asked.

She nodded once.

I scrunched my nose in annoyance, but had to let it go, "Do me a favor. Have him drop you off at the Midnight Raven. I'll pick you up and bring you back here."

The light seemed to return to her eyes for a moment and the world around us softened as the dark cloud that had grown over her was kept at bay. I smiled and ushered her to follow me out the door and to the garage.

The car ride was a sleepy kind of quiet, and as we approached Mags' apartment, Becca turned to me briefly, "Is your mom okay?"

I smiled, "She is as okay as she can be, but I am going to

check on her again today... Three-day weekend, and all."

This answer seemed to quell her curiosity for now, and as I stopped the car, she looked down at her hands as if longing for something. I thought I knew what...

I extended my hand and gently squeezed her wrist, "Hey," I said softly, "If he fucking touches you, I'm one message away."

She brightened and then nodded, gently pulling from my grasp as she exited the Cobalt, closing the door lightly and walking barefoot towards Mags' apartment in my fucking shirt and boxers. It excited me to watch her hips sway.

*How could a world so cruel, create something this beautiful?*

I watched her until I saw her safely enter the apartment building, then I sped off towards my gym.

I pulled out a pair of headphones as I entered, scanning the pass on my keyring to open the doors. I started towards one of the first parts of my morning set rotations and then turned the music on full blast in my ears. This drowned out any sensation other than adrenaline and the feeling of a nice burn that wouldn't require stitches.

The more I lifted, the more I ruminated upon the conversation that I had had with Becca last night, and uponhe fact that Lorenzo had been using her as a murderess for his dirty work.

Even *I* had only been made to kill a handful of people.

I may have injured far more and seriously maimed a few again, but if he ever wanted me to kill someone, there was a strict protocol involved. Cole and I were exclusively the butchers. We worked well together as a team, and we knew how to push the right buttons. I thought we were his only harbingers of doom. The girls were merely meant to exist to satisfy the good clients.

A pang struck my core as I remembered how she had cried last night. The way she curled up in my arms like a child seeking warmth. I worry for her as I have never worried for any other. I wondered if she even knew what love feels like.

*Am I too dangerous for her?*

*Will I destroy her again?*

My phone buzzed in my pocket, so I put down the curling bar and sat on the bench to breathe, pulling out my phone.

It was an unknown number. The message simply said:

**What are you up to?**

I raised an eyebrow and shoved it into my pocket, resuming my workout. When I began to wrap up my time in the gym, my phone buzzed again. I dragged a towel across my face to gather the sweat from my skin and stared down at the screen.

**Don't think I don't realize you're up to something.**

I smirked and ignored the message again.

I knew exactly who it was, that little fucking snake of an ex-boss of mine. I pushed my phone into my pocket and turned towards the car.

I stared at it for a moment, acknowledging the easily concealed silver estate car function that my Cobalt had. But maybe I wanted to live dangerously.

The Charger hadn't left the garage since I... Well, since I retired from Lorenzo's forces. It had a massive license plate with the name CA1N on it and was easy to spot. Easy to recognize.

But Lorenzo had fucked with me for the very last time... and perhaps today might just be the perfect day to wreak some havoc upon his life; perhaps bring it down in shells of hellfire and make him question whether he is in this to win it at all...

And then... reality struck me. I am not some massive crime syndicate. I can't make his life anywhere near the kind of hell that he could make mine... at least... not while Becca is still under his thumb.

Five bricks...

I could manage five. I could manage ten if I needed to.

Ideas began to race through my mind as I cranked the ignition and began to drive toward my mother's nursing home... something in me stirred. It was a confidence that I hadn't felt in myself for quite some time.

I kept picturing Valentine. The way her long blonde hair looked as it was tied up. I wanted to grab that ponytail in my fingers.

Despite every ounce of resolve I had, there was a burning in my belly. This *need* to see her completely and totally surrendered to me and nobody else. Mental images that I didn't realize were stored in the recesses of my mind, of all the different ways I had seen her so close to naked that naked felt like an impossible goal.

*I'd achieve it.*

*Fuck, what am I thinking?*

This drive that she has given me, it feels like my limbs are on fire, like the world around me is mine.

When I think of Valentine... of Becca... this world full of bullshit and pain and annoyance feels bearable. She makes me feel powerful.

Since I had dropped her off this morning, I noticed this hum throughout my body, an energy that buzzed in my core. I think it's anticipation. Waiting for her to call. Waiting for her to message. Wishing to see her face, hear her voice.

I had cast her away.

Manifested this horrible beast out of a woman who was only doing her job. The anger that I once felt so intensely, was now something else entirely. I longed for her… probably more than she knew. More than she could comprehend.

Maybe that is cruel of me.

The nursing home grew nearer, and with it swelled a resolve. I knew what I needed to do… Now all that is left is to do it.

I opened up my messages to Cole and typed out a message.

**Me: Hey, I need your help with something.**

He responded almost instantly.

**Cole: Go on.**

**Me: How quickly can you print passports?**

\* \* \*

# VALENTINE

I peeled myself away from the throbbing hard-on of the man underneath me. The sound of soft pulsing music matched my gyrations as I slipped away from the far corner of an old club's spare room.

My hips hooked left to right as I swayed towards the central point of the room where Mags stood holding a massive black silicone dildo. My eyes flicked over my shoulder to the customer of the day, a scrawny, mousy kind of man with a sharp nose and square-shaped glasses.

I blew him a kiss and fluttered my eyelashes as Mags took a few steps towards him and then ordered him to get on his knees.

The customer, a man named Peter Richie, was a simple man with simple pleasures... If you can call a domination kink and a morbid obsession with being pegged by a gorgeous black woman, to be simple.

As I stood, I could sense the menacing heat of King's eyes locked onto my frame. He stood at the entrance of the room with his arms crossed, a deadly threat etched in his eyes.

'Don't you dare try to fucking run', they tell me.

*Don't you fucking worry, bro. I know better than to run away from a job.*

I sat on the ground, legs crossed. This was really a call for Magnolia. All Peter really wanted was Mags. I was just a bonus bimbo with big tits that he could squeeze if he was bored. But I was more than happy to volunteer my distance. This job was tiring enough as it was.

I sat silently, watching Mags approach Peter and flip him onto his back as she danced for him.

Then a shadow fell over me, eclipsing the soft fluorescent light of the club room's corner lamp to my back.

"Get up." King demanded.

A stitch of annoyance, or perhaps fear, found itself between my eyebrows. I motioned to Mags and shook my head. We don't fucking leave girls alone.

Cain would have known that.

King's hand grabbed the base of my neck, and he forced me to stand. I bit back a yelp of pain from his gesture. I didn't want to alert the customer. The large black man pulled me to a dark, hidden corner of the room and dipped down to breathe in my scent. "You ran away from me last night," He growled.

A shiver coursed its way through my spine, settling at my core. Eyes glazing over in a lust that I wasn't sure was entirely authentic. My lips pulled into a smirk, and I nodded, "I know how much you love a chase."

He bared his teeth and plunged his hand down between my legs, "You're really fucking wet right now, Valentine. It isn't matching up with the visuals of our guest." King peeled my lips apart and rolled his middle finger along my clit. A surge of enjoyment peppered my skin with goosebumps.

"You like that?"

A blush rose to my cheeks as I stared back towards Magnolia. Her performative moans and Peter's gasps of pleasure as she sodomized him with a silicone appendage. I felt every instinct in me to pull away from King, but he had gotten me exactly where he knew he needed me to be.

King's finger rolled in circles along my clit, and he gripped a chunk of my hair like he always did. You'd think he would get more creative as we progressed... But this time, I felt my heart ache.

This felt wrong.

King plunged his finger inside and I bit my lip to hush a moan. My body was giving into the temporary pleasure that it become accustomed to receiving from him. Destructive, harmful, disappointing pleasure that left me begging for more after he finished early.

He pulled his finger out of me and removed his cock from his pants, slipping the denim down just enough to remove the length.

I looked down for a moment, confused as to what I actually

wanted in this moment. The temporary ecstasy that was scattered around each job I did with King was punctuated with a resounding ache of emptiness.

He stood over me, dipping his fingers back between my legs, "Why do you feel so tense, Val?"

I hated it when he called me that. I gritted my teeth, baring down on the eclipsed sound of words I refused to spill.

"You know you are mine. I claimed you. Lorenzo gave his approval. I can do whatever the fuck I want to do to you." He dipped his lips close to my ear as he hissed his vile words into my ear.

Rage coursed through me, but King's fingers on my labia dulled my convictions and I fluttered my eyes closed. I searched the recesses of my brain to find something that may distract me, but all in all... I knew I wanted King to fuck me. He pissed me off. He was nasty and abusive. But I craved the little pleasure he could give me in his disgusting little way. If he was going to treat me like an object of his own pleasures, I was going to sap every ounce of pleasure I could from him... however disappointing and selfish that was.

I reached down to stroke his cock, moving my fingers along it with a soft touch.

"You don't own me," I growled lowly, "Don't you ever fucking forget that I can slice your dick off if you ever fuck with me." I dug my nails into the skin of his shaft.

He reeled back his hand and slapped me clean across the face.

I felt the shock as my jaw twinged with pain. I immediately let go of his manhood and lifted my hand to my face. The world stood frozen as every single cell in my body was inflamed with rage.

King had just *hit* me.

He *actually* fucking hit me.

Suddenly, the shouts of Peter's climax rang out like a perfectly timed bell that allow me to pull away from the situation before I could inevitably make it significantly worse.

The driver's eyes narrowed, and he shoved his cock back into his pants with a huff, then pressed his back against the door where he was supposed to be this whole time, pushing me back towards my friend.

Mags slipped the dildo out of Peter and smirked as he crumpled to the padding beneath him, covered in his own sweat and cum. Her handy work was beautiful when completed.

I caught her eyes as they flashed to me, concerned. She walked over with a stern expression, "Where the fuck did you go?"

I narrowed my eyes, and she seemed to read my expression, but her gaze settled on the redness that was beginning to glow at the base of my jaw. She turned to King and frowned, "Don't you dare fuck with my girl." She warned, her arms crossed in front of her gorgeous body shining in the dim lighting with her artificial glitter.

King grew visibly annoyed, his eyes fixed on me, and even though I was facing away from him, I could tell that his eyes were tearing me apart.

Being almost entirely naked in a room where you are expected to behave as little more than an object for another person's pleasure is daunting enough, but I think that anyone under these stressors would crack. That familiar feeling of wanting to end everything here and now encroached and the annoyance on my face slipped into this expression of hopelessness.

Mags grew closer to me, wrapping her slender arms around me as she pulled me into a hug. She glanced over her shoulder to Peter, who was beginning to grow lucid again. Her eyes flashed to him, "Thank you for a wonderful night, Peter. We will be going now."

Peter's hand lifted and he waved weakly, sated.

The woman to my side intertwined her fingers in mine and pulled me toward the door, shooing King out as she did.

Once we were alone in the dressing room, Mags handed me her phone. A message typed out on her notepad:

**Is he picking you up?**

I stared at the text on the screen, then looked at her and nodded slowly.

Her eyes brighten and the worry on her face fades slightly... but only very slightly. She retrieved her phone and pulled me into a tight hug, "I knew he would come around." She whispered.

Magnolia pulled away from me to turn and get dressed, so I planned to do the same. I removed the lingerie that was clinging by thin straps to my body and pulled on a pair of black leggings and a t-shirt dress that covered my ass. Red with an Iron Maiden graphic on the front of it. Unzipping my duffel, I retrieved a hair clip and swirled my hair into a lazy updo.

King waited impatiently outside the door, and as we emerged, I could hear him grumbling something to himself about me that I didn't care to entertain.

"King," I said flatly.

He turned to look at me, shooting me a glare.

"I have a shift at the club tonight. Can you drop me off there? I'll walk back to Mags' afterwards." I asked innocently, making sure that there was a soft smile on my face.

He narrowed his eyes at me but glanced down at the duffel bag. "Is that your stripper shit?"

"Exotic dancer," I corrected, "I don't strip. I'm already mostly nude anyway."

He bobbed his head in a mocking motion and then rolled his eyes, "Whatever."

I could always rely on one thing with King, he operated in a way that set him completely apart from Cain. As much as King enjoyed using me for my plethora of fuckable holes, he didn't actually like sticking around for my dances, and even if he did like sticking around... King *always* dropped *me* off first.

As the Midnight Raven came into view, I felt my heart leap. That ice pick of anguish that had grown in my belly no longer felt so crushing. I saw my escape. My temporary sanctuary.

King pulled up out front and idled the car, wordlessly demanding me to leave his presence. I did. I blew Mags a kiss from the backseat and crawled out from where I was sat, duffel in tow, and then sauntered toward the back entrance of the club.

Cain always stayed until he was sure I was back inside, or at least under the cover of safety.

King didn't care.

As soon as my tennis shoes hit the ground, his tires were rolling.

Thank fuck for his genuine thickness.

I stepped along the side of the club until the alleyway dissolved into a back parking lot. There, waiting for me, was not the Adam that I expected. No Cobalt with a glasses-wearing, flannel-having, day-job looking man. No, my heart swelled as the growl of the Charger's engine struck my core with direct precision. The driver, that man of mystery, clad in tight leather and black. His hair was concealed beneath the black knit threading of that horrible fucking beanie.

This was not Adam. This was Cain.

My heart raced as he revved the engine for me, calling me forward until I materialized in the passenger seat.

Within an instant of being inside, I felt the energy in the car wash over me.

It was soothing.

Safe.

The smell of freshly detailed leather and a hint of some sort of musk filled my senses with a concocted melody, brought peace to my mind. I placed my duffel bag on the floorboards between my feet and breathed out a long sigh of relief as my back pressed into the seat.

Cain's lips turned up at one side into the softest smirk, breaking apart the shadowed stoic expression into one that was more friendly. "Hey, Becca."

I lifted a hand and shooed the name away, "I'm still Valentine for now." I muttered, my eyes closing to take in the calmness of the setting.

He chuckled, a soft and kind sound that drove the thrum of my heart. "Alright, Val." My heart leapt.

My nickname sounded perfect when it came from his lips. His eyes settled on my face, and I could feel his energy tense and the warmth that had become a dull throb warm once more as his eyes settled on the light bruising. He was silent, taking it in.

I reached my hand to cover the area, the slight sting summoning a wince as I tried desperately to mask the expression from him.

"What happened?" There was a biting tone in his voice.

My heart raced, maybe I liked it when he was angry… as long as he wasn't angry with me.

"I fell…," I lied.

Cain rolled his eyes and turned to face me head-on, his fingers slipping around the wrist of my left hand that pressed against my jaw. He pulled it from my skin, his own face mere inches from mine as he inspected the injury.

"Who hit you? Was it a client? Why didn't King stop them?"

His questions fell from his lips in quick succession, the concern falling around me as I felt my eyes soften.

"It wasn't a client." I muttered, trying to pull my gaze away by turning my head, but Cain's other hand moved to gently cup the skin of my neck, his index and middle finger guiding my gaze back to him.

That fucking rush.

With his hand secured with the gentlest pressure on the outer edge of my throat, I found that his blue eyes met mine intensely. Something burned there in his eyes… and it made me fucking wet.

"Who hit you, Valentine?" His voice morphed into the low growl that sent shivers through my spine, and I found myself glancing down at his lips.

I wanted him to kiss me.

I pulled my bottom lip between my teeth and nibbled lightly at it, my eyes settling back into his. "You already know who hit me, Cain," I growled in response.

The electricity between us was palpable, and I wanted nothing more than for him to tear my clothes off right then and there. I wanted to feel his skin against mine. I wanted to feel the throb of his cock.

He pulled away, just when I thought that I may be graced with some semblance of reciprocation. The warmth of his touch slipped from my throat, my wrist.

It left a cold desperation in its wake.

His right hand pulled the gear stick into drive, and we were off in an instant, the pull of the Charger's horsepower pinning me back against the seat.

"Where are you going?" I asked, the thrill on my chest dissipating into a tremor of confusion.

Cain glanced at me, a few of his brown curls pushing their way from beneath his beanie's hold, but he didn't speak. He returned his eyes to the road. I knew exactly where he was going. Cain had a vengeance to exact, and there was only one place that he could possibly find it.

# Pistol Whip

# CAIN

My foot felt like a brick as it pressed itself into the accelerator. The engine offered heavy hums as I sped through the Atlanta streets. There was a burning in my chest that felt like literal flames. They lapped at my heart as it pounded with seething rage.

I couldn't even turn to look at Val. The fact that some asswipe's handprint showed so clearly on her face, made me absolutely sick. She was quiet for once, but I think she knew I needed the silence right now.

Lorenzo's mansion came into view, the sparkle of his porchlights erupting vibrantly through a sea of trees. Cole's

Scion was parked out front, right next to a luxury Range Rover that I had half the mind to just ram directly into.

Luckily, I realized that I spent a fuckload of hard-earned money on this beast of a car and I wasn't prepared to damage it simply because I disliked someone. I parked directly behind it, though, thoroughly blocking him in.

"Cain, you don't need to go in there," Val pleaded, her hands moving to clasp around one of mine.

I glanced over to her, intent on listening to her reasoning, but the bruise that was turning colors on her jaw sent more shocks of anger through my system.

I stared at her for a moment, taking in how she looked.

For a split second, I debated doing this at all.

To just turn around and drive home. But then I saw that mark again, and the rage took a hold of me again. I reached across into the glove compartment and retrieved the pistol. It was unmarked and untraceable.

The sound of a single, shaky breath escaped from Valentine's lungs as she looked to my hands, tears building in her eyes, "No… no! Cain, I hurt him… It was reactional!" She pulled her hands over her jaw, covering the mark, "Please… let's just go back. You know you'll be outnumbered in there."

I slid open the magazine of the gun and checked that it was loaded before arming the safety and holstering the weapon in its holster beneath my jacket. My eyes locked upon hers. Puffy and red from the tears she had yet to shed.

She was so beautiful.

I always thought that seeing her genuinely happy was one of the most beautiful things, but to see the raw emotion on her face… The desperation in her words… She was stunning.

My heart pounded in my chest, so I made a leap of faith.

I leaned across the car, the act pinning her to her seat.

*She was so fucking beautiful.*

The thrum of my heart grew so loud that I could actually feel the shaking of my ribs as the organ beat against it.

"Do you remember what I told you ages ago?" I asked, hovering inches from her face.

She blinked at me, confused.

"I would show up for you... That I would protect you. Whether it was my job or not."

"I will never break that promise." I stared into her eyes for a few seconds, but ones that felt like an eternity... and then... I crashed my lips against hers.

Part of me worried that she would push me away, but as I leaned into her soft lips, she beckoned me closer and deepened the kiss. This insane burst of courage filled me to the brim, and I felt like I was walking on air.

She was mine, and absolutely nobody was going to fucking take her away from me.

As I pulled away from her, I opened my eyes, and I witnessed her in all of her raw beauty.

Her forehead beaded with sweat as her brown eyes stared at me, hungry for more. Her shoulders moved up and down slowly with each heavy breath as she stared me in the eyes. I cupped her cheek gently and whispered, millimeters from her lips: "Do you trust me?"

Her eyes darted past me toward the house, and I can't lie when I say that I looked over my shoulder too, if only for a millisecond before they fell back to her once more. She nodded softly, resolve growing in her face as she lessened the grip on her face.

I moved my hand to brush a strand of her blonde hair out

of her face, tucking it gently behind her ear. "You are so, so beautiful, Becca." I muttered, pulling away from her slowly to sit properly in my seat. "If I don't come out, don't leave with anyone other than Cole." I said softly.

A pang of grief struck my core as I thought about never seeing her again...

But, if this was the last time I'd ever see her, I wanted it to be the best. I turned to look at her one more time and smiled at her kindly. "Keep the car running. When I come running out, we need to be ready to go."

She nodded once, affirmatively, and I reached over to squeeze her wrist.

"You're my pain in the ass, now, don't you dare forget that." I grinned.

I took a deep breath and climbed out of my car, walking toward the front door. I felt like I could run the world right now. The warmth of her lips still lingered on my own. I hope this works.

I stepped forward and lifted my knee high before delivering a swift kick to the front door, smashing the lock and sending the door flying open. Crappy American plywood. The realization of how easily I could storm a castle was thrilling.

As I emerged through the entryway, a figure approached me quickly, running before skidding to an immediate stop, curly brown hair bouncing against his forehead. His eyes widen as he realizes who the fuck I am.

"Hey," I said simply, offering no threat to my friend.

Cole nodded once, with a stern narrowing of his eyes, "Hey." I smirk, "Look at you with your gun drawn."

He chuckled and spun the pistol in his hand before holstering the weapon, "You know I'd never shoot you." He chuckled with a light-hearted grin, "Where the hell have you been and why did you kick the fucking door in?"

"Oh, Zo didn't tell you he was expecting guests?" I asked, a cheeky grin growing on my face.

"No, actually." Cole said matter-of-factly, "In fact, he said that you fucked off and weren't coming back."

I chuckle, "I'm sure that's what he hoped would happen."

Cole's eyes narrowed suspiciously as he touched the grip of his holstered pistol, "Is that so?"

My head bows in a slow nod, "Yeah… that *is* so…"

I took a step towards him, waving my hand dismissively toward his gun, "I didn't come here to get shot by you, though. You may actually wanna fucking hear what I have to say."

Cole's eyebrow raised and he relaxed, turning to walk at my side, "Is it about the new guy who has been set with your girls?" He asked.

I laughed, shaking my head lightly, "Oh my dear friend, you have no fucking clue." The din of laughter and conversation grew louder as Cole and I approached the dining room.

Lorenzo spotted me at the very same time that I spotted him, a mixture of fear and entertainment growing in his eyes. He snorted, rapping his hands across the table with a joyous laugh as he motioned to me, "Fucking, Cain." He said audibly, "I wondered when your sorry ass was going to come crawling back for your job."

I felt my blood run cold as I noted the faces around the table. Other drivers. Some who had been in the business far longer than I had. They knew Lorenzo better than anyone else. But there he sat at the head of the table; legs outstretched like a mediocre monarch. My eyes fused to him in a menacing, burning stare.

"Nah, nah, Zo. He ain't here for you." King smirked, pushing himself from the end of the table and standing upright with a boisterous stretch, "This motherfucker is mad because I slapped his bitch."

Lorenzo looked between us, his eyes settling on me for a moment before he leaned back in his chair. Amusement scratched onto the faces of everyone else in the room as King sauntered his way around the table.

"*You* slapped *Valentine*?" Cole inquired, his brown eyes widening with anger.

King smirked, "Hell yeah I slapped Valentine." He spat, and then stepped closer to me until our chests touched.

"She runs into you and then suddenly she doesn't wanna put out anymore. She grabbed my dick and dug her big fucking fingernails into it. So yeah, I slapped her. Real good too, my hand still hurts."

The hairs on the back of my neck stood up as my eyes narrowed. This piece of shit deserved every second of the hellfire I was about to reign down on him, but I wanted him to sing. Sing like a fucking bird. *Never interrupt your enemy when they are making a mistake.*

"And you know what, Cain," King said, shoving me backwards once, I let myself step back, "Until you showed your sorry ass yesterday, she used to beg me to fuck her until she screamed. You should have seen what I did to her. We'd get high and I'd send her to fucking sleep with my dick, and then once she was asleep, I had even more fun with her."

My eyebrow twitched, hands tightening into fists as I stared him down with just as much intensity as I when I walked in. *This fucking piece of shit was going to pay.*

King pressed his hand to the center of my chest and

grinned widely, "And you think you are gonna get somewhere? Coming in here? With my boss at my back? You think you're gonna fucking win this fight?"

That one got me, the pure absurdity from his cockiness.

I laughed.

I rolled my head back in a massive fucking howl.

He narrowed his eyes, shoving me back again, "What is your fucking problem, dude?" He snarls.

I laughed again, allowing myself to step backwards once more.

"But you see…" I clapped my hand over my forehead, "It's just that… you seem to be under the impression that a single one of these fuckers actually gives a shit about whether you win or lose."

King's eyes narrowed and he looked at Cole, then back at me.

Then it happened, in an instant. I sank my hand into the leather of my jacket and withdrew my firearm.

Safety off.

One quick shot, straight to his kneecap. The scent of sulfur and smoke filled the air as the pop of the barrel echoed through the room.

King hit the floor, a resounding wail escaping his mouth as he swung one of his tree-like limbs in my direction. Blood spewed from his knee, and his arm still very narrowly missed my stomach as I whipped around and collided the butt of my pistol with his temple.

Flat out.

King's unconscious body struck the floor, and I rolled my eyes.

"Go get me some rope, Cole." I snapped, stowing one swift

kick to King's ribs. I looked up at Lorenzo with an annoyed scowl, "Sorry you've lost two fucking drivers in a year. Maybe you should hire someone that isn't a fucking dickhead next time."

Lorenzo smirked and waved me away dismissively, "He hit my best girl. My punishment would have been far worse." He said with a look of languor, "Just get him out of here before I realize I liked him."

I smirked and turned to see Cole returning with a bunch of bungee cords. His signature. I retrieved the bindings and dipped down to tiethe giant of a man. "Grab his feet," I instructed my friend.

"You could say fucking please," Cole grumbled, but he was smiling as he bent down to grab King's feet. His shoes were luxury. They had once been white but were now stained red by the blood that pooled out of his eviscerated kneecap.

I signaled a pause, then walked over to Lorenzo's dining table and snatched one of the thick napkins from it. I returned and quickly wrapped his bleeding knee. No fucking way was this motherfucker going to bleed all over my trunk.

"Okay, grab his feet, please," I felt the hiss of the 's' on my tongue as I enunciated the word. Cole nodded resoundingly and we both hoisted the huge man from the ground. We managed to carry King's limp body toward the Charger outside.

When we emerged through the door, I motioned to Valentine to pop the trunk, and she moved to do so without hesitation. Cole and I stuffed the unconscious body in the back and realized that he was beginning to rouse once more. So, I delivered a decent punch to his temple, which arguably could have roused him faster... but luckily it did not.

Cole laughed and clapped his hands together to dust off his imaginary dirt from the incredibly arduous feat, "What a fucking dick! I hated this guy."

"He is still alive," I reminded him, slamming the trunk's lid closed with a resounding thump.

"Yeah, but not for long." Cole smirked, his eyes shifting to glance through the deeply tinted windows of my car. It hummed softly in the evening air, "he deserves it. Sasha quit because of him."

My nerves flare, how had he destroyed my team in such a short time? "Thank you for your help, ass-hat." I said, clapping his shoulder with a heavy hand, "Meet me at the safehouse tomorrow?"

Cole nodded quickly, and a sly grin appeared on his blood-thirsty face. There was a reason that Lorenzo kept him around...

Cole was a talented butcher by trade.

The human trade.

We started at the same time under Lorenzo, but Cole was always so much more sadistic than I was.

That is why I needed him.

I acted out of anger.

He... well Cole acted out of pleasure.

"I've got an appointment with our old friends, the Sharpe's, tomorrow. It'll have to be quick and easy," Cole smirked as he turned back towards the path.

I stepped past him before sinking into the front seat of the car, he turned briefly to wave, and I returned the gesture.

Securing my seatbelt, I turned to look to Valentine. Her face was streaked with tears, and her eyes avoided me.

The sight broke my heart a bit, and I reached out to take

her hand into mine. She accepted it with no dispute, tangling her small, well-manicured fingers between my tattoo-ink-covered digits. I delivered a gentle squeeze and pulled the car from the driveway.

Even as I drove, I kept a gentle hold of Valentine's hand.

Her silence was normal to me.

It was welcome.

Eventually, we arrived at the safehouse that I mentioned to Cole, and I pulled to a slow halt in front. I turned to her to see the worry painted on her skin.

"Is he dead?" she muttered, her eyes glistening from a film of tears.

I sent a gentle squeeze to her hand, "No," I said truthfully. "I won't kill him, I give you my word." I brushed my thumb across her knuckles, "But he is going to learn a very valuable lesson. Would you mind helping me take him inside?"

Her eyes narrowed, but she glanced at the door of the house. It looked normal. Like any other house. She nodded strongly, unbuckling her seat belt.

I popped the trunk and the pair of us... mostly me... hoisted King from the trunk and into the building. There was a distinct emptiness to the building. Nothing but a chair in the center of the main room, and a door that led to a cell. I directed Valentine toward the cell, and she placed his feet down on the end of a mattress, the only piece of furniture in that room.

Val stepped past me quickly, standing in the doorway of the cell as I secured King's loosening bungee cords. I stood and joined her outside before closing the door and securing the lock. Cole and I were the only cleaners with access to this safe house. Lorenzo made sure that partners stayed loyal to one another. It doesn't matter how insane he is, there's good reason as to why he is still in business.

I turned back to Val and smiled, extending a hand to brush a hair out of her face, "Shall we go back to mine?" I asked.

She leaned into the touch of my fingers, and I could feel her warmth travel down my hand into my wrist. The stain of black beneath her eyes from her smudged eyeliner was so alluring and beautiful. I wanted to make her eyeliner run like that from pleasure...

I secured the front door of the safe house and drove back to my apartment, sliding into the garage and returning Valentine to the safety of the duplex.

She stepped through the threshold of the garage to the living room and placed her duffel bag on the floor beside the coffee table.

I stared at her from the doorway, watching the way her leggings gripped her curves. My erection was solid in my trousers, as she dipped down to grab a pair of pajamas from the bag. Her hair fell over her face as she turned back from her position to look at me, her cheeks flushed with light embarrassment and she stood once more, pulling the folded clothing against her chest.

"Not like you to be sheepish," I chuckled, closing the door to the garage.

Valentine smiled timidly, brushing a strand of hair from her face as she stepped towards me, "Not like you to be so forward." Her feet pattered lightly with precision, swaying her hips perfectly. She stopped in front of me, an arm's length away.

My eyes deepened and I hungered for her, desperately.

"Did you mean what you said earlier?" she asked, rocking

on her feet.

I tilted my head, "What did I say earlier?"

A million things crossed through my mind as I searched her eyes for hints. She teased me, biting her lip and standing on her toes to grip the lapel of my jacket. "You told me I was your pain in the ass."

I smirked, "Yeah?"

"Did you mean it? Am I yours?" she coaxed, lingering near enough to tempt me.

I nodded once, a deep, lusty sparkle in my eyes, "I absolutely meant it, Val." I groaned lowly, dipping my head lower.

Her face brightened and she seemed to sway on her tip-toes, but the joy on her face shifted to mischievous as she leaned back to stare into my eyes, "Then prove it." she said breathlessly.

My eyes widened and I felt my erection twitch painfully against my zipper. I leaned over and pressed a deep, passionate kiss onto her lips, pulling her body as close to mine as possible.

I wanted to breathe her in and hold her deep inside of my lungs. I wanted to feel her course through my blood. As our lips crashed together, I slowly guided her backwards toward the couch, where she pulled from me and shoved me down upon it. I gasped at first, but she was quick to straddle me, and I felt all my reservations begin to fade away.

The pressure of my cock against the tight denim of my jeans was growing unbearable, especially as Val started to grind lightly over the surface, her lips falling into mine with a ferocity that felt unreal. I wanted her so badly that it was hard to put into words.

I felt the passion in our kisses soften and Val pulled away, peering down at me with an excited smile, a blush now wide across her face.

A chuckle rolled from my chest as I stared at her, "I've never seen you smile like that," I muttered softly.

The red on her cheeks grew darker, and she pressed her palm to my chest, "I've never felt like this after someone kissed me before," She admitted bashfully.

My eyes widened slightly, and I reached up to cup her cheek. She leaned into my palm again and I felt my heart flutter in my chest. *I don't care what I have to do in this life, but I'll be damned if I ever let this gorgeous fucking woman out of my sight again.*

"Becca…" I muttered, holding her gaze, drinking in the honey brown of her irises.

She responded wordlessly, a soft flutter of her eyelashes as she leaned in closer, pressing her chest to mine and sealing her hand between our ribcages. "I am so… so unbelievably sorry for how I treated you that night."

Her eyes deepened and she pressed her head into the crook of my neck. I wrapped my arms around her to hold her close, "I can't believe I let Lorenzo and his stupid games, turn me against you."

She giggled and then nuzzled my chest lightly, "You're a pain in the ass," she muttered and pushed herself from off of me. Her hand moved to press lightly on the couch cushion beside my head, "I forgave you when you picked me up dressed like your sexy alter-ego tonight." She said with a grin.

I felt relief lift from my shoulders and I clapped a hand to my forehead, "I really wish I had taken you on that date." I told her softly.

"Me too," She admitted, then teasingly rolled her hips

against mine, "But you can make it up to me by taking me out on one tomorrow." She smirked.

Tomorrow. Shit… Tomorrow was Tuesday. I have work… and I have to take care of King… It looked like that would be a four-a.m. job.

I smiled at her, moving a hand to her hair and watching as my dark ink disappeared and sank into her bright blonde waves. I searched for the back of her skull where the scar from her roommate's attack had since healed. I felt my heart thud at the thought of him still being out there somewhere.

She giggled and peeled away from me, standing up. The look of disappointment that I had must have been explicit, because she giggled and leaned down to press a quick kiss to my lips, "I need a shower before I feel comfortable letting you touch me. I've got to put Valentine away.

I nodded softly and smiled, "Shall I put Cain away as well?"

She turned back to me with a sly grin, "Hmm, I like Cain. Just lose that horrible fucking beanie."

I let out a laugh and peeled the knit from my hair, throwing it in her direction. She squealed and dodged.

"There we go," she teased, "Now he can stay."

# Scalding Hot

# BECCA

I pulled the shower curtain closed and stepped beneath the heavy stream of hot water. This luxury still felt unreal to me. Rivers of water droplets cascaded down my body, curving over my hips and swirling down my legs before pooling between my feet.

The electricity of Adam's lips remained on mine.

There was a rush in my body... an ache that longed for him. I couldn't believe that he actually kissed me. Still so overwhelmed by the worry of what may happen to him that I almost didn't register the hints if there were any.

I pressed the tips of my fingers to my lips and felt the warmth of a blush growing. My time with him felt so different than sex had felt in a long time. I remembered the night that he told me to get my roommate to finish me off, and the way that I fucked him in my head. I wondered if it would be anything like that.

The relationships you form as an escort are never positive, and mine have clearly been reminiscent of that idea. I had become incredibly self-destructive in Cain's absence, and I formed relationships that served to only fuel my addiction to sex. There was no positive... only an occasional orgasm.

And the thing with orgasms is, when a man is getting with a sex worker, her pleasure goes out the window as long as they experience the pleasure they seek. It was that way with Finn, with King... with all of the men who operated as my clientele.

But Cain was always... Different. He didn't view me as a sex worker. He didn't think of me as disgusting. He was always good to me, even when I was an absolute bitch to him.

He fucked up, twice, and I hated him for both. I really, truly, hated him. At one point, just being in the same room with him after the frat party felt like enough torture to push me over the edge.

Looking back, I understand why he didn't come... I mean, I wouldn't have rescued someone who had just called me worthless and stupid.

My chest began to ache, and I pulled the water over my face to wipe free the makeup that had dried in streaks down my cheeks. I scrubbed my fingers in circles over the soft skin and sighed.

*What am I doing?*

*Why does his presence feel so safe? Why do I search for him in seas of people? Why does his touch light a flame within me that burns so vibrantly that I feel invincible?*

*And... why does it terrify me?*

*Why do I feel like the only outcome of this is heartbreak? Will I fuck this up too?*

I slathered a dollop of soap across my body, scrubbing everywhere. I felt filthy... disgusting. My skin reeked of all the hundreds of men who had used my body, sending this itching burn throughout my flesh. I scrubbed until all of my skin was red and raw, tears pooling in my eyes. This overwhelming heat burned in my chest.

I'm wasn't sure that I wanted this...

I want to run away and hide, to go back to the normal where sex was a means of making money... money I never saw, but money, nonetheless.

No strings attached, no heartbreak, no pain.

I stood there in the water and let it continue to cover me in its warmth, and then I even reached forward to increase the temperature. Scalding water now cascaded over me, and even though I winced, I felt the relief of the pain existing somewhere other than within me. It helped me to breathe, slowly, fully.

The steam within the bathroom deepened and I could feel the jaws of anxiety pulling at me. I don't want to stay here. I don't want to do this.

I placed my hands against the cool tile of the wall and searched for air, failing to fully pull in a breath that didn't fully consist of my own self-harming steam. The air was thick and moist, suffocating.

A soft knock sounded from the door, but I couldn't answer it.

The sound of my heartbeat throbbed in my ears, and I

placed my head against the tile, the heat enveloping me in its suffocating grips.

Suddenly, the temperature decreased in the room, and a swell of cool air pushed in as the door to the bathroom opened and Adam entered. He stepped towards the shower and lowered the temperature slowly until the water had shut off completely, and a large fluffy towel soon encircled me.

I whimpered, finally able to catch a breath that wasn't steeped with moisture. As I turned around, Adam's features were soft, they were kind. He extended his arms to me slowly.

I stared at him for a moment, the leather jacket that I had seen him wear for two years, dark jeans and a thick belt. Eventually, courage built up within me and I stepped forward, leaning into his chest and allowing him to wrap his arms around me. Those feelings of confusion and uncertainty drifted away, and all I felt was safety.

Adam nuzzled his nose into my wet hair, placing a soft kiss on the damp skin of my forehead.

"Penny for your thoughts?" He asked.

The comfort I felt in his embrace eclipsed my reservations. I would give anything in the world to make sure I could stay in these arms forever. I hesitated to express myself, but his reassuring silence actually encouraged me to speak.

"I'm just scared, Adam." I muttered, hearing the tremble of my voice between my words.

"I heard you hyperventilating, and you didn't respond when I asked if you were okay," He muttered.

*Saving me again.*

I closed my eyes and buried my face in his chest, "I don't want to hurt you," I whispered, "But I am absolutely terrified of you hurting me."

Adam placed a gentle hand on the towel covered small of my back, his other hand moving up to stroke my hair gently, "I'll go as fast or as slow as you want me to," He whispered.

His words soothed that burning inside like a balm, and I pulled my head back so I could look up at him. I *did* want this. I wanted him to hold me. To kiss me. To look into my eyes with those stunning blue orbs.

He met my gaze and smiled lightly, "We can stop here for tonight if you want," He assured, placing a gentle peck on my lips.

I shook my head, "No, I want to…" I muttered, a blush settling on my cheeks in a dusty pink, "Can we just take it slow? Let me lead?"

Adam's eyes softened and he nodded, "Whatever you need," He took a step away.

"Get dressed, I've ordered us a pizza. It will be here soon. You don't have to rush yourself into anything, Becca."

My heart fluttered, and this time I *knew* it was with affection. I nodded, though the distance that grew between us drenched me in chills. Adam left me in the bathroom, pulling the door closed behind himself as he returned to the lounge.

I glanced down at my skin, burned a bright pink from the heat of the water. It showed clearly against the stark white of the fluffy bath towel. I didn't understand what drove me to that extreme. To my feeling so absolutely out of control.

*Maybe that's what I needed: control.*

I haven't had a say in who or what comes in contact with my body since I turned twelve, and experience has manipulated my sense of normal. Adam was reserved, and kind. He treated me like my agency was acceptable and encouraged.

My pajamas sat in a neat pile on the counter, and I stepped

out of the shower to pull them on. The soft silk of the camisole blouse soothed the heat that still radiated from my skin, and the matching shorts pulled up nicely around my waist. I felt comfortable.

I fluffed a towel through my blonde hair, drying as much as I could before pulling a brush through it.

A knock sounded from the front door, and brief chatter could be heard. Then the door closed. Adam's footsteps alone sounded from the lounge.

I pushed the bathroom door open, and the scent of fresh pizza filled my senses, and my stomach growled loudly.

Adam grinned in my direction; his glasses perched on the end of his nose. He had changed into a pair of flannel pants and a Jimi Hendrix T-shirt, and was now sitting in his usual spot on the couch, "Hello, lovely."

I blushed and stepped towards my seat, Where my blanket had already laid out, and a bottle of Coke and a paper plate laid on the coffee table for me. I sank into the cushions and breathed a sigh of relief as the panic from earlier finally washed away.

He opened a box of deep-dish pepperoni pizza and dished me out a slice. Excitement grew in my eyes, and he seemed to notice this, delivering a gentle peck to my forehead as I accepted the slice onto my plate.

I giggled, retreated back to my corner of the couch and began to nibble at the slice. Adam started to search through Amazon Prime for something to watch and stumbled upon a film called 'The Escorts'. He shrugged and turned it on.

After we finished eating, I felt the arms of comfort calling to me, and I found my eyes wandering to Adam on the other side of the room. I pushed myself up from my spot and took a few steps towards him, "Is this seat taken?" I motioned to the empty space directly beside him.

He grinned, shaking his head, "No, absolutely not. Even if it was, I'd never deny such a beautiful woman her rest." He said sweetly, then encircled a hand around my wrist to pull me gently into the seat. His arm lifted and fell around my shoulders to pull me lightly against him, his hand settling on the bare flesh of my thigh for mere seconds, before he moved it to rest on the silk of my shorts instead.

Chivalry is sexy as fuck…

I nibbled the back of my lip as I found it increasingly difficult to pay attention to the movie that was playing in the distance. I could smell his scent. Feel his warmth. Out of the corner of my eye, I could see his soft features.

I reached to gently grab his hand from my hip and move it to rest on the warm skin of my thigh. Goosebumps travelled up my body and I hitched a soft breath.

I was certain that this was what *I* wanted.

Adam sent a soft squeeze to my thigh, and I flashed back to his hands gripping my waist as I ground my hips against him at the club on his birthday. I felt my core ache softly, slowly, and I turned my head, extending my hand upward to cup his cheek, guiding him into a gentle kiss.

He obliged, his hand slipping from my thigh to slide beneath the fabric of my shirt.

Our kiss deepened as I removed my hand from his face to pull back the fabric of his pajama pants.

His cock was already hard, pressing against the restricting hold of his boxers. As I pulled them down, his dick popped right out, nearly all by itself. My fingers began to circle his tip as I continued to kiss him, both of us growing hungrier by the second.

A soft whimper of enjoyment escaped his lips as I started to stroke his shaft in slow desired-filled swoops. While I stroke, I peeled my lips from his, but his free hand came up and gripped my throat lightly, pulling me back to him.

*Drenched.*

I was fucking soaking.

I could already feel my pussy begging.

I stroked his cock faster, reaching my other hand down into my shorts to stroke my clit.

After a few minutes of this, Adam pulled away from me entirely and tucked his dick back into his pants. I stared at him, confused and worried that I'd done something wrong, but he smiled at me. His hand raised to usher me towards his bedroom, and without a second of hesitation, I obliged.

He guided me inside and I stepped quickly to sit at the edge of his bed. Adam's eyes lulled in a lusty stare as he took in my appearance.

"Do you trust me?"

My heart fluttered, and I nodded slowly.

Adam smiled and pulled open a drawer to his side, retrieving a pair of handcuffs. Genuine police-grade handcuffs. "You promise me that you will use your safe-word?" he asked, walking toward me with the handcuffs dangling to his side.

I felt the tips of my fingers twitch as excitement grew. I nodded, but he shook his head.

"Use your words," He demanded, his voice low and raspy.

I felt myself choke for a second on the air in the room, but then smirked, "Yes, sir."

"Wrists," He demanded.

My nipples formed stiff peaks beneath my silken blouse,

peeking through slightly, as I lifted my hands from my lap and extended them, palms facing the ceiling.

Adam clipped one of the cuffs around my wrist. It clicked three times until the cold metal pressed lightly on my skin. Contrast to the burning warmth of my arousal.

"Crawl," He ordered, pointing to the metal bars of his headboard.

I glanced at him for a moment, and his eyes were dark with lust, but that familiar feeling of safety lingered beneath it all. I obeyed his order and turned to give him a full display of my ass as I crawled to the top of the bed.

Adam climbed up as well and threaded the other cuff through the metal bars above my head. then he gently took my other wrist and pinned it to the headboard. He dipped down, pressing a ferocious kiss to my lips as he secured my other hand in the cuffs.

He then pulls from my kiss with a grin, "Sorry they're not fluffy."

I giggled as I stared up at him, "It's okay," I muttered, "I like it rough."

His eyes glazed over, and his lips pulled into a smirk, "You're so used to giving pleasure. I'm gonna show you that I refuse to take and not give."

His fingers started travelling to the buttons of my blouse and then slowly opening them, placing a kiss underneath the skin where each button had been until the blouse popped open, fully displaying my breasts.

Adam smiled, and then dipped to roll his tongue over one of my hard nipples, squeezing my other breast lightly. I shuddered as his lips grazed the sensitive nerves on my breasts. *This man was going to destroy me.*

230

He pulled away from my breasts and hooked his index fingers under the waistband of my shorts, "Up," he said softly.

I lifted my hips for him, watching intently as he slowly pulled my shorts down my body and eventually off my legs. He placed the silk shorts on the bedside table and smiled at me, his eyes fully meeting mine.

"You're so beautiful, Becca." He murmured.

My heart still raced, and I narrowed my eyes to shoot rays of lust toward him, "What did you say earlier?" I asked.

Smirking, "That you're my pain in the ass?" he asked, dipping to hover over me, his lips brushing lightly against my chin.

I gasped lightly, "That I'm yours?"

He chuckled in a low growl and nodded, nipping at the skin on my ear, "You're all mine, Becca." he purred.

I shivered and shifted as I felt my core craving for him, my eyes fluttering with desire.

Adam pulled away from my ear and then smiled down at me, "You say the word and it stops immediately." He reassured, awaiting my confirmation of a nod before he reached his inked fingers between my legs to push them open, his middle finger being the first to touch my throbbing clit.

I hissed in a breath and pulled at the handcuffs as I felt the warmth of his fingers. Adam placed gentle kisses on my breasts and rolled his fingers around my clit, allowing me to grow accustomed to his touch.

"Your body's so perfect," He muttered, pushing his fingers lower to press against my entrance. I craved him... I wanted his fingers deep inside of me.

He obliged, plunging the art covered digits into the depths of my sex and then pulling them out slowly, "You're so wet. I must be doing *something* right."

I shivered, spreading my legs wider as he continued to slowly stroke my pussy with his large fingers. They were bigger than mine, and much more fulfilling. He stroked along the inside wall until he stumbled upon a certain clump of nerves that summoned an audible moan from deep inside of me.

He smirked and continued to target this spot, increasing his speed as he pulled his fingers in and out.

I rolled my hips against his fingers and my head back into the plush comfort of his pillows. He felt so *good* inside of me.

Adam sent in another finger and dipped his head between my legs to place a gentle kiss on my clit. I whimpered and tugged at the cuffs, wanting to cover my mouth, but I couldn't.

He massaged m g-spot with his fingers while his tongue was running circled around my clit. All I could do was squirm beneath him, helpless.

"Fuck…" I muttered breathlessly, sweat beading on my forehead. The ecstasy was real, I could feel it coursing through my very soul, crawling from the depths of my core to reach my nipples.

Adam must have taken this as a personal challenge, as he sped his fingers up and began sucking on my clit.

It was the absolute perfect rhythm to send me right over the moon.

I arched my back, "Fuck, don't stop!" I whimpered, feeling the crescendo of the orgasm growing near.

Adam kept his pace and pulled his mouth from my clit to rub it quickly with his other hand.

I called out in pleasure as I felt the buildup of pressure and fluid finally release from within me.

My body vibrated in warmth as Adam ever so kindly escorted me into another fucking dimension, and I repaid him by completely drenching his bed in a sopping pool of my own fluids.

Adam smirked and removed his fingers from inside of me. He lifted my hips and pulled the comforter from beneath me, tossing it to the floor as his lips crashed hungrily into mine.

It was a deep, passionate kiss that made my toes tingle.

I was just coming down from my high when Adam flipped me onto my stomach, my ass now pointing directly into the air.

He pressed his hard bulge into my throbbing entrance and ground it there.

"Do you see how fucking hard you make me?"

My eyes closed tightly as I managed to produce a quiet, "Y-yes."

"Do you want to feel my hard cock inside of your soaking wet pussy, Becca?" His voice carried through the entire room with a damning rumble.

I quivered, "Yes… Yes Adam… stick your fucking cock in me, now!"

His bulge twitched against my entrance, and then he pulled it free. "Contraception?"

"Always," I responded shakily, the need for his dick over-whelming.

He angled his tip to my entrance and slowly pushed inside of me. He wasn't as big as King, but he still filled me to the brim. I let out a *genuine* moan of pleasure as he adjusted himself inside.

Adam pulled his hips back, pulling his tip all the way back to my entrance, "You like it rough, do ya?"

"Fuck yes!" I turned my head back to look at him.

"Good," He smirked, then plunged himself deep inside of me all at once.

I winced at first but found my body tingling in need. He reeled back before thrusting again.

Soon he built up a steady rhythm.

He filled my pussy with his length.

He slammed it into me, over and over.

"Nnng," I arched my back and rolled my pelvis to assist his angle, and his hands secured themselves to my hips. He gripped at the flesh like his life depended on it, using the grip to hit me at just the right angle to ensure that I melted against him.

"Fuck me, Adam!" I called, pulling against the handcuffs like I had just been sentenced to life.

He rolled his head back, pounding his hips into mine, his balls slapping perfectly against my clit.

I whimpered and felt my legs shaking. The whore in me began to break through as I noticed his staggering thrusts, he was close.

"Yeah, baby. You like my tight pussy?"

He stuttered in his rhythm for a moment, "Yeah, I fucking do."

I moaned loudly, "My pussy is all yours. Fucking fill me with your cum, like the fucking slut I am."

He groaned and his muscles tensed as he tightened his grip on my waist. "You want me to fill you up, Becca? To breed you?"

*Well, that is a kink I didn't know I had.*

He had found a way to make me stutter just the same, and for a moment I lost all sense of my faculties, "Yes!" I groaned,

"Fucking fill me up. Make me yours!"

Adam's face twisted into that of release, and he slammed into me a few more times before he let out a loud moan and his body convulsed.

I could feel the shift as he dumped his load deep inside of me.

That was enough for me.

I came a second time.

Adam slowly pulled out, shivering. I could feel the dripping of his cum as it seeped down my twitching pussy.

He collapsed beside me on the bed, and relief washed over the pair of us.

He reached across to the nightstand to grab the key for the handcuffs and released my wrists. I pulled them close, rubbing the sore redness. Adam pulled them to his lips and placed comforting kisses on the hot skin.

I smiled at him softly and curled into his chest, seeking out his warmth. One of his hands tangled gently in my hair.

"Was that... okay?" his blue eyes fell over my body as his other hand moved to gently stroke my exposed skin.

The fear and confusion that I had felt were now completely banished to the back of my mind, and I nodded, "Yes, Adam." I muttered as I buried my face in his chest.

He smiled at me brightly and nuzzled my hair, "That was amazing," he whispered.

I giggled and reached to intertwine my fingers with his, "Never slept with a prostitute before?" I teased.

Adam's eyebrows furl and he shook his head, "You're not a prostitute."

"I am," I smiled, "Not that I get anything for it."

Adam pressed his lips to my forehead and sighed, "I will

never see you as a prostitute."

The smile fell from my face, "Prostitution isn't a bad thing." I urged.

He nods, "I agree, but you don't want to be a prostitute. You are doing it for justice, not desire."

He was right. The only thing that kept me going was the hope of seeing the motherfucker who killed my best friend finally repaid. I snuggled into his chest and sighed; the weight of the world seemed somehow quite bearable in this moment.

"Becca," Adam hummed softly, brushing his fingers against my cheek as he pushed a strand of hair behind my ear.

I searched his face for a moment before landing on his eyes.

He smiled, pushing himself from the bed, and then he began searching for his pajama bottoms, "Thank you for coming back into my life."

# When The World Comes Crashing Down Around You

⚜

# CAIN

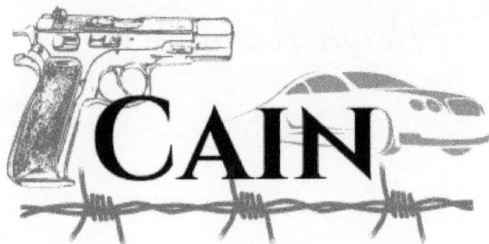

The safe house was a quiet little ranch-style house in the Georgia hills. Nestled in a small woodland neighborhood that seemed welcoming enough.

Not suspicious at all…

Except for when two muscle cars pull up in the driveway at five in the morning and carry in a load of power tools.

By the time I had arrived, Cole had already gotten to work setting up our selection of fun tools. A table contained the various implements with which things could be removed from other things. I placed my own bag of tools to the side and walked toward the padded cell door.

I pulled it open to see King sitting up against the wall, the bungee cords now removed, but he was still chained. I never understood why Cole swore by these fucking bungee cords.

King stared up at me, "You gonna fucking explain this shit, man?" He spat, "Why the fuck am I in some Jigsaw-ass dungeon kinda shit?"

I crossed my arms and leaned against the cell's door frame as I stared down at him, "Do you really wanna start talking shit?" I asked.

King sucked his teeth and groaned, "You're fucking annoying, bro."

Amusement fluttered in my chest and I nodded, "Yeah. I fucking am, aren't I?" I dipped to grab the chain on the wall and pulled the opposite end, King's hands pulled toward the wall abruptly.

"Fuck!" He snapped, "This is a bit fucked, bro. All I did was slap her. It was self-fucking-defense."

I rolled my eyes and wrapped the line of chain around my hand, "I don't think you have a leg to stand on, here." I said, reeling the chain back and striking King's bloody knee.

He howled, pulling his hands aggressively in an attempt to slam me into the wall, but the locking mechanism kept his wrists in place. He stared at me with a murderous grimace, his bright white teeth shining with stains of crimson between them.

"You're a lucky man, really." I said with a soft hum, "I have done far worse to people who have treated her far better than you."

"I cut off a man's tongue!" Cole called from the main room, a grin on his face.

I raised my eyebrows as I nodded my head in Cole's

direction, "He cuts off most people's tongues, really."

King's face twisted into disgust, "What the fuck is wrong with you crazy-ass motherfuckers?"

A laugh built within me, and I shook my head, "The thing you'll learn about working for Lorenzo, is that he doesn't fucking hire sane people." I stepped toward him and stomped on the edge of his ankle.

When his scream was good and loud, I smirked and stepped closer, pulling his arms behind his back. I unhooked the chain from the wall and grabbed him by the shin of his broken leg, dragging his thrashing body into the main room where Cole was prepared with his table of oddities.

Cole stooped down and grabbed his chained arms, "It is really better if you just shut the fuck up and stop moving. Cain gets trigger-happy when ya'll squirm," Cole's thumb juts back to point at me, and King's eyes narrow again.

I chuckled and pulled a pair of black gloves over my hands, allowing the vinyl to snap against my ink-covered skin. I dipped to retrieve my large knife from within my black bag.

By the time I turned back to face them again, Cole had already stuffed a ball gag into King's mouth.

I grimaced, "Did you even wash it after the last guy?"

King's eyes widened in fear as he gagged around the ball, swearing behind the silencer. Ever since Pulp Fiction, the ball-gag was when they *really* started to freak out.

I shared a look of disgust as Cole shrugged with his stupid shit-eating grin.

I shook my head and tapped the knife on the fabric of Lorenzo's napkin that acted as a tourniquet.

With a swoop of the blade, I sliced through the fabric, and it fell to the ground. The fear in King's face deepened in line with a muffled groan of pain.

"I promised Val that I wouldn't kill you. Count this as your lucky fucking break." I snorted, digging the tip of the blade into his kneecap and searching around.

King thrashed, the sound of muffled protest.

"Stop it, dumbass. There's no exit wound. I have to get the bullet out." I kept digging until I struck metal.

I extracted the bullet with pliers and then reached into my bag to retrieve a genuine tourniquet and a bottle of hydrogen peroxide. I dumped a load of the peroxide on his knee with a smirk as I watched him squirm some more, then I placed the tourniquet and began to work on bandaging King's knee, "You're the only person I know who will complain about having his medical care done for free."

Cole snorts out a laugh and grabs a few of his tools, making quick work of removing the hair from the man's head.

When done, I pulled away and crossed my arms in front of myself, now standing over him.

"How does it feel, ay?" I asked, "Watching your body be used without you having any say in what is done?" A smirk burned bright across my face as Cole dug a blade into King's shoulder, meticulously carving the words *Cain's Bitch* into the flesh of his skin.

"Not as skilled as Atticus, but pretty fucking nifty," Cole sneered with an evil grin.

King stared at me with an unwavering level of confidence in his eyes as he hardly flinched at Cole's carving. This asshole made me want to kill him and then just lie to Becca… but I couldn't do that to her…

I had made a promise.

My phone started buzzing in my pocket, so I turned to allow

Cole to continue his twisted little deeds as I checked to make sure it wasn't Becca.

It was my mother's nursing home.

The blood in my veins ran cold. Why would they be calling me at six in the morning?

"I'll be two minutes," I said to Cole, then slipped out the front door.

Cole smirked at King, "It's just us two now." He let out a menacing laugh.

I slipped out the front door and walked toward my Charger, leaning against the hood as I slid the answer icon across to answer.

"Hello?" I said into the receiver softly.

"Hi, Mr. Hunt?" A man's soft voice asked through the phone.

"Speaking…" I waited on bated breath for a response.

The man cleared his throat, "We have gone to check in on your mother this morning, but she isn't doing very well. She seems to have a chest infection and with her asthma and her heart medications… she is really struggling."

My heart beat hard in my chest, and I allowed a shaky breath to fall from my lips, "Is she suffering? What can I do?" I asked softly.

"Well, at the moment she seems stable, but every time we go in to check on her, she is breathing slower, and her chest is more congested."

I gripped my gloved hands into tight fists and choked back a sigh, "Do you think she will be okay until this evening?" I asked, worried about Roy and work.

The man hummed, a not-so-hopeful sounding hum. "I think we can try to keep her comfortable for as long as we can, but… I think it would be best if you came as soon as possible."

I leaned against the hood of my car, horrified at the thought of a world without my mom. A million thoughts rolling through my head, "O-okay." I found myself saying softly into the phone, "I will try my best. Please keep her comfortable." I hung up the call.

Rage and sorrow bubbled inside me. *Why was nothing ever easy?* I gripped a tight fist around my phone.

I walked back into the house with a new sense of just how fucking angry a broken man could become.

I set my phone down on our table of trinkets and grabbed Cole by the scruff of his neck to pull him away from King, but somehow, the bound man managed to reel back his head and thwack me good and hard in the mouth with his forehead.

I growled, ripping King from the chair by the fabric of his tattered designer shirt.

I threw him to the floor and put my full weight on him, hammering my fists into his jaw and temples until his face was as good and pummeled as it could get without being too far gone. I only then forced myself away from him, kicking him twice in the ribs as I went, for good measure.

I pulled my gloves off and threw them down onto King's stomach as I wiped a hand across my face where the sweat was dripping.

Cole looked at me with concern spelling out of his face. Seeing my split knuckles he asked, "Whoa dude. What happened?"

I spat blood from my split lip to the floor between my feet and shook my head quickly, "Fucking clean this asshole up and drop him off at Lorenzo's. I have to go."

"Cain, what's wrong?" Cole asked, his hand settling on my shoulder, but I shoved my friend away.

"Fuck off, Cole." I snapped, "Take this fucker to Lorenzo and tell him that I'm coming for his ass next."

With that, I stormed out of the front door and toward my car without a second thought.

The engine screamed as I peeled down I-75 toward my apartment where I had left Becca asleep.

I pulled the car into the garage and pushed through my front door, hardly bothering to close the garage.

Becca was still asleep in my bed, but when I stormed inside to grab clothes to change into, her eyes fluttered open and she looked up at me with confusion in her eyes.

"Hey... you don't look so happy." she said softly.

I felt annoyance bubbling in my head, but had to bite it back to focus on the fact that she had literally no idea what I had just been through, so I took a breath.

"I've got to call out of work today, my mom is really sick," I explained, rifling through my drawers to find something suitable.

Her eyes softened and she pushed herself to stand, "Your lip is bleeding, and your knuckles are busted. What happened?"

I sighed, pushing a drawer closed and turning to look at her.

The instant that my eyes fell fully upon her, the anger in me twisted to the true emotion that my anger had been masking: Fear.

I choked back tears as I shook my head, "Becca... listen." I struggled with my words, "I know you're worried, but I really... really need you to do me a favor and just let me get through this."

She stepped closer and placed her hand on my bicep, gently curling her fingers around the muscle, "Can I please be there with you?" She asked.

I looked down at my feet and shuddered for a moment, "I don't think it would be good for her to meet a new person she doesn't know or trust on her deathbed…"

"I can wait in the car," Becca stands on the tip of her toes to cup my cheek. She pushed her thumb across the bits of crusted blood beneath my lips and frowned, "I can be there for *you*."

The fear bubbled inside of me, but I nodded slowly, "O-okay. Get dressed… I need to call Roy… Fuck." I searched for my phone, but it wasn't in my pocket. Panic flickered in my mind, but I knew there was no time to waste. I'd have to stop by the office on the way to see her.

My mind raced as I threw on a pair of clothes and dashed out the door to the garage. I poked my head into the Charger to see if my phone had fallen out of my pocket there, but it hadn't. It was nowhere to be seen.

I grumbled a number of choice expletives under my breath before climbing into the driver's seat of the Cobalt.

Becca slipped down the stairs from the house, closing the front door behind her. She climbed into the passenger seat and her eyes warmed my cheek. I reached a hand across the car to place it on her thigh, and when her fingers wrapped themselves around my hand, I felt my stress ease.

I leaned my head against my headrest and let out a long, heavy sigh, "I can't find my phone," I muttered.

She smiled kindly and rubbed the back of my hand, "It is okay. Only a phone." She said softly, "We can retrace your steps when-"

The buzz of her own phone cut her off and she glanced down to see my name painted across the screen. My eyes widened as she slid the icon across the answer and waited for a voice to come through.

"Valentine?" Cole's voice called through the receiver. A burst of relief poured through me.

"Hi, Cole," she called back, putting the phone on speaker.

"Oh, good! Is Cain with you?" Cole asked.

"Yeah, he is right here beside me. Which is odd considering you have called me from his phone."

A shrill chuckle resounded, but it sounded tense, "Something happened before he left here... I don't know what, but he is in a foul mood. Check on him please... tell him that there has been a... small issue."

"What is it?" I broke through the silence, my voice sharp like a blade.

"Erm," Cole sighed, "I found King with your phone. He was speaking to someone named Roy..."

The whole fucking world stood still.

I blinked in slow motion and a distinct ringing sounded in my ears. "What did he say, Cole?"

"I don't know, but when I managed to take it off of him, he looked far too pleased with himself." Cole sighed, "I've knocked him out for now."

"I'm going to fucking kill him," I growl, "If he has fucked with my life, I am going to fucking murder him."

Cole let out an uncomfortable laugh, "Um, You should really not say that shit over the phone."

"Fuck off! Keep his ass locked up until I am finished with what I need to do. Hold onto my phone."

"You're being a fucking dick," Becca whispered, "Thank you for your help, Cole. I'll keep an eye on him. We will see you soon."

"He *is* being a fucking dick," Cole agreed, then hung the phone up.

I sighed and pressed my fingers to my temples as a migraine exploded in my skull.

"Listen, Adam... you are allowed to be angry and upset, but you not allowed to treat people like shit when you feel those things." She crossed her arms.

I bit back the desire to fire back a statement that would have launched us into a major argument, but I opted to start driving instead.

Towards the office first... luckily the buildings were similar in proximity.

As we got to the worksite, I noticed Roy getting out of his car.

I quickly pulled up to park near him and got out of my car, but his face already told me everything I needed to know.

"You're part of a street gang that pimps out girls?" Roy asked me, sounding as though he was already disgusted with my existence.

My eyes widened, "No, no, no. That isn't true, Roy." I said, holding my hands up.

"Really? Because the man on your phone had a different tale to tell." Roy snapped, placing his coffee mug on the roof of his car as he crossed his arms and leaned against his door, "I didn't believe him at first, but he told me that this morning you beat him within an inch of his life, but he was able to headbutt you and split your lip. And now your lip looks pretty fucking split to me, Adam."

I tensed and looked down at the ground, "Listen Roy... I want to tell you the truth because you have helped me so much..."

"Save it, Adam. I can't have people like you under my umbrella. I shouldn't have excused the fact that you were always exhausted. I thought Conor's death was just really bogging you down. Now it all makes sense."

Roy shook his head, and I could see the defeat in his eyes, "I introduced you to my *family*... you met my *kids*."

I stiffened, pulling my shoulders back to straighten my posture, "Please, let me explain."

Roy shook his head with a soft sigh, "I think you need to leave, Adam. I'll have your belongings packed and sent to your address... Your final pay-check will come at the end of the month. I'm giving you full pay... just please leave." Roy turned away from me and grabbed his mug, drawing a big sip of coffee.

Resolve emptied from my faculties, and I nodded slowly, taking a step back towards my car and then getting in silently. A stoic demeanor fell over my face as I sped out of the parking lot with fury behind my every breath.

"Adam," Becca muttered, her hand reaching to hold mine, but I gripped the steering wheel until my knuckles showed white despite the ink that covered them. Her arms went limp, and she returned her hand to her lap.

I was almost entirely silent until I pulled into the carport of my mother's nursing home, parking in the same spot I always did.

Once I had disengaged the engine, I pulled my hands to cover my face and breathed a heavy, shaky breath in.

This was far too much to cope with right now.

Becca unbuckled her seatbelt and placed her hand on my chest, "You really need to breathe, Adam. You're holding it inside and you're gonna pass out."

She was right, but I couldn't manage. I pulled my hands from my face and looked over at her, trying to disguise the fact that I was very... *very* unwell at this moment in time.

"Hey," I muttered, "I'm sorry for being a snappy dickhead all morning... This isn't your fault, what I am going through... thank you for being here for me."

Her honey-brown eyes softened and she leaned across the seat to place a gentle kiss on my cheek, "I know that look in your eyes," She whispered, placing her hand on my cheek, "I used to see it in my reflection all the time. I am going to be right here waiting for you when you come out."

I bit down on the edge of my tongue as I stared into her eyes for a moment, "Fuck..." I shook my head, looking at the door of the nursing home.

"I wish Conor was here. He was always fucking stronger than me. He would have been able to do this without shedding a fucking tear."

Her eyes soften with a gentle sadness, "I'm forever sorry for taking him from you..."

My eyes settled on her once more and I shook my head, "don't you *dare* blame yourself."

I shook my whole body, trying to toss away the frustration and anger and fear, "I've got to go inside... will you be okay out here?"

She nods, "I'm going to call Sasha. I haven't talked to her in a while."

I leaned over to press a soft kiss to her lips, and then squeeze her thigh lightly as I removed myself from the car. I placed the key fob in her lap in case she needed to signal me.

The receptionist beamed as soon as she saw me enter, her eyes soft and comforting, "Morning, Mr. Hunt. We have made her as comfortable as possible in the Tea-room." she explained, pointing down the hall to a quiet little private room.

I pushed through the doors and saw my mother there.

The wind felt as though it left my body.

She was laying there in a bed, with wires and gadgets plugged into her from nearly every angle. A steady beep could be distinguished over the sound of electrical whirring and the shaky, raspy breaths of my mother.

She looked like a ghost.

It had only been two days since I had seen her last, but it seemed like she had aged thirty years. Her skin was now pale and blotched and purple from lack of oxygen. Her plush cat rested on her chest, a hand gripping firmly to the fur of its back.

The tea-room was a quaint little room that had a wall full of exotic teas that residents could enjoy, but most notably, there was a wall-length window that peered out over a stunning water feature behind the nursing home. The capitol building could be seen in the distance with its dome of gold.

I stepped into the room and quietly moved to sit by her side. Her eyes fluttered as they followed me, a nasal cannula perched at the entrance of her nose, though it didn't seem to help too much.

They say that patients with dementia can slip away from us faster than we realize. One day they are here, kicking and screaming, causing trouble... and the next day they are catatonic.

My mother looked at me with the deepest, kindest blue eyes I had ever seen. Her breathing was shaky as she stared intently at me.

"My Adam," She whispered, a sharp whistle at the back of

her throat.

My heart sinched, and I felt a pang of joy at the recognition. I reached for her withered hand, holding it close, "Yes, mama. I'm here." I said softly.

Her thin blue lips pointed up lightly into a soft smile, "Conor told me you'd come. That I had to be patient." She said slowly.

"Did he?" I asked, feeling an ache in my chest, "He knows I am always late for the important things."

Her eyelids fluttered shut for a moment, then opened again to stare at me intently, "You're unhappy."

I shook my head, "No, mama. I am so happy to be here with you. You have no idea." I laid my head on the edge of her bed like a child would. It probably looked absurd. A massive muscly man lying on the bed of a sick old woman, but I didn't care. Mama reached her other hand out to gently stroke my hair.

"Don't worry Adam," She whispered. "Conor will keep me safe."

The heartache in my chest increased, and it was becoming harder to hold back the waves of emotions that flooded my senses. I sniffed lightly, breathing the scent of medicine and some sort of lotion.

"I'm tired, baby."

I clamped my eyes shut and gently squeezed her hand, breathing in slowly to regulate myself, "It is okay mama... you can sleep. You can rest..."

She curled her fingers lightly through my brown curls and then allowed her eyes to fall closed.

I relished the moment, feeling her chest slowly moving up and down, the gentle pull of her fingers through my hair. I imagined we were at home, curled up in her big bed, surrounded by pillows.

"I love you, mama." I muttered, sealing my eyes shut so I could preserve this memory of her. This peace.

Her chest raised as she pulled in a long squeaky breath, "I will always love you,"

And then, the raspy whistle slowed, the whirring stopped.

The beep of the monitor grew silent.

Her chest ceased its cycle of rising and falling with great effort… and her hand slipped slowly from my hair to rest on the blanket.

Her body was still warm, I could still smell her scent… she was still here with me… if even for a moment.

I squeezed her hand tighter now, feeling the bones in her hand move with ease now that her life force no longer held them together.

The sting of tears burned in my eyes as I pushed myself from her bed and I turned away from her lifeless body. Trying to push the tears to the back of my mind, I traced the artwork on my forearm obsessively to distract myself.

A doctor came in a moment later with a solemn look on her face, "She waited for you."

I nodded slowly, then finally allowed myself to look at her.

She was simply asleep.

Peaceful.

I dipped down and placed a gentle kiss on the top of her forehead, and then thanked the doctor for her help.

She offered me a supportive handshake and told me that they would be in touch with funeral arrangements within the next few days. I knew where she wanted to be… she wanted to be right next to Conor.

The world didn't feel quite real in that moment.

As I stepped through the front doors, the sun shone brightly in the sky.

Birds sang.

I could her the sound of children laughing.

Yet each step toward the car felt like I was wading through water. Time moved in slow-motion around me, and I felt well and truly bled dry.

I pulled open the door to the car and sank into my seat.

"I've gotta go, Sash. I'll call you later," Becca said, putting the phone down quickly.

We sat there in the silence that befell us for what felt like an eternity.

The weight of the world slowly hanging over my shoulder as I stared at the steering wheel with a vacant expression.

Becca permitted the silence, her eyes respectfully falling to her hands as she rested them in her lap.

I lifted a hand to touch the texture of my steering wheel, but my arms hung limp and heavy from the wrist down. At the moment, I felt absolutely nothing. A numbness that filled every crevice of my soul with a soft vibration of absolute ice.

Soon, Becca's hand reached to gently pull mine from the wheel. She pulled that hand into her lap. Her warmth began to soothe the throbbing vacancy of sensation in my hand at the very least.

I turned my head slowly to glance at her, and her eyes met mine with voracious support beneath the concern. Her soft features felt irrationally bright against the darkness that was slowly eating away at the corners of my vision.

My left hand reached for the wheel, and I slowly pulled my right hand from Becca's grip to turn the key and start the car.

"Are you going to be okay to drive?" she asked softly, but

I simply nodded once and began the slow drive towards the safe house.

Cole's Scion was still there, but this time he was sitting inside of it. His head shot up as he noticed me pulling up in the unfamiliar car. The door opened and he stepped out, greeting me with a confused expression.

I pushed my gear shift into park and emerged from the Cobalt, walking to Cole.

"I need your gun." I said flatly.

Cole's eyes widened and he looked past me to Becca in the car, then back at me. "Why?"

I sighed flatly and shook my head, "Do you need me to explain what we use guns for?"

My friend's face fell to a look of sadness, "Are you going to use it on yourself?"

My eyes narrowed, "Why the hell would I do that? I have shit to do."

Cole turned to his car and dipped inside to retrieve a Glock from the center console. He turned to me and sighed, "Did he fuck your cover?"

"He fucked more than my cover, Cole. Give me the gun," I snapped.

"It doesn't have a silencer," Cole tried to stall.

I scoffed, "And?"

He nodded once and handed the weapon to me. His eyes once more moved to look at Becca in the passenger seat of the car.

When she noticed my receipt of the gun, her door opened, and she rushed to my side, "Adam, no." She gripped the fabric of my black button up dress shirt.

I looked at her for a moment, but the emotion in my eyes

was null and there was no hope of sending her a reassuring expression. I simply shook my head with a near imperceptible motion and turned away.

She tried to follow me, but Cole placed a hand on her shoulder to cement her in place. He also shook his head "You need to let him do this, Valentine. He'll resent you for the rest of his life, if you don't."

Her eyes fell and she nodded slowly, pulling her hands to her chest anxiously.

I stepped through the front door of the safe house.

Cole had cleaned up the tools and left King bound to the chair with proper binds this time. None of that bungee bullshit.

"Hey man!" King tried desperately, looking at me with a hint of terror in his voice that matched his bloodshot eyes, but I wasn't here to play games.

This man didn't deserve the pleasure of being tortured. He didn't deserve to feel as though he had a choice. He didn't even deserve the satisfaction of knowing that he was about to fucking die.

I pulled back the safety and aimed the Glock directly between that maggot's eyes, "Fuck you."

The words fell from my lips with the most intense, completely raw emotion that I could muster.

My finger pulled against the trigger, and I watched as the muzzle flashed, and I watched as the bullet imbedded into King's terrified skull.

An explosion of blood, bits of skull sprayed over the bare wooden flooring of the main room.

The release was raw.

Everything came flooding to me at breakneck speeds and I

gagged at the taste of bile as it filled my throat.

Death was fucking disgusting, but at least I could control this one.

The burning stench of flesh filled the room as King's body finally collapsed to the ground, his hands were still bound to the chair, even as his weight capsized it.

Tears flooded down my face as I ripped open the door to the rudimentary kitchen that had never been used. I turned the gas release valve on the gas stove and left the room when I could hear the soft hiss.

I gave the gas time to reach everywhere in the house before-walking back to King's body and retrieving a pocketknife to saw through his bindings. His hands fell to the ground, and I grabbed him by the ankles, feeling that same familiar click of bones with no muscle tension as I dragged him to the center of the room. Then I grabbed the chair by the backrest and launched it at the wall with an angry howl that embodied all of the burning rage within me.

The chair practically disintegrated against the exposed brick.

Wood chips fell upon the ground like fucking morbid confetti.

I was beginning to smell gas, so I walked to the front door. Now on the porch, I turned and fired another shot at the spark igniter for the fireplace and hoped to God that it worked.

Fucking hell, did it.

I had approximately three seconds to react as the echo of the gunshot ceased and the ticking of the firestarter began. My body turned from the house, and I locked eyes with my Valentine just in time to feel the shockwave from the explosion knock me forward onto the grass.

Darkness.

Temporary solace.

And then the ringing in my ears grew, the sting of my face in the sharp blades of grass. Four hands hooked beneath my armpits, pulling me further from the house that now burned in glorious vengeance.

I lifted my head to see the blurred outlines of Cole and Becca.

Cole threw my back against the bumper of the Cobalt and started snapping in front of each of my ears. Slowly, the percussion on his middle finger on the pad of his palm cuts through the heavy ringing in my ears, I lift my eyes to meet Cole's and nod slowly with a raise of my hand.

"Adam!" Becca called, throwing herself to her knees at my side.

"We don't have time to wait, Becca. Help me get him in the car before the cops get here," Cole snapped.

I shook my head, "no," I muttered, pushing myself to stand shakily. "Take Valentine to Mags's place."

Cole grabbed her by her upper arm and pulled her toward the car, but not without plenty of protest from her. She was able to rip herself away from Cole, and came rushing to me, pulling my face to look at her.

Her eyes were so beautiful… I realized just how much I appreciate the spectrum of her emotions.

"Please come with us, Adam," she begged, her voice breaking between her breaths.

My hands dipped to hook into the belt loops of her capris as I pulled her against me, crashing our lips together. She whimpered at first, but then she melted into the kiss.

When I finally pulled from her, I cupped her cheek "I will

be okay. I need you to trust me, and you need to go where you will be safe"

Becca whimpered again, biting back tears as she nodded slowly, but tried to pull away from me. I grabbed her wrist and held her in place, reaching to brush a strand of hair behind her ear, "I love you."

Her eyes widened and she nodded resoundingly, leaping to throw her arms around my neck and pull me into another kiss.

My knees buckled.

I tried my best to find my balance as I kissed her in front of the furling flames of the safe house.

The kiss ended and she fell back, stepping towards Cole's car and sinking into the seat.

I waited for them to disappear down the road.

Still not even the slight call of distant police sirens, so I gave myself a minute to adjust to the pain that was settling in my bones, the ringing that still shown present in my ears.

I took a deep breath and climbed into my car.

I had shit to do, and this ringing in my ears wasn't going to stop me... or the migraine that pierced through my skull... or the stench of singed blood on my black shirt... not even my whole world crashing down up on me was going to stop me now.

# A Deal with the Devil

# BECCA

I stared down at my phone, waiting anxiously for it to ring. For a message. Nothing.

It had been six hours since Cole had dropped me off here at Mags' apartment, and those six hours felt painfully slow. I could feel every second in the thrum of my heart. Panic eating at my bones.

"Girl, you need to take a breather," Mags said with a soft chuckle, her deep brown eyes drifting over me like a pleasant wind.

My stomach churned loudly, signaling my already concerned friend to the hunger that gnawed at my gut. She stepped in front of me and crouched down, pressing our foreheads together.

"Two days ago, you would have screamed at me if I said his name, and now here you are," She chuckles, placing a hand over my device and pulling it from my hands, "Now you can't last an afternoon without him."

The panic in my eyes must have startled her, and she released the hold on my phone and sat down, legs crossed before her.

She was right.

I had spent the past three months drowning myself in disgusting habits. Attempting to drink away the void that I felt inside. I hadn't wanted to feel the pain of Cain's absence in my life. Even though I had always acted so fucking bratty, he had always put me first. *Always.*

I remembered how obsessively he cleaned his house. As if the idea of leaving a drop of water on the glass of his coffee table would shatter it. The panic that grew on his face when I had nearly forgot to use a coaster. I wondered if he kept his life so neat because it was the only thing he could control... because that was the polar opposite of what I did.

My body craved the cortisol.

It craved the danger.

Feeling on edge...

I think it is because I was so scared that if I let myself stop... if I let myself break down... I'd never be able to get back up.

I watched as Adam twisted and turned into Cain.

They aren't the same person.

Adam is kind and respectful, understanding. Adam laughs, places gentle kisses on my face that make me feel like I was floating... but Cain...

261

Cain was brutish.

Broody.

He embodied the darkness as though he was forged within it, and he was capable of so much hurt.

Cain hurt people... because Adam was hurt.

I think there is some sort of Jekyll and Hyde kind of metaphor here, one that made me realize that I had embraced this shadow which eclipsed all of my light. This world made me feel so alone. I chased the highs that kept me right here where I was. A slave to a man who would never let me go, a life that would never lead anywhere but darkness.

But Adam made me feel at peace. That's why I am so fucking scared of him. That's why when he told me that he loved me... I froze.

Mags' phone began to ring across the room, and she quickly pushed herself up to grab it. I saw her eyes darken as she slid her finger across the screen to answer. I hyper-fixated, trying to listen.

*Was it Cain, or was it Adam?*

"How the hell am I supposed to get her there?" Mags snaps, her voice pitching up into a shrill sound of annoyance.

It must have been Lorenzo... requesting me?

I pushed myself to stand and stepped slowly towards Mags, my hands trembling. He wouldn't dare try to make me do another fucking job right now, would he?

"You're sending who? Maxwell? Isn't he the motherfucker who almost took out a girl's eye?" Mags continued. Suddenly, her eyes fell flat, "You want me to send her alone?"

Panic suddenly washed over my whole body, and I felt my heart lurch at the idea of being alone with Lorenzo. Alone with *any* of his goons.

"T-Tell him to fuck off," I snapped anxiously, but my friend slowly shook her head.

"No, girl. You need to go."

I choked on the shock that filled my lungs, a burst of insubordination rumbling behind my eyes as I saw Mags point to the door. I stamped my foot, but she only sighed and ended the call.

Mags turned her phone around to show me a picture sent to her from an unsaved number. It was Cain's Charger, empty and in perfect condition… to the naked eye. It was parked in Lorenzo's garage.

Fear began to flow through me, and I grabbed my slippers before running out the door. I clutched my phone tight to my chest and began to hyperventilate. There was a blue Ford Mustang idling outside of Mags' block, and I seemed to somewhat recognize the face of the man. He definitely recognized mine.

The man nodded to me from the driver's seat and pointed to the back door nearest me, ordering me to get in.

I have done far stupider things than getting into some random creepy man's muscle car in broad daylight. Honestly, it could be worse… at least, that is what I tell myself as I slip into the car.

It smelled like an escort's bag.

A stinging chemical scent of lube and silicone.

A hint of sex still lingered in the air.

Every time I have the unfortunate pleasure of riding with another one of Lorenzo's goons, I am more and more thankful for the cushy, respectful driver that I used to have.

Maxwell slammed his foot onto the accelerator and peeled away from the curb, a squeak of what I can only assume to be some sort of turbo revving loudly. He isn't much of a talker, not that I minded.

I would honestly rather stab my own eye out than speak to this greasy gremlin.

My phone vibrated against my chest, and I flinched at the feeling. I quickly unlocked it to see a simple pin drop from an unknown number. Anxiety began to bubble in my chest as I stared at it, trying to work it out. Then a message came through from the same number.

**Unknown: Focus**

For a moment, I didn't know what to do. This had to be Adam. It had to. Nobody outside of the Vixens even considered our safe-words as anything slightly meaningful.

I typed out a message quickly.

**Me: Maxwell driving. Lorenzo.**

Nothing for a moment. There was a subtle stench that rose through the air like the spray of a skunk. I glanced down to see a basket full of tiny bags of weed. My nose scrunched at the realization that I was in a dealer's car barreling up the interstate at Mach fifty.

Maxwell turned a dial on his radio, searching for something to fill the silence that he didn't seem to be too accustomed to. Music was the ride from then on.

When we arrived at Lorenzo's house and I could see the garage door open, the Charger's hood sticking out just slightly. Lorenzo was seated on the shiny front.

His smirk was sickening.

The Mustang stopped in front of the mile-long driveway and Maxwell pressed the button which sounded the unlocking of my door. I looked over my shoulder at him for a moment, expecting him to be looking straight ahead, but his bulging green eyes were beaming directly into my neck with a hungry stare.

My stomach dropped and I quickly pulled at the handle to free myself, feet finally colliding with solid ground.

For the first time in quite a while, I think the reality of solitude was actually apparent to me. Maxwell's car pulled away from the curb, speeding off toward the metro area. I could see Lorenzo at the very end of the driveway. He was perched with a knowing grin on the hood of Adam's car.

The world around me felt eerily dark.

Eerily cold.

One foot in front of the other.

My breath hitched in my throat as I conquered the monster of a drive through. I hoped to see Adam step out from inside of the car. Round the corner to stand guard, but there was no sign of him. There was only Lorenzo and his beady black eyes staring into my soul from another dimension.

An energy that consumed me.

He devoured me alive.

I hadn't felt this raw of a fear from him in six years. Not since I showed up on his doorstep begging for information. Desperate... Willing to sell my soul to understand why my best friend was shoved in front of a train.

Alexia has been the world's brightest light... at least, she was the brightest light in my world. She was three weeks from giving birth to my godson, Aubrey. I was so fucking excited to hold him in my arms. She was so excited to be a mother.

Then in an instant she was dashed to a million pieces. Gone. Ripped from this world.

It should have been me.

I wished every fucking day that it had been me. For some reason, I feel Alexia would have coped better with my loss. She would have been able to live her beautiful life with her beautiful baby boy and I would have finally been able to fucking rest.

The past six years have been torturous.

Addiction and abuse.

I was given such a beautiful escape with Adam… but now I didn't know what was going on.

My steps come to a quick halt about a yard from Lorenzo's slouched stance.

He blinked, one eyelid at a time, and smirked.

"I assume that you're quite curious as to why I have invited you here alone," Lorenzo hummed, his palms folded together in front of him.

The air in my lungs felt heavy, but I stiffened my spine and squared my shoulders, hoping to make myself stand straight enough to avoid the caustic effect of his stare on my psyche.

"I would most definitely appreciate an explanation," the shakiness and uncertainty in my voice was blatant.

The fear seemed to thrill him. He was like a hunter stalking his prey… and I was right there in fucking front of him. Lorenzo lessened his grip on his hands and slicked the sweaty meat of his fingers through his greased hair. His smirk dissolved into something mixed between annoyance and deliverance.

"I have been outbid," he said simply, shrugging.

"Outbid?" I repeat cautiously, observing his expression closely.

Lorenzo nodded once, swiftly.

A pit grew heavily in my stomach, and I bit back the taste of bile…

"You're severing my contract?" This was not so much in relief as much as it was genuine fear of who had fucking paid off my debt.

The vile man stood before me grinning, but then shook his head and his hand snaked out so that it was now resting on the hood of the Charger.

His fingers began tapping rhythmically along the metal.

"I worried this would happen. It was only a matter of time, really." Lorenzo says flatly, "I hope you know that I did try my best to avoid this outcome, but he was so insistent. Even after I explicitly explained to him that you killed his brother."

My eyes grow wide with curiosity and confusion. *What was he talking about?*

"Cain?"

"Cain doesn't exist. He hasn't existed for months." Lorenzo snapped.

I tilted my head, pulling my arms across my chest, "Adam?"

His smirk returned, but there was an air of factitious intent behind it. He rocked on his heels and then pushed himself to stand.

"He came to me three months ago with the proposition of paying off your contract. I had attempted to thwart his plans of trying to play at being your knight in shining armor. I told him half a million was the price of your soul and…" Lorenzo motioned to the Charger, "He has made the deposit."

I narrowed my eyes, "Do you mean that Adam has paid off my contract?"

Lorenzo laughs, "no, Rebecca. He hasn't completely paid off your contract. That's why you are here, so he can't try to whisk you away to avoid the rest of the fees."

The pit in my stomach dropped slightly and I felt tears well in my eyes. Lorenzo called me by my name.

My *actual* fucking name.

From behind Lorenzo, the screen of his phone lit up bright against the slick black coat of Cain's car. He turned to glance at it and smirked.

"He works fast." Lorenzo snorts, "crazy what desperation and depression does to a man." He practically cackled.

My heart began to race, and the soft rumble of thunder peeled across the grey skies above me.

Lorenzo scoffed and rolled his eyes. "You're free to go."

*Free? What the fuck does that mean?*

"I'm confused," I muttered. There must be a catch. There was no way he was just going to let me go. "What about Alexia?"

Lorenzo sucked his teeth in annoyance, "You stupid bitch," he rubbed his forehead, "She killed herself. I reviewed the footage twice and can tell you that much."

Anger struck me in the hardest possible way, "You're fucking with me."

There was no way she would have killed herself…

Alexia loved life.

She loved living.

"Her son had cystic fibrosis. She couldn't live with the diagnosis." Lorenzo stepped closer to me, his round belly stopping just before it could touch me and he leaned forward, "She walked straight off of the platform without a second thought."

A single frustrated tear glided down my cheek and I wanted nothing more than to shove him away.

Then realization donned on me…

"When did you come to this conclusion?"

The mischief returned blatantly to his eyes and he laughed maniacally, peeling away from me, "you never asked, so you'd never know."

I growled and gritted my teeth, "you fucking psychopath!" I snarled, balling my hands into fists.

Lorenzo's laughter bubbled from him like he was a teapot left on too high of a heat. His cheeks were red with pure exhilaration. This twisted motherfucker pimped me out for six fucking years.

He watched as I became a fraction of the person I used to be, for his own gain… and he offered me pennies in return.

I couldn't even afford to live in an apartment without a roommate. I could hardly afford the lingerie that I bought to continue his fucking charade.

I pulled in a deep breath through my nose and tried my best to regulate my body.

This was all *far* too much.

Lorenzo shooed me away with his hand. "You should leave now. I have a supreme distaste for retired employees being present on my property. It would be a shame to have your lover boy's heart dashed as he cleans you off the pavement."

My phone buzzed once in my pocket, but I dared not lose sight of Lorenzo. My eyes glued to him until I could find the courage to break the weld between my feet and concrete.

*Run.*

That's all my mind told me.

*Fucking run.*

*Don't stop.*

*Just get the fuck out of there.*

I turned on my heels and ran.

Fucking faster than I had ever run before.

The adrenaline in my blood made a quick haze of my surroundings and all of the shackles that bound me to this fucking despicable man's side, broke away behind me.

The heavens above opened, and the patter of heavy raindrops fell against my skin until I was drenched. The sweat on my forehead beaded together with the onslaught of falling rain.

I ran until my feet ached and my chest pounded. I tasted bile in my mouth again and doubled over to steady myself. I didn't recognize where I was, but I knew that this road was straight.

I searched the recesses of my mind to piece together the route that I had taken in the passenger seat for years, but nothing was perceptible beyond the racing thoughts.

My phone buzzed again. Long, slow buzzes. A call.

It was that unknown number.

I slid my thumb along the raindrop coated screen and pulled it to my ear. My hair clumped in cemented strands against my cheeks and my breath was ragged, but I called out over the deafening roar of the rain.

"Adam?" I called.

A soft chuckle, enough to shake me to my core, "you know... you're a real pain in my ass sometimes," his voice said. I could hear the smile in his voice.

My heart leapt and I felt the release of tears as my fears were muted instantly, "Fuck!" I shouted, "I- I don't know where I am, Adam. I just ran... I just... I fucking ran."

"Check the pin I sent you, Becca," he said softly into the receiver.

I pulled my phone from my ear and swiped back through to find the messages. I tapped the pin and it grew in size, filling the screen. A small blue dot pulsed my current location. The pin was dropped about three hundred yards from me.

"Is that you?" I asked, lifting my head and searching the perimeter.

Adam didn't respond, he only allowed me to calculate. Once I found my bearings, I made my way toward the dropped pin.

"I can't believe you," I said softly into the receiver, tears matted my cheeks, but you'd never know behind the raindrops.

Adam's soft laugh echoed in my ears for a moment, "In regard to what, exactly?"

I spotted him. The silver Chevy Cobalt with peach state plates. I smashed the end-button and rushed to the passenger side of his car.

The rain had soaked me through. My T-shirt clung tight against my skin and my blonde hair was now at least two shades darker beneath the weight of the clinging rain.

I glanced over at Adam, looking him over. His bottom lip was busted from his altercation earlier on, and there were distinct marks on his forehead and chin from his collision with the rough ground as the safehouse exploded. The expression on his face was a blend between exhaustion, annoyance, and relief.

He smiled at me, nonetheless.

"Hey, you," he said softly. His voice sounded heavy with all that he wasn't saying. His right hand reached over to grip my thigh.

I shuddered beneath his touch, but also felt a pang of sadness in my chest as I noted the split skin on his tattooed knuckles, "and you say I'm a pain in the ass," I muttered, my own hand reaching to gently stroke along the back of his hand.

Adam chuckled, "what ever could you mean?"

"You bought my contract off of Lorenzo?" I asked, feeling the weight of that statement as it settled on my shoulders.

He nodded once, slowly. His blue eyes avoided my gaze.

"And… you gave him your favorite car," I said softly.

Adam's eyebrows bounced lightly in a silent admission, but he nodded again.

My bottom lip quivered, and I rested my hand against his, feeling a rush of emotion collapse over me like a wave.

"Why?" I asked, pressing my head flush against the headrest behind me.

Adam pulled his hand from my knee and used it to turn the key in his ignition, he had still not answered my question.

As he drove, the silence was beginning to eat at me like it never had before

I press my tongue to the roof of my mouth and sigh, "Adam."

"Don't get snippy with me, Miss Valentine," he responded in quick succession, "Patience is indeed, a virtue."

Adam pressed his foot to the accelerator and turned from the main road. This time, I didn't recognize where we were going. He was driving in the opposite direction of where we would need to go to get back to his duplex.

I sat back in silence and pulled my arms around myself. Before long, we emerged in a beautifully manicured cemetery. Adam parked on a mound of dirt, which seemed to serve as a parking lot, and got out of the car.

He walked around to my side and pulled the door open, reaching inside to take my hand.

I looked at his hand for a brief moment, then raised my eyes up to meet his gaze, "You still haven't answered my question,

Adam."

His blue eyes soften, and the large man stooped down to fill the doorframe. He pressed his palm to my cheek.

"You don't seem to get it," He muttered softly, pushing his thumb along my cheek, "I've told you numerous times now, that I will protect you whether it is my job or not."

My heart fluttered to the tune of his words. His skin was warm against mine, and I leaned into the touch to seek out that warmth.

Adam pressed a kiss to my lips gently, "You have no idea how much I wanted to throttle Lorenzo." He grumbled, the low pitch of his voice careening down the back of my neck, rising goosebumps as it sank. "But I couldn't do anything to him until I knew for a fact you would be safe." He placed another kiss on my jawline.

Everywhere he touched erupted in sensation and as he moved on, ached for his presence. I wrapped my fingers tight around the front of his black dress shirt and pulled him onto me, now essentially inside of the passenger side seat with me.

His eyes flickered with hunger, but there was a deeper emotion in his eyes. I couldn't quite decide whether it was ennui or depression. He pulled back against me, his hands squeezing tight around my waist as he hoisted me from inside of the car and placed me on my feet.

I nibbled my lip, feeling the cold air of the night and the soft patter of still-falling raindrops. Adam's hand wrapped around my wrist and guided me away from the Cobalt toward the entrance to the cemetery. He seemed to be able to pinpoint exactly where he needed to go, and we headed directly there.

Before I realized what was happening, we were standing in front of a grave with the name Conor Hunt inscribed into the stone facing.

My chest tightened.

"I wanted to come here one last time," Adam muttered softly, his eyes now downcast and hidden from my view.

"One last time?" I asked, rocking on my toes anxiously.

Adam knelt down and whispered something imperceptible under his breath to the well-tended plot before us, his head dipping low.

He was a quiet man, but today was obviously hard on him. I couldn't begin to imagine what he was feeling at this moment.

After a few minutes of kneeling at his brother's grave, the patter of rain grew heavier and Adam's shoulders began to shake. I watched silently as he put his hands to his face, shielding his tears from view as he allowed himself to properly feel the pain that had piled up inside of him.

I stepped closer and placed my hand on his shoulder, leaning down to press a gentle kiss to the top of his head. He seemed to appreciate the gesture, but his sobs grew louder, filling the space with the sound of grunts of agony.

It hurt to see him so broken…

He had truly lost everything in a single day, and nothing could ever return his mother to him.

Pain demands to be felt, and when the world seems to be against you, the hardest thing in the world is coming to terms with it.

After a while, Adam's cries softened. He raised his hand to wipe the tears away from his face. He sighed, leaning his head back as he pressed his weight backwards. His head touched my thigh, and I reached down to move a strand of wet hair from his face.

His eyes finally opened to look up at me, and I got a sense of some sort of resolve finally growing inside of him. His hand extended upward, a silent request to draw me nearer to him. I obliged, leaning down to press another gentle kiss to his forehead.

Adam's fingers wrapped gently around my wrist, and he pulled me to kneel next to him, holding me close to his body.

"I came here often when you and I weren't speaking. This is where my mom wants to be buried, right next to Conor." He pressed his palm to the earth with a solemn sigh, "It's unfortunate that I probably won't get to see her grave."

I nuzzled further into his chest, but frowned at his words, "You keep speaking as if you are going to vanish into thin air," I said softly.

Adam turned his gaze to meet mine, his eyes were soft, guarded.

He *was* going to disappear.

"I left too much evidence at the safe house. They're going to find my old phone… it has all of my personal details… enough to make a case from which I can't escape." Adam said softly, his knuckles running across the damp fabric of my leggings, "I have been planning this for months now, really… I've just never executed the beginning until now."

I hold my gaze on him, my heart aching with confusion, "Where are you going? What about your life here?"

He chuckled and closed his eyes, shaking his head, "I don't have anything left, Becca. I've lost my job. My family are now all gone. My house has been bought."

"What are you saying, Adam?" I whimpered.

"I have made plans to leave the country," He finally announced, his eyes settling on his brother's gravestone.

"What?" I pushed myself away from him and stood up.

He quickly rose, "I pulled everything from my savings to get you out of Lorenzo's grasp and to buy my plane tickets. I have enough to get me through a few months, but I can work-"

I cut him off, "You're leaving me again?" I shouted, clutching tight to my chest with one hand, "After everything we have been through, you're just gonna fucking walk away and leave me to rot in this hellhole of a city."

Adam's eyes finally moved to meet mine, but there was something new there.

*Was he smiling?*

He turned away from me again and pointed to the car, "Open the glovebox in front of your seat."

I narrowed my eyes, the heat of anger beginning to surface on my face as I stomped towards the car. I pulled open the storage compartment and froze. A passport and a ticket.

Tears welled in my eyes as I threw them onto the seat, "You're fucking despicable, Adam!" I cried, gripping at my long hair.

Adam rolled his eyes and slipped his hand around my waist before pinning me to the car door. He crashed his lips against mine in a ravishing, silencing kiss. I could feel the desperation in his touch, but I pulled away as best as I could. He chuckled and grabbed the passport from the seat inside of the car.

I froze as he opened it and showed me what was inside.

I stared at it for a moment.

It was definitely my picture on the passport, but it wasn't my name. It had been changed to Scarlett Crue.

"What- what is this?"

He grinned, "You really are a pain in the ass, Becca." He leaned in and placed a kiss on my forehead, "But you are MY pain in the ass... Come with me, please."

My mind began to race with all of the possibilities, and I grabbed the passport from him, inspecting it.

"But it is obviously fake… they'll catch us, right?" I asked.

Adam's smile picked up at the corners and turned into a smirk, "I have my connections."

I stared at the navy-blue booklet in my hands, it felt so real. Then I looked up at Adam.

His eyes softened, "Please, baby," He dipped down to press his forehead against mine, "We will start a brand-new life. I'll work on building sites until I can save enough money to help you open a studio…You… You can teach people how to dance."

My heart raced. *Nobody* had ever done anything so kind for me. The way he held me made me feel so safe and secure.

"Yes," I muttered, not even sure I believed my own words.

Adam's face brightened and he bit the back of his lip, "You mean it?" he asked, "You'll come with me?"

I placed the passport on the seat and then turned my attention back to him. I reached both of my hands to rest on the thick muscle of his biceps and stood on my toes, baring down on his arms to hoist myself high enough to kiss him. Our lips locked together in a crash of passion. Adam's hands fixed to my hips, pushing me back against the metal frame of the car.

When I pulled away, Adam's eyes fell to my mouth as though he wanted more. I reached to press my thumb to the broken skin on his bottom lip that had scabbed over now. My heart leapt in my throat as I blurted out the only thing I could think to say in that moment.

"I love you, Adam," I muttered anxiously.

In an instant, he had me deep in the throes of another

passionate kiss. His eyes closed tight; our bodies pressed against each other like we were pieces of some crazy fucked up puzzle.

He soon stepped back, the blue in his eyes shining through the darkness of stormy skies above.

I meant it.

I really, truly fucking meant it.

I absolutely fucking loved this man.

# I Fuck You in My Head

# ADAM

If you told me yesterday that the next 24 hours of my life would send me through every single broad emotion known to mankind in swift kicks, I don't think I would have believed you.

If you told me a week ago that I would be speaking to Becca again after discovering that she killed my brother and ultimately threw her to the curb, I would have laughed in your face.

Now, as I drive back down toward metro-Atlanta, I can feel the clarity in my mind. I had freed Valentine from Lorenzo, and now we get to run away together.

Becca sat smiling in the passenger side of the Cobalt. Her long blonde hair was crinkled by the slow drying of rainfall that had soaked both of us completely through our clothes. My hand rested on her thigh, holding her there as if I was worried that she may vanish into thin air if I even breathed too hard.

She had told me that she loved me… words I never in a million years believed would come from this fan-fucking-tastic woman beside me.

I pulled into the duplex's garage and undid my belt. The garage felt so empty without my Charger… but I had no regrets. I did worry how she might react when I opened the door to my house though.

Once inside, it was clear that I had made my decision to leave long ago. Everything that wasn't bolted down was already gone save for one large suitcase and Becca's duffel bag. The living room furniture was part of the house, so that too remained the same.

Her eyes widened, "That was fast… you were only gone six hours."

I chuckled, "I keep personal effects to a minimum, really. I knew this was coming."

There was still a sense of sadness in her eyes as she stepped through to the living room and bent to rifle through her duffle bag for a pair of dry clothes.

I closed the door behind me and stepped closer to her, "Becca," I said softly.

She glanced up at me, her gorgeous brown eyes searching my flesh. I knew she was worried about me, and she had every right to be. Today I was erratic. I made some very bad decisions, and I hurt people… bad people, but people, nonetheless. I lost the only things that used to make me feel whole.

And yet, at this moment, as I am standing here with her in my almost empty home, I feel at ease.

"Thank you for waiting outside while I was with my mother," I said softly, "I don't think I could have coped so well if you hadn't been right outside."

Her features soften and she stood on her toes, throwing her arms around my neck to cling to me, "You must have loved her."

I felt a pang of true sadness as it grew in my chest.

She was right... I absolutely did love my mother. And even though I had spent years grieving her, nothing will ever compare to how it feels when you feel the life drain from someone you love.

My eyes closed to brace back the rush of emotions, but I soon opened them again, and Becca was still there, smiling at me with those beautiful full lips.

"Thank you, by the way," she whispered.

I tilted my head to ask what for, but she continued.

"I never actually said thank you for taking care of my contract. I'll never forget that."

The warmth of a smile lifted the corners of my lips, and I wrapped my arms around her waist, pulling her into a tight hug, "You deserve to be happy, and you deserve to be free."

She giggled and pressed a soft, loving kiss on my lips, her palm caressing the skin of my cheek as she did.

I moved my hands to rest on her hips, hooking my thumbs beneath the waistline of her leggings. I leaned into her, smelling the salt of rain on her skin. As I breathed in the mix of petrichor and the floral tones from her perfume, I felt my heart crash heavily in my chest. I placed a kiss just behind her ear, "we should get you out of these wet clothes," I muttered, my thumbs peeling the black fabric away from her skin.

Becca hummed into my ear, pressing herself flat against me, palms resting on my chest. "I think you're right," she said.

My breath hitched as Becca began placing small kisses along my collarbone, pushing back the fabric of my shirt for better access. I felt my dick swell instantly, pressing against the back of my jeans. I stepped away from her for a second and she giggled, pulling the fabric of her t-shirt away from her body and lifting it off over her head.

The skin beneath the shirt was cold but painted in blotches of pink and red from the blush that was beginning to spread. I bit down on the back of my bottom lip as I took her in.

She was gorgeous. I had seen her in every sort of lingerie known to man, and yet nothing looked more captivating on her than a standard lace bra that accentuated the generous size of her breasts.

Now a pace or so away from her, I started to unbutton my shirt, but she stepped forward and placed a hand over mine.

"You showed me so much respect last night, now it's my turn." She said, as she moved to unbutton my shirt. As she pulled the buttons free, she placed kisses along my skin, sending shivers throughout my body. It was hard to hold back the desire to moan for her.

Becca slipped my shirt off over my broad shoulders and it fell to the floor behind me. She then smirked at me as she dipped to her knees and began removing my belt.

My cock ached, begging for release from its prison behind the tight denim of my jeans.

Very soon, though, she permitted this release, pulling my length from within the confines of cloth. These too fell to the ground in puddles around my ankles.

Her hands both wrapped around the length of my cock as she began to slowly stroke it, "Crazy how hard you get when all you've gotten to see are my tits in a bra,"

I laughed wryly, "I think I could get hard just hearing your voice."

She hummed in satisfaction, stroking my cock in long, gentle strokes with just the perfect amount of pressure. "You remember that night that I begged you for help getting off?" She asked, her eyes glassing over with a sultry sheen, "The night that you told me to have my roommate do it for me?"

A blush rose to my cheeks.

I *did* remember.

That was fucking stupid.

I nodded, "Yeah, I remember."

A spark of deviance grew in her eyes, and she licked the tip of my cock, swirling her tongue around it enough to drive me mental. But she abruptly pulled back and returned to the stroking. It felt really nice, but God did I miss her mouth already.

"I couldn't get you out of my head that night," Her voice sounded like fog rolling, dangerous and slow, "I touched myself that night and imagined that it was you. Your tattooed hands gripping my throat. I fucked you in my head."

My cock twitched from excitement, and she smirked again. *This woman was a demon.*

She dipped her head to the tip once more, taking it into her mouth and guiding the length into her throat until I could feel her gag lightly.

That thrilled me and I reached down to tangle my hands in her frizzing hair. Becca took this as a positive sign and pulled back, then slid my tip along the roof of her mouth as she started to deepthroat me.

I whimpered with pleasure, already feeling the buzz in my toes. When I managed to open my eyes long enough to glance down, I could see that her eyes were locked on mine as she took my cock deep in the back of her throat. My knees buckled, and I nearly collapsed right then.

Her lips pulled away from my cock and she points to the couch. I obey wordlessly, kicking off the puddle of jeans and boxers from my ankles and sitting down with my throbbing cock hard between my legs.

She smiled and hooked her fingers under the waistband of her leggings, slowly bending over as she removed them, her panties sliding down along with them. Her ass was now on full display, and I couldn't help but touch myself. A soft moan escapes my lips, "Fuck, Becca. You're so hot."

The look in her eye was knowing, and she practically jumped to straddle me, her legs on either side of my own, my hard cock exposed between us, begging for her attention.

She smiled, "You called me baby earlier," she said flatly, placing kisses on my neck.

"S-sorry,"

Her golden hair bounced as she shook her head, "No, I liked it."

I bit down on my lip, "Yeah?"

She nodded, "I did."

A shudder raced down my spine, and I lifted one of my hands to her throat, encircling the flesh with my tattooed-covered hand and squeezing only enough so that I was able to pull her toward me and mash our lips together for a hungry kiss.

The soft whimper of a moan that left her lips sent me spiraling, and I reached my hand between her legs to softly play with her clit. I pulled my lips from hers, but kept her face there so that she could feel my words against her lips as I spoke, "You like to fantasize about me touching you, baby?"

Her eyes roll back with a flutter of her eyelashes, she nodded lightly, "Y-yes."

I smirked, "You imagine my cock deep inside of you?"

The nod was faster this time, begging. My finger swirled quickly around her clit.

"You need to climb onto my cock right now," I demanded in a low growl.

Becca bit her lip and reached forward to grab the shaft of my dick in her hand, pumping it slowly. I release her throat from my grasp as she lifts her hips forward and positions my tip at her entrance.

She was soaking-fucking-wet and I was *rock* hard. I could feel the precum leaking from my tip, and in an instant, she lowered herself onto my cock.

We moaned in unison, and Becca began to slowly roll her hips, moving strategically up and down on my dick like the hardcore professional that she was. I could feel every ounce of her soaking wet pussy as it squeezed tight around my cock. All I wanted was to fuck her until she couldn't walk straight anymore.

I gripped the soft skin tightly, guiding her hips along.

"Take my bra off," she ordered, her eyes locking on mine.

As if I would pass up *that* opportunity. I moved one hand up from her hip and made quick work of undoing the fastener.

With the release of the strap, Becca rolled her hips to signal a good job, and I pulled the lace free.

Suddenly, she stopped and pushed herself to stand, my cock pulling out of her and greeting the cool air. I watched in confusion for a second, but as she turned around on my lap, I knew she was about to rock my world.

Becca backed her ass up to me, then quickly found my cock again and slipped down onto it, facing away from me. I groaned, my hands moving to settle on her ass as it bounced in front of me.

She was slowly dissolving into a moaning mess, but I couldn't quite tell if it was theatrical or not. I wanted to make sure she felt every ounce of pleasure that she could, so I placed one hand on the front of her stomach and the other around her throat, I stood, using the position of my hands to stabilize her until I had her pinned against the couch.

I plunged my cock deep inside of her, my hand on her throat pulling her backwards slightly so that I could nibble her ear, "You better not moan unless you mean it," I warned. Her walls tightened around me, and I whimpered, "You want me to fuck you till you can't feel your legs?"

"Y-yes," She struggled beneath a moan.

I nipped at her ear, slamming into her once, deep and hard. "What did you say to me earlier?"

She thought for a moment, her hand moving between her legs to circle her finger around her clit, but I grabbed her wrist.

"Say it, or else you'll never cum again," I ordered, both of her wrists securely in my hands, I pinned them to the wall behind the couch and pulled out of her entirely. She was pinned there, shaking. I fucking loved to watch her tremble in need for me.

Her voice was shaky as she choked her words out, "I-I love you," She whispered.

I chuckled and placed my tip at her entrance, "Sorry, I didn't quite catch that."

She whimpered in need, "I lo-love you," She tried again, this time clearer.

"I am not quite sure I believe you," I muttered into her ear.

Becca pressed her ass backwards to encourage me deeper, but I pulled my hips back.

"Not until you say it like you mean it."

"I fucking love you, Adam. I love you and I want you to fucking fuck me!" She said in a voice clearer than crystal.

That was all I needed.

I reeled back and plunged my cock deep inside of her, thrusting hard and fast.

I pushed my own fingers between her legs and lips, circling the lump of nerves.

"Fuck!" She moaned out, her hands pressed flat to the wall as I ravaged her pussy. "Fuck yes, baby! I fucking love you!"

My entire body convulsed with her words as I slammed into her. I started to feel the spasms in her pussy, and I knew she was getting close. I wanted to cum with her so badly.

"You want me to cum inside of you, Becca?"

She nodded, "Yes, baby. Fill me up. Breed me!"

That was definitely it.

I felt the knot of pleasure build up behind my abs and within seconds I was unloading my cum into Becca.

But she hadn't cum yet.

So, I just kept thrusting through the overwhelming sensation until eventually she wavered in her strength, and I could feel her walls squeezing around me.

The feeling launched me into another realm of perception, and I came again, almost as hard as the first time.

She slumped forward and I collapsed against her back, using the wall to hold myself steady as I floated down from the blinding high.

Soon, my cock slid out of her, and I watched as my cum dripped from her pulsing core. I admired my handiwork with an exhausted smile, but I wanted to care for her too. I didn't even know if she had *ever* experienced aftercare before.

I slowly stepped toward the kitchen and grabbed a bottle of water from the fridge, bringing it to her along with a towel. I knelt down beside the couch where she now sprawled, handing her the items and pressing a kiss to her forehead.

Becca blushed as she accepted the stuff and cleaned herself up.

She then looked at me and patted the space on the couch beside her. I climbed into the seat with her, pulling her tight to my chest and peppering her forehead with soft kisses, "You're so beautiful, baby," I muttered, a hand brushing through her hair soothingly.

For a moment, I could have sworn that I saw a tear roll down her cheek. She crawled further up on the couch so that she could bury her face in the crook of my neck.

"I really meant it, Adam," She muttered.

My heart fluttered and I reached to intertwine my fingers with hers, "I know, Becca. I know you did."

"You haven't said it back," Her words struck through me like a bolt of energy, and I instantly placed a tender kiss on her lips.

"What is your full name?" I asked softly.

She pouts, "Rebecca."

"That's your first name," I chuckled.

Her nose scrunched, "I don't like my full name."

I chuckled, "Well, I didn't ask that did I?"

She rolled her eyes, "Rebecca Cassidy."

I nodded slowly, "Right then, Rebecca Cassidy… I love you with every fiber of my being. With every cell in my body. With every ounce of my soul."

I placed another gentle kiss on her lips, "I will love you until my love for you is unbearable, and then you can tell me to fuck off."

Becca grinned and blushed lightly, "Hey…"

I pinched her chin to bring her eyes to my level.

"I like the name you chose for my passport." she muttered.

A chuckle rose in my chest, and I nuzzled her, "Mine is Sebastian Crue," I explained.

Her eyes flickered, "You've made us siblings?"

That chuckle morphed into genuine laughter, and I shook my head, "No, you dummy." I kissed her jawline, "I made us married."

"Married? I never agreed to that!"

The flutter of elation inside of me dropped off lightly and I rubbed the back of my neck, "It isn't legal… It's just for the passports…"

She pouted, "I never even got a proper proposal…"

I tilted my head, then felt a grin overcome me, "I still have to take you on a proper first date," I said softly.

Her eyes glimmered with a bit of hope, and she smiled, "Does that mean it might happen?"

"Anything is possible." I grinned, holding her close.

Anything and everything felt possible when I had her. Every shit decision I had ever made culminated to this point where

I was here, holding the woman of my dreams… and we were about to start our new lives together.

# A Friend on the Other Side

~ひ⁕♡~

# BECCA

I pulled at the strap of my duffel bag that slung over my shoulder as my feet pattered softly across the smooth marble flooring of Hartsfield-Jackson International Airport. My mind was filled with absolutely everything that could very easily go wrong so very quickly. Adam seemed far too confident in his belief that these fake documents would work for us.

The past few days were a whirlwind of chaos.

Adam organizing things for his mother's funeral, which he would unfortunately never get to see. He had to clear all of his things from his apartment before the new buyers came to take over ownership, and he just barely managed to sell his only remaining car.

And then, there he was standing in front of me in a queue for Delta's customer services.

He seemed far too calm, but I couldn't be certain that he wasn't absolutely shitting himself beneath all of the broody masks he typically wore. We had arrived with only carry-on luggage, our documents, a bit of cash that would serve us for a fair amount of time, and the clothes on our backs.

We stepped forward to the self-service check-in booth where Adam pulled out his passport and pressed it into the sensor. I felt my heart in my throat as I watched the circle on the screen turn at the slowest, most agonizing pace possible. Then the screen brightened and flashed with a check mark, "You are now checked in!" It told him in a hushed tone. He smiled and ushered me to mimic his actions.

I anxiously stepped forward and placed my face page against the scanner. The machine buzzed and whirred beneath me, and now my heart was fully lodged in my throat. I could have sworn that it was moving even slower this time.

Adam placed a hand on the small of my back, nuzzling his nose into my hair, and as the soothing sensation of his touch arose, the machine granted me the same favor that it had granted to him.

I felt the air return to my lungs and my anxiety slipped back into normal travel frustration as I retrieved my document and sighed a breath of relief.

He smiled at me and extended his hand, "I'll keep the passports and tickets in my bag so we don't lose them," He explained.

That made sense. I felt so frazzled today that I probably

would have misplaced my phone if… wait… I patted myself down, searching for my phone. The panic shown plainly on my face, but Adam chuckled softly and unzipped his jacket pocket, "You left it on the seat of the taxi," He retrieved my phone from his pocket, and I felt the wash of relief rain over me.

"Shit… sorry. I'm just so nervous." I muttered.

Adam hooked a finger under my chin and leaned in to press a gentle kiss on my lips. He smelled of coffee; deep and rich. "I know you're anxious, but you gotta trust me." He told me softly, his hand falling from my face to gently intertwine his fingers with mine.

With a gentle tug, we were moving towards the TSA lines.

Oddly, this was the least terrifying part of the endeavor. The line moved at a snail's pace, which allowed me to focus on the people in the crowd. A plethora of souls from all walks of life: from families going on vacation to suited businessmen.

Adam shifted on his heels as we grew closer to the security lines and looked down at me, "I don't want you to panic. Just stay calm."

Fuck. He knew something was going to happen here.

And he was right. As the pair of us walked through security, we made it through the initial checks perfectly fine, but we were pulled aside by two agents before we could collect our carry-on luggage.

I bit down hard on my lip. I forgot everything Adam had told me to say if something happened. He had coached me through this before and now I felt like I was going to fuck this up.

Adam turned to me as we waited against the wall for the agent, his eyes settled on mine as he brushed a strand of hair from my face. "I can't wait for our honeymoon in Greece, Scarlet." He spoke as though he knew I needed him to refresh my script.

Fuck me, he knew me too well.

I nodded once, slowly, "I just hope security doesn't take us aside for too long."

I knew why he insisted on speaking like this. It was far too easy for us to blow our cover right here and now.

An agent approached us, beckoning me away from Adam. A pain burned in my chest, and I bit down on my lip as I looked back at Adam. He was being guided in another direction.

Fuck. Fuck. Fuck.

He told me nothing like this would happen.

How could I be so stupid?

The agent, a woman with deep tanned skin and curly brown hair, ushered me to a room where I was now completely and totally isolated from everyone else.

This felt far too inescapable.

"Mrs. Crue?" The woman with a thick Hispanic accent asked.

My ears perked up, and I threw on my brightest smile. I needed to act the part. "That's me," I said softly.

She smiled kindly, a stack of papers in her hand. She locked the door and joined me at the table.

This felt like a full-on interrogation.

The woman stacked the papers against the table to straighten them, then smoothed them down against the table with her hand, "My name is agent Louise Silva. I'm waiting for my supervisor to join us, but I wanted to go ahead and get started with some basic questions."

I choked back the sensation of panic as I nodded slowly,

plastering a look of concern on my face, "Have I done something wrong?"

"Have you?" Louise tilts her head.

"I- I don't think so," I muttered.

*I fucking have.*

"Do you have your passport and boarding documents on you, Mrs. Crue?" Louise asked.

*Oh, this was all part of his plan.*

I shook my head, "Oh, no!" I said sweetly, "My husband… it feels so weird calling him that," I giggled, pulling a strand of hair behind my ear with a gentle blush on my face, "My husband always holds onto my things when we travel. I'm like a space cadet when travelling!" I placed my hands on my cheeks. They were warm. Could she discern between the anxiety and the absolute terror that was racking my brain?

She studied me for a moment, looking me over. Her chestnut-colored eyes searched every inch of me. I wanted to absolutely fucking die.

"When did you get married to your husband, Mrs. Crue?" She asked.

Fuck…

I searched the recesses of my brain for an answer, but I couldn't remember this being something he coached me on. "Last Monday, Memorial Day Monday. I remember because I was lucky that I didn't have to call off of work for the ceremony." I giggled, "We are going to Greece for our honeymoon. I've never been before."

Her eyes narrowed as she inspected the papers before her. We never actually got married, so how the fuck would there be a record of it?

"Mrs. Crue, do you go by any other names?" She asked.

I shook my head succinctly, "No, well… my maiden name was Bell." I felt the hairs on my arms stand up, she was asking far deeper questions than I was prepared to answer.

Her eyes narrowed lightly, but before she could process these thoughts any further, the door to the room opened and a man entered the room.

"Right, Lou, I'm here now so you're free to return to your duty."

I recognized his voice in an instant.

Holy. Fucking. Shit. No Way!

I turned my head up to meet the figure who had entered the room. He was tall, stocky, and buff. His hair was brown and pulled back tight into a knot at the back of his head. The only thing that was missing was his unbuttoned Hawaiian t-shirt.

It was fucking Cole!

Louise pushed herself to stand and nodded, "Everything seems to be in order, sir. It is just the main investigation now."

"Beautiful work, Lou. I've just finished in the other room with Mr. Crue," Cole said, retrieving the papers from her and guiding her out of the room.

Heat prickled along the back of my neck as I fused my eyes onto Cole. When he returned inside of the room, he pulled the door closed and locked it. His eyes fell on mine, and he had the audacity to smirk at me.

"Surprise!" He teased.

I didn't say anything. I was terrified of trusting him. *Do I drop the act? Am I caught?*

Cole stepped over to the chair Louise had been sat in just a moment ago, "I know you're probably very confused, but I hope you know that my loyalties lie with Cain." He chuckled, tossing the papers lazily onto the table. "You two are a little bit unlucky, your faces are plastered everywhere in the metro area. Seems the police were given a heads up by some slimy motherfucker with a God complex."

"What?" I muttered softly.

Cole leaned forward with his elbows pressed to the table, "You, my dear Valentine, have a warrant out for your arrest. It seems that your years of debauchery are catching up to you. Somehow, records of your silent killings have been leaked. You're officially one of America's Most Wanted Criminals."

My heart pounded in my chest, and I felt a tingling sensation growing in my head and fingertips like I was going to faint.

"Don't you worry though; I have already cleared both Sebastian and Scarlett Crue for travel. I can't risk you missing your honeymoon, can I?" He grinned.

It felt unreal to be sitting here with a man that I had only ever seen with a woman of the night under his arm, staring at me with such mischief. I looked down at my hands anxiously, "Does- does that mean I can go?" I muttered the question.

He nods slowly, "Yes. You two should be fine for a few days, but I only have so much power. You need to get off grid as fast as you can and stay that way for a while."

My heartbeat began to correct itself and I felt relief wash over me, I nodded quickly, "Yes- Okay! We can do that."

He pushed himself from the chair and motioned for me to lead the way out of the room.

I stood, moving to the door as he unlocked it. Adam was waiting just beyond with a soft smile on his face.

"Alrighty then, Mr. and Mrs. Crue," Cole said with his paperwork clasped firmly in his grasp, "Enjoy your honeymoon!" He winked at Adam, then turned away from us to walk down the hall to an office.

The air returned to the atmosphere around me, and I glanced over at Adam. He smiled softly and reached his hand over. His fingertips graced the skin of my forearm, slowly moving down to part my fingers and intertwining our fingers together. He gently tugged me toward the security desk where our belongings waited.

We didn't speak for what felt like an eternity, but the silence between us felt comfortable, safe. Adam never once dropped my hand, even when we were seated at our gate, awaiting our flight.

A TV was mounted above us, displaying the news.

I found myself fixated on it in the buzz of the airport, staring at the shifting colors but not actually taking any of the information in. That is, until I noticed something familiar pop across the screen. A white marble mansion with gold accenting. Lorenzo's house. I sat forward, focusing in hard on the display.

"Atlanta firefighters responded to a heartbreaking scene in Cherokee County this morning as the home of philanthropist, Lorenzo Gonzales, goes up in flames. What is believed to be a mechanical issue is now being resolved, but the initial explosion resulted in three fatalities at the home. Mr. Gonzales himself has been transported to the hospital to treat injuries sustained during the event." The news anchor said flatly, a resounding tone that provided us with this incredibly important detail as though it was nothing.

I turned my head to see that Adam's eyes were also fixed on the display. When he noticed the shift in my gaze, he passed me a knowing grin and shrugged, "I might have left something in the Charger's trunk for him."

This warmth grew in my chest, but it didn't resemble fear

or anger… *was it elation?*

I bit my lip for a moment as I held back the waves of joy.

"You fucking car bombed Lorenzo?" I whispered.

His lips lifted into a smirk, "I always fucking hated that house."

I giggled and threw my arms around his neck; he hoisted me from my seat and pulled me to sit across his lap as he placed gentle kisses along my cheeks.

We sat like that, pressed together in peaceful bliss, until the boarding gate opened, and we stepped aboard the plane, leaving this fucking disgusting life behind us. I had never really liked fairytale endings before…

But this… *this* I could definitely get used to.

**The End**

**Maybe…**

# Bonus Chapter: The Dancer and Her Beau

# BECCA

*One Year Later*

I turned the lock on the heavy glass door to my studio, feeling the resistance in the pins as it bolted shut. I was now closed for the night.

Jumping, I retrieved a pull tab from above that would bring a security screen down over the door and small square window of reception.

Behind me, I heard a soft bang. *Someone had just entered through the back door.* My breath hitched in my chest as I grabbed my keys tight in my hands, walking to the office nearest me and pulling open a drawer where I stored my can of mace.

Footsteps, heavy and strong, approached the office as if they knew exactly where I would be. My heart pounded, but I held out hope, "A-Adam?" I called out, my finger poised on the trigger for the mace.

The footsteps stopped, sending the world into darkness and abject silence.

My heart raced.

"Do you have the mace?" Adam's voice suddenly boomed through the silence like a knife. I practically jumped out of my skin when he spoke.

Relief.

"Fuck... You nearly gave me a heart attack!" I whimpered, stepping out of the office to see him standing there at the entrance to the studio. He had a shit-eating grin plastered on his stupid face.

Adam's lips parted and he stepped closer to me, moving his hand to gently disarm me of the pepper spray. He placed in on the shelf beside us that displayed all of my certifications, then dipped to wrap his arms around my waist. He pulled me into a gentle kiss, "Sorry for scaring you, baby."

I blushed lightly and pushed his face away playfully, "Why are you even here?" I asked with a giggle.

Since we had left America, we had settled into a quaint little Dutch village. Adam had taken up work in a construction company and they right away noticed his prowess in the industry. He had moved up to work essentially the same job he had worked under Roy in the States.

After a few months, he surprised me with the studio. It was small, but it was my everything... and I adored it almost as much as I had grown to adore him.

He pouted, "Do you not want to see me?"

My brown eyes rolled, and I moved to throw my arms around his neck, "There is literally nobody else I'd ever want to see."

Adam's eyes brighten and he pecked my lips with a quick kiss, "It's dark out, and I just wanted to make sure you got home safely."

I giggled and rubbed our noses together, pulling away slowly so that I could finish turning everything off in up front.

"I still have to clean up, so you'll be waiting a little while." I explained, dipping into the studio room where five stunning silver poles stood. One in each corner and then one at the very center of the room.

Ceiling-to-floor-length mirrors covered each wall, and the softest pink lighting cast down from the LEDs that Adam had installed above each reflection. The atmosphere in this room was stunning, and I felt like flying every time I was here alone.

He chuckled, "I can start with the floors if you want help."

I smiled back at him and nodded, pulling a microfiber cloth from a bucket on a nearby rack of cubbies and then tucking it into the waistband of my shorts.

"That would be nice. I need to wipe the poles down while you do that."

Adam nodded and dipped into the utility closet where he retrieved a broom and dustpan as well as a mop and bucket. He stooped to fill the bucket, adding in my favorite scented lemon cleaner.

I stalked towards the pole nearest to myself and retrieved the end of the cloth, soaking it in an alcohol-based solution. I then climbed to the top of the pole and removed the cloth from my waist, wiping the pole down in its entirety, and slowly pulling myself down the pole as I cleaned.

"You're like a little monkey," Adam teased, pulling the broom across the floor.

"That's insensitive to monkeys," I fired back, glancing down from my place at about seven feet in the air to see him standing below me.

He always worries about me, even when he knew I was quite competent. He was there to make sure that he could catch me if I fell.

My comment brought out a snort as he shook his head, "I don't think anything compared to you could be considered insensitive." He snickered, moving away once I was closer to the ground.

He finished sweeping, but he refused to mop until I was off of the poles. Now focusing in on the final pole, I noticed that his eyes were settled upon me. Even though his face was blank, I could see the desire.

I smirked and hooked my leg around the pole, leaning backwards into a Duchess. My hair fell out behind me as I locked eyes with Adam.

His lips had fallen apart slightly in concern, but as I held myself there, I could see the wheels in his head turning.

Engaging my core, I pulled myself up gracefully and crossed my legs one over the other to sit on the pole.

Adam stepped closer to me, "You fucking scare me up there," he chuckled, his hand reaching to gently hold one of my bare feet.

I smile, "But you love it when I scare you."

He nodded, "Oh, absolutely. It makes me want to rail you against your desk."

A blush snapped into my cheeks, and I threw my hands over

my face, "You dick," I muttered, "you know I have to clean everything before we go home."

Adam smirked, his hand moving from my feet to gently trace the skin of my legs as they sealed me to the pole. His touch was to die for. "We aren't in a rush," He reminded me, winking.

I nibbled the skin of my lip and nodded slowly, "You go in the office, I need to finish this one first." I muttered.

"No," His eyes deepened, "I want to watch you clean it."

A shiver tickled my shoulders, and I nodded slowly, moving to unlock my grip from the pole and wipe the rest of it. Once I had reached the bottom, my feet touched the ground and I bent myself in half, allowing him to see how my shorts had wedged themselves in my ass while I was in that seat. I then crouched as I wiped the base of the pole down, and theatrically pushed myself to stand.

Sweat beaded on his brow and Adam grabbed my hips, "You are disgustingly gorgeous," He hissed into my ear, dragging his two front teeth along the skin of my shoulder.

I felt my core ache, and I pressed myself back against him, allowing my head to fall back as I stared up into his eyes. His hands began to trace my body, paying special attention to the curves of my hips and the muscles of my upper arms.

"You're fucking irresistible," He muttered, dipping down to place a kiss on my lips upside down.

The little slut inside of me began to churn and I pulled away from him, peeling my crop top off and throwing it at his feet, "You think so?" I asked, slipping the booty shorts away to reveal that I wasn't wearing anything beneath either of them.

I saw his knees waver, and I smirked, walking towards my office with a sexy sway in my hips. He followed close behind me like a hungry animal, ready to ravage me to my core.

Before I could even make it to the office, he had grabbed my waist and pinned me against the door frame, I felt my heart race as he hooked his index finger under my chin and angled my face up so that I could receive a passionate kiss from him. His tongue crashed through my lips and surveyed the inside of my mouth.

My nipples hardened as his other hand brushed across them, squeezing and massaging at the skin of my breasts. He pulled his lips away from mine and immediately suctioned them to my neck, sucking at the sensitive skin at my shoulder line.

I whimpered, tangling my hand in his hair and gripping to it lightly, "Mmm."

Adam grabbed my hips and lifted me, pulling my legs around his still clothed waist, "I want you to hold onto me like you hold onto those fucking poles," He growled into my ear.

My legs instinctively tightened around his waist, and I pressed my exposed entrance against the denim of his jeans. Now eye-level with Adam, he continued to attack my neck and shoulders with kisses, eventually coming to a stop at the meaty flesh of my shoulder, where he sank his teeth into the skin just enough to make me tighten my legs further. I moaned out softly and bit down on my lip.

He smiled as he pulled his teeth from my skin, an imprint was left behind that didn't bleed, but it was highlighted it in a pink color that glistened with a decent layer of his saliva.

"Are you just gonna tease me?" I asked in a sultry tone, pulling his face to meet my eyes. I breathed against his lips, "Because you threatened to rail me, and at present there isn't any fucking railing happening."

Adam chuckled darkly, reaching to tangle his hand in my

hair. He pulled at the locks of blonde, forcing my head to tilt as he covered my throat in soft kisses.

He eventually landed at my ear and hissed, "Patience is a virtue."

I whimpered from excitement, I could feel how wet I was already, and he was only torturing me at this point.

"Patience is reserved for people who weren't promised anything." I grit my teeth, pulling the fabric of his t-shirt away and lobbing it across the room to land somewhere that I would worry about later.

That haunting chuckle was summoned again, and Adam braced my back with his hand as he pulled me from the door frame, pressing out bare chests together as he carried me through the threshold of the office door and placed my ass on my desk that was surprisingly tidy for once.

I made decent work of the skin on his own neck, pressing love bites and kisses along the skin until he tugged once more at my hair, this time staring me in the eyes.

My own eyes fluttered lightly, and I locked into his stunning blues.

"Undo my belt, Becca." he demanded while staring directly into my soul. He was seeing straight into all of the disgusting things I was thinking in my head, but right now in this moment... all I wanted with his cock.

I slipped my hands down the front of his chiseled chest, never once removing my eyes from his, and I undid the buckle of his belt, pulling it until it had slid completely free of his trousers. I placed it on the side, but he apparently had other ideas.

His hand fell from my hair and grabbed the leather length, wrapping it diligently around his fist until only the end hung down, "Drop your legs," He demanded, "Turn around and present your ass."

I felt my resolve weaken and my skin prickled with hairs that stood on end, as soon as I released his waist, he stepped back and watched as I bent over the desk, shoulders up, but ass on full display.

Adam stepped behind me with a smirk, "You're so fucking sexy," He reassured me, pressing a few kisses along the center of my spine. I could hear him unzipping his trousers, then the woosh as they fell to the floor. He kicked them away and his hand that was free of his belt's coil slipped between my legs, plunging into the wetness that he himself had created.

"Mmm," He hummed, "Good girl." He reeled back his hand and with a swift crack, I felt the sting of his belt as it struck the skin of my ass.

I whimpered, biting down on my lip. My legs shook from the sensation that the leather left behind.

He pressed kisses along the back of my shoulders, "You have been teasing me for a few days now. It is so hard to control myself," He growled, "I can't wait to sink my cock inside of you.

My eyes glazed over with need, and I nodded, "Yes, baby, I want your cock inside of me."

His eyes flickered with lust, and he struck me again with the belt, this time on the other cheek.

"I love the way your skin glows for me," He positioned himself directly behind, angling his tip at my entrance. Both hands gripped at the flesh of my ass, and I could feel the wrapped leather around his right hand as he pushed himself inside of me.

"Mmmm," I grit my teeth, the sting from his belt playing a

medley of sensations that made the temporary sting far more worthwhile. And now, his cock was buried deep inside of me.

Fuck… yes…

Adam began to thrust, but his movements were calculated and slow. The need for him grew deep inside of my belly and I pressed my ass back into him to encourage him to hit just the right spot. He chuckled, "Don't get too excited. I'm going to give you all the cock you want. Savor it as it is, for now."

It was fucking amazing, that's what it was.

The way his length perfectly contoured to the inside of my pussy, stroking along all of the right places. He had mastered the art of fucking me, and he now knew where absolutely every single nerve ending was. He knew how to drive me wild, and he was intentionally avoiding that space.

I shuddered beneath him, leaning forward more on the desk. He seemed to like that, as he began to pick up his pace. He thrust deeper now, and I could feel the slap of his balls as they strummed against my clit.

My pussy craved him.

I felt myself descending into genuine pleasure, my moans became louder.

"Mmm, you like that baby? Tell me what you want me to do to you." Adam cooed, throwing his belt to the ground. He delivered a thick slap to my ass, rocking his hips into mine.

I whimpered, moving my hips against his strategically, "I want you to fuck me harder, Adam," My voice was stern and commanding.

His thrusts were long, smooth, and then suddenly, more aggressive.

"You want me to destroy your pussy?" he asked, delivering me one hard thrust before returning to the normal gentle pace he had been at before.

I moaned loudly in response to the thrust and bit down on my lip, "Yes!" I whimpered.

With that, Adam pulled out of me entirely and flipped me so that my ass was on the desk, I leaned back on the heels of my palms and stars entered my vision as Adam slammed his cock deep inside of me.

Over and over, deep and fucking hard.

I could feel him banging against my cervix, the tightening in my belly grew warm and I threw my head back as I moaned loudly, "F-fuck me, Adam!" I whimpered breathlessly.

He wrapped a hand around my throat and pulled me forward for a hungry kiss as he absolutely ravaged my pussy.

I squirmed on the length, feeling the surge of electricity that was growing in my belly, creeping through my nerves until I finally felt the release crash over my shoulders and a full-scale orgasm sent my legs trembling. He smirked, staring down at me as he pulled from my lips, "Fuck yes, baby. Cum all over my cock!"

My orgasm came to a simmering buzz and I felt release as Adam pulled his length from inside of me, the cold air instantly chilling the mixture of juices that clung to my labia.

Adam stepped back, "On your knees," he ordered.

Still trembling, I slipped down from the desk and fell to my knees before him, I knew exactly what he wanted, and I was damn well going to do it. I wrapped my hands around his dick, feeling the stick of my own juices as I pumped away. My eyes shot upward in his direction, and I smirked as I leaned in to wrap my lips around his tip.

For a moment, he allowed me to do my own magic, sucking teasingly at his tip and then removing my hands so that I could take his cock to the back of my throat.

That is when he shifted. He grabbed me by my hair again and held me still, thrusting his hips into my mouth. My eyes rolled back as I felt him in the back of my throat, and I relished my taste on his skin.

He absolutely fucked the life out of my mouth until I could feel my jaw beginning to ache, but it wouldn't be too much longer now.

Adam's head rolled back and he groaned aloud, "F-fuck, Becca! I am gonna cum."

I took control again and slid my tongue along the sensitive nerve endings beneath the hood of his tip, paying special attention as the salty taste of precum became more prominent than my own juices. I took all of his length in just as he finally released, filling my mouth with his cum. Adam mounted loudly, his own knees shaking as he unleashed load after load into me.

Tired and shaky, I pulled myself from his cock, but not before I swallowed his cum, staring up at him with satisfied eyes as I did.

He reached down and pulled me to standing, pressing a kiss to my lips between attempts to catch a solid breath. The room around us felt electric; buzzing with the energy that we had just created.

Adam pulled me against his chest, his hand rubbing soothing circles in the small of my back as he glanced down at me, "Was that, okay?" he asked softly, as if nervous.

I laughed, pressing my skin against his as though peeling away would leave me aching, "That was perfect," I responded, pressing a kiss to his collarbone, "*You're* perfect."

He smiled and held me for a moment in absolute silence,

his chin resting on my forehead as he closed his eyes.

The peace that I felt in this moment was something that I had craved my entire life.

And yet, this past year had been so full of that feeling, of that peace, that I was terrified of sinking into out of the fear of getting hurt.

Here, we were safe.

Here, we didn't have to worry about the cops knocking at the door in the middle of the night, wanting to whisk us away to prison.

I felt so free with Adam.

He saved my life, despite all of the shitty things I had said to him, and despite all of the heartache that we had felt, he was still there for me throughout everything.

Occasionally, I'd check my phone or google my old name. It would come up with a BOLO and my picture.

The idea that I could never go back made me beyond anxious, but I knew in my heart that as long as I was with Adam… everything was going to be okay.

# COMING
## Soon

### Ask for Ellis

## A TALE FROM THE MIDNIGHT RAVEN

9 781068 787201